# The Artist's Special Touch

River Wild

River Wild
www.riverwildusa.com

This book is dedicated to my wife.

She is my inspiration.

PROLOGUE

# Young Love and A Promise

Have you ever been in love? A kind of love that overwhelms every part of your soul. Nothing you do quiets that ache inside except to be with the one you love.

If ever they become separated, their hearts will lead them back to each other. They won't rest until they're together again...

CHAPTER ONE

# A Special Gift

Jackson Henderson wiped the tears from his eyes as the door opened that led up the stairs to his art studio. The familiar creaking of the steps in just the right spot told him it was his only daughter, married several hours earlier. Before she made it to the top of the old staircase, he stood up from his easel and gazed out across the beach and into the ocean. He tried his best to regain his composure before she saw him. He loved this special corner of the upstairs loft. It was his haven.

Most days you could find him toiling over a canvas, looking for inspiration for a new project or just standing there in solitude. Whatever the occasion, this little nook brought him much-needed peace. He often slept on the small couch along the back wall.

The studio sat in the corner of the upstairs, facing the beach. The living space, kitchen and bedrooms took up the rest. Below, on the first floor stood the famous Seaside Grille restaurant. It was a favorite spot on Folly Beach for locals and visitors to Charleston, South Carolina. Scores of beautiful paintings lined the walls, competing with the floor-to-ceiling windows for the best view.

Long ago, Jackson had put in custom made curved windows in the front corner that gave an unobstructed panorama of the coastline. He always said a clear blue sky and a few hours by the seashore could do wonders for the soul.

His daughter Faith reached the summit of the stairs and stared at her father without uttering a sound. He was still looking out the window and running his fingers through his hair as she watched him. Jackson's "little girl" looked stunning in her light blue and white polka dot dress. Her long sandy blonde hair framed her beautiful face perfectly. Her warm, tanned skin glistened in the sunlight coming off the window.

Jackson turned to her and smiled. "You look so beautiful; you look just like your mother."

Faith smiled and looked around the room.

Jackson spoke up. "Faith, honey what are you doing here? Shouldn't you be on your honeymoon?"

She kept looking around the room, "Our flight doesn't leave for a few more hours, and I wanted to see you one more time before we left. How are you doing?"

"I'm fine, honey."

The art studio revealed a different story. It had been so long since Faith last visited her father's art studio. Faith turned away in anguish when she realized how long it had been since she last visited him here. She had been so busy finishing her master's degree in North Carolina, finding a job and planning a wedding. When she had finally looked around the entire room, her eyes widened in disbelief. Hundreds of damaged canvases lay littered on the floor and in every corner. They were all torn apart or painted over. When she focused on each one, she realized they were all the same familiar painting.

The art studio had never been in such a mess. Jackson had always been meticulous about keeping things neat and clean; she couldn't believe he let it get like this. Jackson had scores of custom cabinets built to store all the paints, brushes, and canvases and each one had its specific place. The cabinets and their shelves were in terrible disarray as she took it all in and tried to make sense of it. He noticed her looking at the condition of the studio when their eyes met.

"I know it's a little messy around here, but I've been a little tired lately, and I haven't been able to keep everything cleaned up."

Even though the wedding reception ended several hours earlier, Jackson was still wearing his black tuxedo. He was a handsome man of 49, graying a little on the sides of his thick brown hair. His skin glowed from his daily dose of sunshine. Every morning, he ran the five-mile trek down the beach to the old Coast Guard station at the end of the island and back. The smell of the ocean breeze and the glow of the sun helped him think. His 6' 1" 190-pound frame was as fit now as he was in high school.

"Faith, you didn't have to come here... Dad's okay."

She said to herself, "Yeah, I can see you're okay."

"Daddy, I brought you something... I'll be right back."

As she disappeared back down the old staircase, the visions of her whole life ran through Jackson's mind. Teaching her how to paint, swimming lessons at the YMCA and the first adventure on her bike. He was there for every single one. Every moment played through his memory like the slow winding frames of a movie, each with bold clarity. He was so deep in thought, he didn't hear her return up to the loft.

She walked over and placed the large brown package down on the worn, gold pine floor in front of him. He picked it up and slowly ran his hands along the edges. He sat down and removed the packaging, revealing its contents. When he slid the last of the covering away, his heart sank as his eyes met her gift. He stared at it without saying anything. Faith stood close, waiting for his response. As tears trailed gently down his cheeks, a smile broke across his face, and he looked up at her.

"How did you know?"

CHAPTER TWO

# The Journey Begins

## Thirty-eight years earlier...

## June 7th, 1977

Mrs. Sally Mitchell's 5th-grade classroom was noisy and hot on the last school day of the year. Early June came so fast, and the kids were climbing the walls to be free for summer. The students had just returned from recess and the classroom smelled like an old locker room. Sally heard their conversations about their upcoming vacations as their young voices filled the room. Each one told a different story.

She glanced up at the clock; school didn't let out for another two hours. "What can I do to keep these kids entertained until the bell rings?" She wondered.

Sally turned the TV on, but the children weren't interested. After a few outbursts from the less than impressed 5th graders, she switched it off and searched the room for something to occupy their time. She walked to the back of the room to a set of grand old storage cabinets that held their books and school supplies. Her father had built them thirty years ago for her when she began teaching. He was meticulous and careful to sand every square inch smooth and round the corners, so no little fingers got hurt. He made scores of compartments and drawers and arranged them so that she could change them around. It was quite a work of art itself.

She opened the decades-old pine door and saw the stacks of magazines she had stored up over the years for different school projects. Mrs. Mitchell kept every magazine imaginable. Sports ones, old variety journals, home improvement, gardening guides, and even a few on cars.

"Surely the kids can find something interesting in here to read," Sally thought to herself.

She turned and stared back at all the bright young faces she helped over the year and smiled with heartfelt admiration. Sally Mitchell had quiet eyes and a gentle spirit that everyone adored. Her first assignment out of college was teaching 5th grade, and she loved the kids so much that she never wanted to do anything else.

"Kids, I have a bunch of magazines back here. Come and take a look."

In an instant, the students dashed to the back of the room and ripped through the piles of magazines she pulled out.

Eleven-year-old Jackson Henderson sat at the front left corner of the room near Mrs. Mitchell's desk. He was a cute young boy with dark brown semi-curly hair. Taller than most in his class, but a little skinnier too. Since he was so far from the back, he got to the mountain of old periodicals last when she had called everyone. By the time he made it back there, the best ones were gone. He filed through over 30 magazines, but none caught his eye. He kept thumbing through the stack, and near the bottom of the pile, he discovered an oversized magazine with a beautiful portrait of the beach on an easel with a handsome young artist next to it. The title read "Learn how to paint anything." Jackson stared at the cover for what seemed like hours. The brilliant colors and detail captivated his mind. He ran his finger across the painted seascape on the glossy cover and was instantly transported to Folly Beach. The sand felt warm between his toes as he ran around at the edge of the water, chasing after seagulls and fiddler crabs. The salt air and the warm breeze made him feel alive as he chased the waves back and forth.

As quick as it started, one of his friends bumped into him and startled him back to reality. Jackson stood there for a moment wondering what had happened. Was it real or did he imagine it? He walked back to his seat and thought about what he'd just experienced and then sat down and studied every page of the magazine.

CHAPTER THREE

# Curiosity Racing

About halfway through the painting magazine, Jackson came to the story from the front cover. The young artist had several pictures on display, but the beach and mountain scenes were Jackson's favorites. Jackson wondered how old the artist on the cover was and how he could be so good, so fast? He had never seen anything like it. Those paintings were something special, and he knew he wanted to paint just like him.

As the young boy absorbed every word of the article, his mind raced. Could he be as good as the young painter? He thought about all the endless possibilities, and his excitement began to build. During the two hours left before the end of the day, he read the featured story seven more times.

Mrs. Mitchell got the classes' attention about 10 minutes before school was out. "Boys and girls, it's almost time for the bell to ring; if you want to, you can take the magazines home with you to keep." Jackson's eyes lit up.

"I wanted to talk to you one last time. This year has been wonderful for me. You all worked so hard and did well during the school year. I'm so proud of all you have done, and your parents are too. Just remember that your attitude decides your outcome in life. If yours is positive, you'll be successful. A person with a negative attitude will find it difficult to succeed, and they'll have a sour personality. Everyone in here is special in some way, and I know you will do extraordinary things in life. Always work hard at whatever you do and be a good friend. Do the right thing no matter how tough it may be."

One student in the back of the room raised her hand and asked, "Mrs. Mitchell, are you going to 6th grade with us?"

Mrs. Mitchell laughed. "No honey, I'm getting "left behind" in the 5th grade."

The class busted out laughing.

"Well, let's get ready to go, the bell will be ringing soon."

Jackson slid the magazine into his book bag making sure not to damage it. He couldn't wait to show his mom Leah. The bell rang, and the children sprang to the door. Jackson waited a few minutes then picked up his backpack and stopped by Mrs. Mitchell's desk.

"Thanks for letting us keep the magazines Mrs. Mitchell. I love the one I got."

She stood up and hugged him. "You're welcome, I hope you enjoy your summer, and I wish you the best in middle school. Jackson, you have been a tremendous help this year. You were so kind to the three new students that transferred to our class, and so brave helping all the kids out when we had the fire in January. There is a difference between you and the other boys; you are an extraordinary young man Jackson. I can't explain it, I just feel it. I will miss you, but I'll keep checking on you. A friend of mine is a 6th-grade teacher at James Island Middle School. I'll ask her to watch out for you. I'm confident you will do something wonderful in life. Have a great summer."

CHAPTER FOUR

# Really Seeing

On the walk home, Jackson's eyes opened to the world around him. Things he used to pass right by without noticing, now seemed so beautiful. Jackson was in awe of the towering Live Oak trees that lined the streets of his quaint neighborhood as he made his way home. He focused on the details of every branch and wondered who planted these living giants, hundreds of years ago. As he passed by the charming little old houses, he enjoyed the picturesque scenery each provided. Many displayed beautiful roses, others had azaleas fencing the property, and many showered their beds with arrays of bright colored flowers. He ventured back in his mind to the field trip his class had taken earlier in the spring to Middleton Gardens, and he remembered how magnificent the dogwoods and azaleas were. The colors so vivid; it was a virtual wonderland of beauty. Spring was his favorite time of year. It was a new beginning of life as the harshness of winter gave way to the birth of spring and the promise of new hope. When his grandfather was alive, he had shown Jackson how to "look" at nature and concentrate on its artistry.

He would say, "Son, don't just walk by and not pay attention. There's a world of wonder out here that's good for your heart and music to your soul. All the worries of the world will fade away if you stop and look at our world. God made this world beautiful for us to enjoy, and it's our responsibility to notice and see his fingerprints on everything around us."

His grandfather's yard was home to every plant imaginable; it was a playground for the eyes. Jackson and his mom moved there after he passed away. Bees buzzed around every flower as they gathered their valuable nectar, their little legs transferring the magic pollen from one blossom to another. On his short trek home, he began really seeing the beauty around him for the first time.

As Jackson turned the corner for the last few blocks home, he looked left to cross the street and noticed three older boys on their bicycles headed his way.

"Hey, let's catch this punk and see if he's got any money," he heard one of them yell. Jackson turned again and realized the boys were racing toward him. He took off in a flash and was still several blocks from the safety of his home. The punks were gaining with every second, and Jackson had quite a way to go. Running with everything he had now, the gang was almost on him. As he dashed into his yard, the derelicts jumped off their bikes after him, and two of them tackled him to the ground. The moment Jackson's face hit the dirt, the air was silenced by the unmistakable sound of a 12-gauge pump shotgun chambering a round.

"Get off him, you little punk-ass kids!"

The gang of kids turned around to find out where those words came from and standing on his front porch with his shotgun pointing straight at them was Roy. Chief Roy Davis, a retired police officer, had moved in next door to Jackson a few years ago. He was a widower and kept an eye on Jackson and his mom.

"I told you punks to take your hands off him before I fill your stupid butts full of lead."

The ringleader of the bunch was a delinquent named Billy Barbatt. Jackson had seen Billy a few times in the neighborhood and saw him get arrested once for shoplifting at a local convenience store. One of Jackson's friends lived a couple houses down from Billy and had told him how Billy's dad was an alcoholic and would beat him during some of his drunken binges.

"I don't know what you boys' problem is, but if you ever come near Jackson again, you will regret it."

The boys slowly backed away from Jackson. "You can't shoot us old man," Billy shouted.

Roy pulled the trigger as he aimed at the ground by their feet. The boys scattered like they were on fire, crawling all over each other, scrambling to escape. They looked like a bunch of angry cats trying to avoid a bath. Jackson laughed so hard; he couldn't catch his breath. The punks grabbed their bikes and pedaled away as fast as they could.

"You weren't gonna kill them were you Roy?" Jackson asked timidly.

"Nah, there's just rock salt in them shells. It would have just given them a nice big welt on their stupid butts. What's their problem, anyway?"

"I'm not sure Roy. I was walking home, and it sounded like they wanted to rob me to try to buy beer. They can't be over 14."

"I'll keep an eye out for them and don't you worry Jackson. They ain't gonna bother you anymore."

"Are you sure?"

"Yeah. I've seen punk kids like that many times, and they are just looking for an easy target with no one around. Jackson, you don't need to worry your mom by telling her what happened out here unless you really think you should."

"She will worry, so I guess I'll wait to tell her unless something else comes up with those kids."

"Ok, buddy. Enjoy your summer. I'll be out here on the porch with my old dog Sam, and we'll keep watch. You have fun okay."

"Thanks, Roy. For everything."

"Don't mention it, kid."

When Jackson got inside, he pulled the window blinds back to make sure the boys weren't coming back. He was shaken and still a little nervous. Knowing Roy was next door helped out a lot. Jackson sat down at the small kitchen table of his old house and pulled the art magazine from his bag and continued to study it. His mom would be home soon, so he did his chores and waited for her to arrive.

Jackson's mom Leah came in after a long day at Dr. Harris' office, a local pediatrician. She was his office manager and overall keeper of the flame. Leah did everything there except prescribe medication. She greeted Jackson with a loving hug and asked him about his last day of school.

"Hey mom, look what I got today."

"What is it?"

"I got this cool magazine from Mrs. Mitchell's old book closet; look at this painting."

"Wow, that's beautiful." She smiled.

"This magazine is all about painting. It tells you everything you need to know. Do you think we could pick up a few supplies, so I can learn to paint?"

"Well it is the end of the school year, and you have made excellent grades, so I guess a little reward is in order. Let's grab something to eat first. We can go to the hobby store on the way home."

They got ready and piled into their old Ford station wagon. It was only Jackson and Leah around the house; Jackson's dad had left when he was in kindergarten. They divorced the next year. His mom worked two jobs to support them. One or two calls a month or a visit in the summer was all he saw of his dad.

"Where do you want to go for dinner Jackson?"

"Can we go to Buddy's steakhouse?" Jackson grinned.

CHAPTER FIVE

# The First Paint Set

Buddy's Steakhouse was Jackson's favorite restaurant on James Island, just a bridge away from the city of Charleston, South Carolina. Since his mom used to work there on weekends, he knew most of the cooks, and they always greeted him with a smile. He watched them prepare his steak as he passed through the line. The steaks were great, but the desserts tasted even better. The shelves were full of so many tantalizing treats, it was difficult to choose. He finally decided on the chocolate cake. They found a cozy table back in the corner and Rosie, their favorite waitress, stopped by to catch up.

"I heard congratulations are in order... someone is on their way to middle school. Fantastic job Jackson, I'm so proud of you."

"Thanks Rosie," Jackson said.

Rosie sat down in the booth next to him and gave him a big hug. He didn't mind at all. She was gorgeous, and her perfume smelled terrific. After a while, Jackson had finally finished his last bite of steak and started on his dessert.

"Hey mom, do you want some of my chocolate cake?"

"No thanks honey, you earned it; you enjoy it."

They finished dinner and headed to the hobby store for Jackson's paint supplies. As they walked the aisles, Jackson saw shelves full of every brand of paint and canvas imaginable, stacked from floor to ceiling. A friendly older lady came up to ask if they needed any help.

"Could you help us find a beginner's paint set?" Leah asked.

"Sure, follow me. They are right on the next aisle over."

"Wow mom, look at all the different sets they have. Which one should I choose?"

"How about this one?"

Leah pulled a large kit from the shelf.

Wary of his mom's finances, Jackson chose another nice, but cheaper one. She smiled and hugged him, realizing what he was doing. On nights like this, she wondered why? Why did her husband decide he didn't want to be married anymore? What happened to forever? What about loving someone for life? Why didn't people honor their wedding vows anymore? His lack of child support and trying to raise Jackson with what she made at the doctor's office was tough. Her face turned red, and she had to turn away, so he didn't see her eyes well up with tears. "Are you sure you don't want the bigger one?"

"Mom, this one is good for me to start with. I can pick that one up later."

Leah sighed to herself when Jackson decided not to get the more expensive set. Thankful; but still angry.

On the way back to the house, Jackson pulled the small paint set out of the bag and studied every word of the instructions. After he got home, he explored it further and realized the young artist in the magazine sold the paint supplies too. It had a detailed instruction book and several practice cardboard prints that were "paint by the number," just to get new painters started mixing colors. The last lesson showed how to take a picture and compose it onto a canvas. This made him more intrigued. Jackson loved all the pictures his mom would take of the Charleston area, and he had a lot to pick from.

Jackson set everything up in the back corner of the kitchen on a small table. He decided his first project would be a portrait of his favorite place; Folly Beach. Searching through his mom's old photo albums, he found a 5 x 7 of the Folly shoreline at sundown in the fall. The autumn sky displayed a beautiful myriad of colors that made him feel exhilarated. During the time he stood there touching the snapshot and reflecting on the scene, he felt the crisp fall wind touch his face. The ever-present seagulls squawked around him in relentless pursuit of their final meal before the sun sank low. There was something dramatically different about the picture now. When he touched it, Jackson felt like he was standing on the beach. After he removed his hand, he was just staring at the photograph. He continued exercising his newfound gift, touching it repeatedly while enjoying the experience of each touch. He touched it once more, but now, nothing. Nothing but the glossy snapshot. No sounds, no smells, no seagulls. He sat down and pondered whether he was dreaming again. This would be it. His first painting.

Jackson loved the beach. His mom took him there all the time. It didn't cost a lot, but a few hours listening to the waves and staring out into the deep blue ocean was healing for the body. As the tides made their perpetual journey back and forth, the landscape changed with every visit.

Leah had taken a shower and got ready for bed. "I have to work tomorrow at the Sand Dunes Club restaurant Jackson. I'll leave you a plate in the refrigerator for lunch. Have fun, but don't stay up too late."

CHAPTER SIX

# The Dream

Jackson worked for hours without stopping. When he finally gazed up at the clock, it was past one o'clock in the morning. He put on a few more last details and set his brush down. The new artist stood back and studied his handiwork. It wasn't quite like the picture, but still impressive for his first time. His thoughts were wildly spinning as he drifted off to sleep with visions of soft, warm sand in between his toes. That night he dreamed of becoming a famous painter. Right before he woke up, the most vivid of dreams played out. The story of his life ran through his mind; what would happen in high school, growing up and getting married and the twilight at the end of his life. Every detail was as sharp and focused as reality. When he awoke, his heart was beating fast, and he couldn't catch his breath. His entire life had just run before his eyes in his dream, but now, he couldn't remember any details at all. He lay still, concentrating, trying to recall.

Nothing.

Not a single detail remained.

His mom was down the hall in the kitchen getting breakfast ready. They didn't always have time for a big meal during the week, but on Saturday she made up for that with a huge feast. The smell of fresh bacon and eggs and buttermilk pancakes filled the air and wafted their way to Jackson's room. He opened his eyes and caught a peek at the clear blue sky outside. Jackson crawled out of bed and headed down to get something to eat. Leah saw a small glimpse of despair on his face and asked what was wrong.

"Mom, I dreamed the wildest dream I've ever had last night. It was about my life. It went through everything until..."

"Jackson...!"

Leah stopped him.

"You're still a young boy. How can you talk about the last chapter of your life?"

"That's just it. I don't know any details, and I can't recall anything specific. I know I went to high school and grew up and then at the end..."

"Jackson, stop."

"Everything felt so clear in my mind, but now I can't recall exactly what happened in my dream."

"Just remember it's just a dream. You have your whole life ahead of you. You don't have to worry about death for a long, long time. At least another hundred years or so. Let's change the subject please."

"Did you see my painting?"

"Yes, I did, it's absolutely beautiful. I can't believe you did all that in one day. What time did you go to bed?"

"It was kinda late, but I wanted to finish it."

"Jackson, Mrs. Weston called and asked if you would cut her grass and rake her yard today."

"Do I have to mom? It's summer vacation and she always makes me sweep that big driveway until every leaf is gone. Her whole house is under oak trees. Do you know how hard it is to get every single leaf? When I clean them off one side, I look over, and there's more on the other side. Those trees are leaf factories."

Leah laughed. "You need money for the summer, and I don't have a lot to give you. Summer is a longtime Jackson. I'll be working all summer. Mrs. Weston said she and her neighbors would keep you busy. You could earn some cash and stay out of trouble. Remember, those paint supplies aren't cheap. If you work hard all week, I'll take you to the hobby shop on Friday or Saturday to get more materials with what you make. You can't forget to save for a rainy day and give some of your money to help others at church too."

CHAPTER SEVEN

# The Art of Cutting Grass

Jackson got dressed and started the three block walk down the street to Mrs. Weston's house. As far as he could see, towering Live Oaks lined both sides of the road, their Spanish moss draping down and blowing in the breeze. Each gentle giant, an old friend to whoever found refuge from the sweltering summer sun under their enormous cover. The road he lived on used to be the grand entranceway to a plantation built over 200 years ago. He always wondered who planted those trees and if they had watched them grow. There's an old saying, "You don't plant oak trees for yourself; you plant them for your grandchildren." Jackson was glad someone planted these trees for their grandchildren. A few of his friends lived along this street too, and he had climbed several of these big Oaks himself.

About once a year, late in the spring after all the trees renewed their beautiful leaves, his mom would take him to the biggest Oak tree around. Just across the Stono River Bridge on John's Island stood the massive "Angel Oak." Visitors come from all over the country to see her sprawling branches. Locals say she is over 500 years old. Long ago, a landowner named Justis Angel and his wife donated the land for everyone to enjoy and that's where she got her name. Still, some tell of the ghosts of slaves that danced around the tree as angels. Her giant branches spread out everywhere in all directions. Angel Oaks canopy covered over 18,000 square feet. She was a beauty like no other. Jackson and Leah would make a picnic of it. They would set out early on Saturday morning, and when they arrived, Jackson would scale the giant tree like a squirrel. His mother would sit and read a book, careful not to look as he continued his ascent to the tips of her branches. After lunch, they would head back home and stop off for watermelon and boiled peanuts at a local fruit stand. They both looked forward to their little weekend trips. A little escape from reality to a place of incredible mystery and beauty. In the short walk to Mrs. Weston's house, his mind raced back to his times at "Angel Oak" and his summers playing along this street. He knocked on her door and waited. Mrs. Weston came to the door and greeted him good morning.

"Come on around to the garage Jackson and I'll meet you over there."

The garage door creaked and moaned as she slowly opened it to get her lawnmower. This wasn't just any lawnmower; this mower was electric. Mrs. Weston insisted on him using it. As he pulled the old antique out of its dusty storage, miles of extension cords followed. One pile was the size of a beachball. Once he got the cords untangled, he got started. If you've ever cut grass with an electric corded lawnmower, then you know what a pain it is. All those cords are enough to drive anyone crazy. He worked hard and was careful not to run over any of the extension cords as he ran the mower across her yard. It seemed like every turn was a chance at disaster. He wondered why anyone would have this contraption. To keep from electrocuting himself, took some exceptional skills.

Jackson finished the grass and raked up all the clippings. Now he had to sweep that long driveway. After what seemed like hours, Jackson made his way to the end of the drive. Still a little nervous from his run-in with the neighborhood derelicts, he stared down both ends of the road to make sure the coast was clear. When he walked back up to the front of the garage, he spotted more leaves on the driveway and laughed aloud.

"See, I told you."

His broom was fast as he swept the few stragglers off and rang the doorbell to get paid before any more fell. Mrs. Weston came out and inspected his work. She wanted him to do a few more things before she paid him.

"This lady is a pretty tough customer," Jackson thought.

As he was getting ready to leave, Mrs. Weston invited him to stay for lunch. She had been a widow for many years. Since she didn't have many visitors, Jackson graciously accepted her offer. Soup and chicken salad sandwiches with sweet tea were the special today. The gentle lady sat down with him at her small table and asked him if he wanted to say the blessing.

"No ma'am, can you do it please?" "Okay, I'll say it.

Jackson took a bite of his sandwich and was surprised how good it tasted. She had never asked him to eat with her before; why was today different?

"What are you going to do this summer?" Mrs. Weston asked.

"Well, I don't really know, I guess maybe I'll go to the beach a few times or hang out with my friends... the usual stuff."

"Are you going to try anything new this year? My daddy always told me I should never be afraid to learn something new. He even encouraged me to do as many things as I could make time for."

"Well, I tried something new last night Mrs. Weston.... I painted a picture of the beach."

"Where did you learn to do that?"

Jackson told her the story of finding the magazine at school and getting his paint set.

"I would like to see it sometime; maybe you can bring it the next time you come."

"Okay, I'll do that."

After they finished eating, Mrs. Weston showed Jackson a painting on her living room wall. It was a beautiful panoramic view of Folly Beach and the boardwalk that used to be there in the 1960's. The painting captured every detail using so many brilliant colors.

"Do you mind if I touch it?" He asked.

"Go ahead, just be careful."

Jackson softly ran his finger over every inch of the scenic picture, lost in all the hues displayed. At once, he felt like he was there. The westerly wind coming off the ocean warmed his face. He saw the lights of the Ferris wheel and heard the beachgoers playing skee ball and other arcade games, and they beckoned him closer. The stingy seagulls searched for a free meal, while two lovers held each other and gazed out into the Atlantic as if no one else mattered. He was there. Mrs. Weston finally interrupted "Well, I guess it's time for you to go. I'm sure you have a lot to do this summer."

Stunned back to reality, he moved his hand from the canvas and shook his head. This time, he wasn't dreaming. Something was happening, but he didn't know what.

"Thank you for lunch, Mrs. Weston. I enjoyed it. Thanks for showing me the painting. It was amazing."

"You're welcome, Jackson. Can you come back again soon?"

"Yes, ma'am."

CHAPTER EIGHT

# The First Commission

Two years had passed since Jackson began painting. His talents continued to improve, and his artwork adorned their home. He often tried to recreate the experience when he touched a finished canvas, but he never felt the same way again. Every day he would slide his finger along his first beach picture that hung in the kitchen, but nothing ever happened. With each project, he worked harder and harder to put as much detail as he could into every painting. He missed that feeling.

One Saturday afternoon when Jackson's mom Leah was working at the Sand Dunes Club restaurant, she brought in her birthday present from Jackson to show her friends. It was a beautiful depiction of the lighthouse on Morris Island at sunset. The Morris Island light had guided ancient mariners to a safe harbor in Charleston for centuries. Now the lighthouse stands a quiet watch, surrounded by the constant pounding of the waves at the end of Folly Island.

"Sarah, look at this painting Jackson painted for my birthday. Isn't it beautiful?"

Sarah Jessup was a great friend of Leah's and a newlywed working on her nursing degree. Leah handed the driftwood framed painting to Sarah. She stared at his landscape, absorbed in the colors and details.

"All I can say is WOW! I've never seen anything like this. The detail is amazing."

Leah spoke up, "He can take any picture and reproduce it on his canvas. I don't know how he does it." Just then, Steve Harris, owner of the restaurant stepped into the kitchen and overheard them talking. Sarah motioned towards Steve.

"Steve, come over here and take a look at this." She smiled as she handed him the painting.

"Who painted this?"

"Leah's 13-year-old son Jackson."

"How long has he been painting Leah? This picture is unbelievable."

Leah told him the story of Jackson's discovery of the magazine and his transformation from a young beginner to an expert.

"Do you think he could paint something for us here?"

"What did you have in mind?" Leah asked.

"Give me a little while, and I'll find something special."

Steve had built the Sand Dunes Club up from a small establishment to a Folly Beach favorite. It was tucked away a few miles from the beach, but still situated on the tranquil Folly River. It was home to one of the most famous places to watch the sunset across the river. The place was packed every weekend. A few hours into Leah's Saturday night shift, Steve returned with a picture one of his friends had taken on vacation to the area. The photo captured the restaurant on a beautiful fall evening with the Folly River in the background and the sun's rays displaying a palette of brilliant colors.

"Do you think Jackson could paint this on a huge 4' x 6' canvas? I'll drive him down to get whatever he needs, and I would pay him a good commission."

"Steve, he hasn't painted anything near that big, but I believe he can do it. I'll talk to him tonight and see if he is up to the challenge."

"Thanks, Leah. I can't wait to see it."

"Hold on a second Steve; he hasn't agreed to it yet."

"I know, but anyone who can paint something as good as your painting is ready to move on to something bigger."

Jackson took two weeks to complete his first commission. He worked on it every chance he got, and when he finished, the vast landscape looked like a window to the outside. It was so real. Not a detail was left out. Steve was so happy with his work he paid Jackson $500 and hung the painting in the main lobby on display for everyone to see. He took a picture of the young painter and posted it and a little biography next to the artwork, highlighting his masterpiece. Steve had never seen or heard of an artist with such an eye for color and detail, especially one who was only thirteen.

CHAPTER NINE

# Reality

"I'm sorry Ms. Henderson, but the compressor is worn out on your AC unit. A new one will cost you about $399 installed." The older, stocky AC technician explained to Leah. Jackson stood there looking at his mom as she slumped over the kitchen sink in silence looking out the window. Fear gripped her face, and the technician saw it.

"Would you like me to give you until tomorrow to think about it Ms. Henderson?"

"Yes Ralph, that'll be fine. I'll call you by 2:00 PM."

"Ok Ms. Henderson, have a nice day."

Leah thanked him and walked him to the door. She trudged back to the kitchen, holding her arms around her and stared out the window again, searching for answers. Jackson ran down to his room and opened his bank and pulled out the money he received from Steve for his painting. When he came back, she was sitting at the worn, round table with her head in her hands.

"Here mom, please take this and fix the air conditioner."

"I can't take your money for this Jackson; you earned this commission with your beautiful painting. I'll find a way to pay the bill.

"We're a family mom. It's just you and me. You've been taking care of me all my life. I should be able to help you whenever I can. God blessed me with that job because he knew that compressor was gonna break. Let me do my part. I'm getting older now." Leah sat at the kitchen table with tears in her eyes. She got up and hugged him and cried on his shoulder.

"Thank you, Jackson; you're so special."

"Mom, what if I can get other companies or businesses to buy my paintings? That was the biggest painting I've ever done. What if Mr. Steve told his friends and customers about me? I might pick up a few more jobs from him?"

"That would be great Jackson; I hope you do. I'll be on the lookout at work."

Within several months, patrons from the Sand Dunes Club restaurant gave him ten more commissions. All the while, Jackson kept getting better and better.

CHAPTER TEN

# The Bully

It must be over a hundred degrees today, Jackson thought as he boarded the aging school bus for the "interesting" ride home. This had been the first week of high school for Jackson in the ninth grade, and a heat wave had blanketed Charleston. Since September had just begun, there would be no reprieve from the stifling temperatures for two more months. He thought about that ride home and how every day ended differently. Some days, he would be left alone to talk to his friends or to think about his next painting project. Other days, Billy Barbatt, the resident bully of the 9th grade would see if he could push Jackson's buttons and get a rise out of him. Billy was that overweight, mean-spirited kid who had tried to rob Jackson back in the fifth grade. He was fresh off a stint in the local juvenile detention center for repeated shoplifting and other crimes. Since he'd failed several grades, Billy was in ninth grade with Jackson now. Over the last few years when he lived in the neighborhood, Billy mostly stayed away from Jackson. Old Chief Roy had moved closer to his children now and didn't live next door to Jackson anymore. Billy was three years older and about 60 pounds heavier than Jackson. Today, he turned his attention again to Jackson.

"Hey painter boy, why don't you paint me a picture for my birthday like you did for ol' Elizabeth here?"

Elizabeth scooted closer to the window.

Billy laughed and glanced around and realized no one else was. His face burned red, and he stared down his little minions. They all looked around, and a few of them half-heartedly joined in with him. Jackson ignored him and looked out the window at the towering old trees that lined the winding road home. He watched the moss that draped them dance in the wind and wished he was climbing one of them instead of riding that tin can bus. Billy continued his rant towards Jackson, growing angrier each time Jackson didn't say a word.

"Hey painter boy, I'm talking to you."

Jackson finally screamed at him, "Don't you and your trolls have a bridge you need to go hide under? Why are you always bullying people? Why do you have to be such a jerk?"

And with that, Billy's face turned as red as the passing fire truck, and he pounced on Jackson trying to land a good punch. The boys were scuffling over the seats when William, the driver pulled the bus over and broke up the fight. Being an old Marine who had fought in Korea and Vietnam, William was a formidable man. After he got back from the war, he had started up a successful "home cookin" restaurant with his wife. He retired a few years back and drove the bus because he loved kids and loved to be around them and help them out.

"Billy, you get your behind to the front and sit down and stop bothering people. You are gonna get your butt suspended again."

William leaned over to talk to Jackson. "Are you alright Jackson?"

"Yes, sir."

William walked up to the front of the bus and shook his head at Billy.

"Boy, when are you gonna grow up and quit bullying people?"

William moved closer to say something to the angry bully, and he looked him straight in the eye.

"Remember this boy; you might think you're tough and big and bad, but there is always someone tougher and bigger and badder than you are. And if you keep up this foolishness, you will learn that a lot sooner than you think."

Billy sighed loudly and sank down into his seat, still angry as a stirred-up beehive. William started the old clunker back on the way home and pointed a careful eye in the rear-view mirror at Jackson and the other students Billy tried to mess with. Billy just stared at Jackson, fuming mad.

They made it to the corner stop, and William opened the door. This stop wasn't just Jackson's; it was Billy's too. As Billy and the other kids walked off the bus, Jackson made his way to the front and frowned at William.

"Jackson, are you gonna be alright?" William asked.

"Yes sir, I'll be okay; thanks."

William stared at Billy on the street and said, "Remember what I told you, Billy."

Billy ignored him looking down at the pavement. The yellow beast slowly rolled out of sight, and Jackson dreaded seeing it disappear. He didn't want to fight; he just wanted to walk home in peace.

"You'll pay for that smart remark on the bus you little pansy."

And with that, Billy landed a right cross to Jackson's left eye. Jackson could taste the blood running down the back of his throat and felt his eye swelling. He dropped his books and yelled at Billy, "I don't want to fight. Why are you such a jackass to everyone? Why can't you mind your own business and leave us all alone?"

Billy threw another punch at Jackson, but this time, Jackson ducked and came back at him with an uppercut to Billy's chin that startled him. The blow didn't have the impact that Jackson had hoped for. Billy grabbed Jackson and wrestled him to the ground and drew back to hit him again when out of nowhere, a football came flying in and nailed Billy in the head. It came in with so much force it knocked Billy to the pavement. Jackson got up and brushed himself off. Billy pulled himself together and looked around to figure out what happened and standing there was Red.

Red was a towering young boy, with a full head of bright red curly hair and twice as big as Jackson. He yelled at Billy to pick on someone his own size. Billy was so surprised and shocked that he picked up his books and ran away promising to finish what he started. As he hurried away, he heard William's voice echoing in his mind as he rubbed his sore head.

Jackson didn't know what to make of Red until he reached out his hand. "Hi, my name's Red. Some folks call me Big Red."

His real name was Jimmy Brown, but everyone called him Red since kindergarten, so it stuck.

"Thanks for the help Red, but I had him right where I wanted him."

Red replied, "Yeah, I know, I could see that."

CHAPTER ELEVEN

# Big Red

"Hey Red, where are you from? I've never seen you around before."

"I just moved here from Michigan with my folks."

Jackson invited his new friend in for an afternoon snack. Since Red wasn't one for turning down food, he agreed, and they enjoyed the leftovers from the night before.

"Jackson, are you in high school here?"

"Yeah, I'm in the 9th grade. This was our first week."

"I'm in 9th grade too; maybe we can be in some of the same classes when I start on Monday."

"That would be great."

Red asked, "Would you mind showing me around?"

"Sure Red, I'll show you everything I know about this place."

Red got up from the table.

"Well, I guess I should get back and help my folks unpack. This is my first day here."

"Hey Red, do you have a bike?" Jackson asked.

"I sure do."

"Ask your parents if you can come over after dinner, and we can ride around the neighborhood, and I'll take you around then?"

"That would be cool, I'll see you later."

Red thanked him for lunch and headed out the door. Jackson began his chores and stopped by to look at a painting of the famed "Charleston Battery," that he started painting the night before. He loved walking along "the Battery" and gazing out into Charleston Harbor. The Battery was a centuries-old, protective seawall that ran along Charleston Harbor and many palatial houses adorned the streets behind it. Those majestic homes had front row seats as the shots rang out over Fort Sumter to begin the Civil War. His painting was dry from last night, and he loved to slowly run his fingers over every inch of the canvas, imagining himself in the scene. He stared for a few minutes looking at the dogwoods and the azaleas in full bloom and all the beautiful houses that guarded the harbor around Charleston. The feelings he once experienced when he touched his paintings before, began to slowly return. Some days, there was nothing. Other times, he was whisked away to where those pictures took him. Today he could feel something. As he was enjoying the breeze, the telephone rang and brought him back. His mom would be home in about an hour, and she asked him to start dinner. Even though he was young, Jackson knew how to do a lot. His mother and grandmother taught him how to cook when he was a little boy.

"That's how we did it growing up," his grandmother would always say. Jackson put an ensemble of traditional southern foods together that would have made her proud. When his mom got home, he told her about everything that happened that day and how he'd met Red.

Around 6:30 PM, Red knocked on the door and came in to meet Jackson's mom.

"Jackson told me about the incident at the bus stop, so I wanted to say thank you for helping him out."

"It's no problem, ma'am. That kid is a real bully. Hopefully, he won't mess with Jackson anymore. Jackson gave him a good uppercut."

Leah said, "I sure hope he doesn't bother him anymore. You boys be safe."

With only a couple of hours of sunshine left in the day, the boys hurried out the door.

"Hey, do you want to go down to the Fire Station and see the river?"

"What's the big deal about a fire station?" Red asked.

"I'll show you. It's an awesome place. You'll see."

The two raced out the driveway and down Plymouth Avenue to the Fire Station. The Fire Station was more than just the local fire station. It was a neighborhood hangout for kids of all ages. "The Fire Station," as the kids called it, was actually the whole area at the end of Plymouth Avenue and it was situated on one of the most iconic pieces of property on James Island. The fire station was there, of course, but there was also a boat landing that allowed access to the inter-coastal waterway on the Wappoo Cut river dug by the Army Corps of Engineers many years ago. Across the street was a beautiful park underneath towering trees where the kids could play. On the side of the real Fire Station, was a field where Jackson had played baseball and softball many summers. If anything was going on in the neighborhood, it would be at the schoolyard or down at the Fire Station. The boys rode down to the water's edge to look at the passing boats headed for Charleston Harbor. The two new pals stopped and looked out at the sun sinking low in the sky.

Red spoke up, "This is great! Is the water warm here?"

Jackson replied, "Yeah, it's like bathwater."

Red looked out across the river to the marsh on the other side. Stretched out in a long row across the water stood high voltage power lines as far as the eye could see.

"Have you ever swam across that river to that telephone pole on the other side?"

Jackson shook his head no. "But I could if I wanted to," as he swallowed hard.

"What do you think about trying to swim across it one day?"

Not wanting to disappoint his new friend, Jackson agreed. The boys watched for a long time, and when Jackson looked back across the river to the bank on the other side, it seemed as wide as an ocean.

Jackson said, "It's getting late, I need to get back home, I can show you some more of the neighborhood tomorrow."

"That would be great; I had a fun time. I think I'll like it here."

The boys headed back down the street and parted ways a few blocks before Jackson's house. Just as a few fireflies lit the night sky, Jackson opened the front door.

"I was wondering when you'd be back," said his mom.

"Hey mom, I showed Red around the neighborhood and the Fire Station."

"Jackson, how old is Red? He looks a lot older than you."

"He's fourteen, just like me. We're the same age, but did you see how big he is? They must feed them something different up in Michigan," Jackson chuckled.

"We had a lot of fun. Red thinks he'll be happy here. I'm gonna show him around again tomorrow."

Monday came, and the kids were back at the bus stop. This time Red was with Jackson, ready for his first day of school in South Carolina. Jackson introduced him to all the kids at the bus stop, and Red caught the attention of a little brunette named Gina Lenty. Right before the bus came, Billy walked up still sporting the bruise from that football to the head on Friday. He took one look at Red and his whole attitude changed. He tried to be nice to the kids at the corner, but they all knew he was faking. Each one turned away to continue their conversations. They all saw what happened on Friday and were glad Billy got a little reality check. The rest of the school year, Red and Jackson remained inseparable. If they weren't working somewhere cutting grass, they were all over the neighborhood playing whatever sport was in season. Some days they would sneak out and get in a few holes at sundown on the golf course. Other times, they fished or played basketball or a pickup game of football. Jackson had wanted to play football for James Island High School, but he had to work to help his mother make ends meet. In the evenings, Jackson continued to paint. He became so involved, that he would lose track of time, and the small clock in the kitchen would sound the bell for midnight, summoning him to sleep. The recession had taken its toll on the economy, and the regular commissions weren't as many as in the past, but he still sold a few paintings every so often. It wasn't enough to help his mom like he wanted to, so he decided he would find a steady job and supplement their income with paintings whenever he could.

CHAPTER TWELVE

# A Real Job

One afternoon, Jackson came home through the back door, but his mom Leah didn't hear him come in. She was on the phone with the mortgage company and didn't notice him.

"I can't pay that much in taxes. That's outrageous. This house is barely over 1200 square feet. How can the taxes go up so much?"

"I'm sorry ma'am, we must go by what the city sends us, I'm sorry."

"Well sorry won't help me pay my mortgage. Is there any way I could get an extension or break up the payments?"

"Well ma'am, you can pay the taxes quarterly, but a small fee is assessed to do that."

"There is no way I'll be able to come up with an extra $200 per month. I already work two jobs as it is."

"You can get a thirty-day extension ma'am, but that will be it, and then you must pay the taxes."

"Well, what happens if I can't pay the taxes?"

"We can give you a little time Ms. Henderson, but if the taxes aren't paid, the city will begin foreclosure proceedings after three months."

Leah's heart was pulsing, and tears rolled down the corner of her cheeks. Jackson heard the whole thing. He didn't mean to, but since Leah didn't realize he was home, he knew this was bad and didn't turn away. By now he was mad but couldn't show it to his mom. Why did his dad leave them in such a mess? He thought, "I've got to do something. We can't lose our house."

Jackson slowly crept his way out the back door and then came back inside again, making enough noise to wake the neighbors. Leah struggled to wipe her face and not let on that something was wrong.

"Hey Jackson, where have you been?"

"I was at Red's playing Ping-Pong with him and his dad. Red's quick for such a big guy. He beat me 3 out of 5 games."

"Are you hungry? I'll fix us something."

"Ok, mom that sounds good. Do you want any help?"

"No, I can take care of it. How about go clean up your room and by the time you're finished, I'll have dinner ready?"

While they were eating, Jackson hinted around to his mom about making more money. The recent commissions for his paintings weren't enough steady income for them. Even though he continued to improve with every artwork, he wasn't as recognized around town as he could be.

"Hey mom, I need to get a normal job where I can make some money to help out. I would like to look for something I can do with good hours and regular pay."

"Jackson, you're not even 16 yet, and you're talking like a man with a family. You're still my only child, and I want your childhood to be normal. We'll make do."

"I will have a childhood mom. Red and I can still have fun and hang out when I'm not working, or he's not working. He'll be working with his dad after school and on weekends too. He needs money just like me. We still need to live, and if I can help you with the bills, then I should do it. I've learned how to do a lot these last few years, and I'm getting bigger and stronger. I just need someone to give me a chance."

CHAPTER THIRTEEN

# Jackson's First Job

Work was nothing new to Jackson. He had been doing odd jobs for all the old ladies in the neighborhood since he could hold a rake. In the wise words of his grandfather, "You work, you get paid. You don't work; you don't get paid. That's how life works Jackson. Hard work makes a man out of you. It puts food on the table, and it keeps you motivated to be doing the right things."

Jackson knew everyone at church and had done many jobs for many of them over the years. He helped put on roofs and build houses working with a local carpenter from the church. All Jackson needed was an opportunity. Most of the regular grass cutting and raking jobs he used to rely on, slowly went away and made it difficult to earn money. New, younger families moved into the neighborhood, and they didn't seem to need any help with their yard work. He wasn't quite 16 years old yet, but he had heard some of his friends found jobs in different areas like construction helpers or tomato packers on Johns Island. He looked in the classifieds and called several companies that were hiring. When he told them his age, they all said sorry, they couldn't hire someone that young. He got turned down by every place he stopped. Jackson finally picked up a small job folding newspapers for the carriers of a local community paper. They paid by the bundle of papers wrapped, and the kids who wrapped papers in the old dark and dank warehouse were derelicts. He tired of the mundane work and the silly comments of some of the workers. Jackson wanted to do something fun and something that helped people. It was the first Saturday of summer and Jackson wanted to get a head start on finding a real job.

The Cracked Egg diner was his favorite breakfast spot, and he stopped in to grab something to eat. As Jackson thumbed through the classifieds, he came across a help-wanted ad at a local garage up the road from where he was. He finished his breakfast, hopped on his bicycle and pedaled his way over to the garage. As he pulled up, he was surprised how clean and well-kept the garage was. The asphalt parking lot looked freshly paved and was neatly painted. Grand, beautiful old oaks and magnolias lined the property. The building was brightly colored, and the windows were clear as a bell. All seven stalls were full. The waiting area was packed with customers, and a local program played on TV. The smell of fresh coffee and cinnamon rolls wafted through the air. He walked to the side of the building and glanced in at the mechanics working. Jackson had done a lot of jobs in his short life, but he wasn't a full-fledged mechanic. His hands were shaking, and he was nervous, but he needed a job. He had been turned down so many times, he was losing hope. Jackson finally got the nerve to go in, and as he opened the door, a little welcome bell rang, and he was greeted by an older black gentleman in his late 40's. His hair and mustache were gray, and the crow's feet around his eyes told a story of a hard-working life. Jackson walked up to the counter and introduced himself to the man and said he came to answer the ad in the paper. The kind man behind the counter introduced himself as Willie, and he smiled at Jackson as he listened to him talk.

"Hi Jackson, you say you're looking for a job, huh?"

"Yes sir," Jackson said, standing up straight.

"How much experience do you have as a mechanic?" Mr. Willie asked.

"Well sir, I have fixed my lawnmower more times than I care to remember, and I've helped start my mom's old Ford a few times too."

"Is that right?" Mr. Willie laughed.

"Yes, sir."

"Jackson, you're a nice young man, and I appreciate you coming in, but I need an experienced mechanic to help out around here. These cars keep getting more complicated to take care of every year."

Jackson lowered his head in disappointment.

"I'm a hard worker and a fast learner. A hundred places have turned me down and said I'm too young. I just need a chance."

Mr. Willie's heart sank, "I'm sorry son; I need someone that can go to work right away. Maybe you can try back when you're a little older?"

Jackson backed away from the counter, thanked Mr. Willie and walked out the door. Mr. Willie watched the disheartened young man through the glass door. He couldn't help but wonder whether he was doing the right thing. Jackson hopped on his bike and turned it towards home, and as he pedaled away, Mr. Willie came running out of the garage.

"Hey Jackson, hang on for a minute."

Jackson stopped and turned around.

"Maybe we can give you a try. This work ain't easy, and you won't get any slack around here. You'll have to pick up everything quickly and do whatever the guys tell you, but if you'll listen and pay attention, you can learn a lot, and it's something that can help you in life."

"Oh, I will Mr. Willie, when can I start?"

"Hold on a minute Jackson, how about you come inside and fill out a little paperwork? I don't even know your last name or where you live."

Jackson put up his bike and almost couldn't contain himself. He filled out the paperwork for Mr. Willie then bolted out the door after Mr. Willie told him he could start on Monday. When Jackson flew out the door of the garage, Mr. Willie picked up the phone.

"Ms. Henderson, this is Willie Brown from the Island Garage. Jackson just stopped by and asked for a job. I have been looking for someone, but he's not experienced, and he's only 15. I told him I needed someone with more experience, but his face looked so sad, my heart couldn't stand to tell him no. Would you mind if he worked down here? We'll take good care of him."

Jackson's mom was silent for a few seconds and then said "Thank you, Mr. Willie, for giving him a chance. He's a special young boy, and he's willing to learn if you'll teach him. He picks things up fast, he works hard, and he's honest."

Leah remembered Mr. Willie from several years ago when her car was having trouble as she was headed to Folly Beach with Jackson. She had pulled in for some help thinking her car was going to break down, and Mr. Willie diagnosed the problem right away. It was a small vacuum leak. He installed a new vacuum hose for her, and she was on her way. He didn't even charge her. She had thanked him profusely and tried to pay him, but he said it wasn't necessary. Leah remembered his kind smile and caring demeanor. Mr. Willie was smiling when he hung up the phone looking at the picture of his family behind the counter. He touched the picture and thought how much he missed them, and then he touched the face of his young son. He shook his head then turned and headed into the garage.

CHAPTER FOURTEEN

# The Garage

"Hey, Mom guess what?" Jackson asked, as he ran inside.

"What's all the fuss about?" Leah smiled.

"I got a job today. Mr. Willie hired me down at the Island Garage. I can start Monday."

"Whoa, wait a minute. You got a job at a garage? You haven't even talked to me about it."

"Can I mom? I have been to so many places, and they all turned me down. Mr. Willie was willing to give me a chance, and I don't want to let him down."

"It's a dangerous place down there. I'm not sure about this."

"C'mon mom, I'm almost 16?"

"How are you going to get to work every day this summer? The garage is almost seven miles from here. I can't take you every day; I have to be at work early."

"I'll ride my bike mom; seven miles is nothing."

"Okay Jackson, but you better be careful and listen to Mr. Willie. I don't want something to happen to you down there."

Monday came, and Jackson pedaled his bike all the way to the garage. In fact, he showed up 30 minutes early. As soon as he pulled up, he saw the lights of Mr. Willie's truck as he arrived.

"Hey, Good Morning Jackson. I see you're ready to get started."

"Yes Sir, I sure am."

Mr. Willie smiled and whistled as he unlocked the door and went inside.

"Hey Jackson, do you know how to make coffee?"

"Sure, I make it for my mom all the time. This coffee pot looks a little bigger than ours, so if you wouldn't mind, tell me how many scoops this time and I'll remember after that."

Mr. Willie laughed and showed him how to make the coffee. As Jackson stood there watching the pot brewing, the wonderful smell brought back many fond memories for Jackson of sitting at the kitchen table in a small nook in his house listening to his grandfather and great-uncle talk over coffee. Jackson would ask for a cup, and his grandfather would pour him a little coffee, a lot of milk and a lot of sugar into the cup. Jackson remembered stirring his coffee like they did and listening to their stories. That small little nook in the house was where everything happened. Meals were shared, games were played, and lessons were taught. It seemed so large back then, but as he got older, it began to shrink. When the coffee finished brewing, Mr. Willie said, "Pour us a cup and let's see how you did."

Mr. Willie put a little sugar and a little creamer in his coffee, stirred it up and took his first sip. Jackson's heart fluttered, waiting for Mr. Willie's approval.

"Hey now, that's a good cup of Joe. Make it like that every day Jackson. That will be your first job when you arrive in the morning. If you make good coffee, you'll get on the good side of the boys right away."

Jackson smiled and promised he would remember. He looked around at everything in the break room and noticed how clean it was. Everything was neat and shiny, everything was in its place, and the room was bright. He thought to himself, "This place looks a lot different than I expected."

"Before everyone gets here, let me show you around the garage and let you know what you're gonna be doing."

Mr. Willie showed him the waiting room, the storage room and finally the main garage. The place was immaculate. Jackson had never seen a garage or any other business so clean. Even the area where they put the used motor oil stayed neat and tidy. Each bay in the garage had its own set of tools. Each one put in its place. As they walked through the garage, Mr. Willie turned on all the lights and walked to the back and started up the big air compressor for all the pneumatic tools. He took Jackson into the storeroom and gave him his uniforms, safety glasses and two pairs of mechanic's gloves.

"These gloves will keep your hands safe and clean. You don't want a pretty girl to hold your hand and get all greasy now do you?" Mr. Willie laughed.

Jackson's face turned red as he grinned.

"Did you pay attention as we went through the garage? All the things we did this morning, I would like you to do every morning. Be here around 6:30 AM, get the coffee going and get the place ready for when the boys show up. They show up around 7:00 AM and we open at 7:30 AM. Stephen will be along in a few minutes; he cleans up around here for us. He's real quiet, but he does a great job as you can see. This place didn't always look like this."

"Who's Stephen?"

"He's a young man I met a while back. Stephen and I first met down at the corner stoplight where he sold newspapers every day. I was in my truck, stopped behind a school bus on my way to pick up a part for a customer's car. These kids hopped off the bus and walked over to where he was selling his papers. They teased him and then one of the kids turned his whole pile of newspapers over and kicked a few of them out into the street. I pulled my truck over and ran those punk kids off then I helped him clean up his papers. He cried, and I was mad as a hornet at how they picked on him. I can't stand bullies. Stephen was 19 then, and he has Down's Syndrome. He is a pretty big boy too, and he could've beat up all those punk kids at one time if he wanted to, but he's a gentle giant and wouldn't hurt a fly. I couldn't stand to think about those kids bothering him every day, so I asked him if he would like to work with me down at the garage. His parents agreed to let him work here. On his first day, he got here an hour early. I asked his folks what he could do, and they told me to teach him what I wanted, and he would figure it out. At first, I had him helping bring parts and tires out to the mechanics, then one day we were all standing around in the garage shooting the breeze when he looked around and said how messy this place was and how he was going to clean it up. Guess what? He did. I got him a few basic cleaning supplies, and he went to town. The waiting area was first, and he cleaned and scrubbed every square inch of this place until it was all shining. He did such a good job he made the mechanics feel guilty that they weren't doing more to clean up. Instead of throwing their tools in the toolbox they would put them back neatly. When before, they would have left drops of oil on the floor, now he had them wiping them up. Before you knew it, everyone pitched in keeping this place clean. He made me really think about this place. The outside of the building and the waiting area were old and outdated, so we did some scraping and painting and put in new lights, and the place sparkled. All the customers commented on how good the place looked and how it made them feel welcome. We gained a lot of customers because of that. Stephen has brought a lot to this garage. He doesn't talk a lot, but he works like nobody's business. I even have to stop him sometimes at lunch to take a break and have a sandwich with us. I buy lunch for all the guys on Friday, and Stephen goes and gets it down at the store on his bike. You'll like him. If you need help to lift something, he's your man. He's as strong as an ox. All the guys here have taken a liking to him, except this new guy I just hired, Bobby. He doesn't seem to care for him too much. Bobby's been here about six months, and I've had to talk to him a few times about how he talks to Stephen. He called him a retard a few times, and when I heard it, I called him into my office and chewed his butt out. I told him there wouldn't be any of that here. He half-heartedly apologized to Stephen, but I'm still not too sure about this guy. I hired him because he just got out of tech school and he knows how to work on some of these fancy new cars. Try to stay clear of him. You should be okay with all the other guys."

The clock approached 7:20 AM and Stephen and the other guys meandered into the garage. Mr. Willie called them all around to meet Jackson. The first mechanic, Ralphie Johnson, was a massive, round, red-bearded mountain of a man. Then came Boots Hart, a skinny Vietnam vet with a thick mustache and old cowboy boots. Next was JD Richardson, a mid-thirties black man with a kind smile and finally, there was Skeeter Miller. Skeeter was a skinny man with long hair who never stopped talking. They all welcomed Jackson, and he shook each one of their hands trying to give as firm a handshake as he could muster. Each one of them "crushed" his hand. The years of work repairing cars had given each one of them a formidable grip. By the time they finished saying hi, he felt like his hand had been in a vice. All the guys headed to their tools and Jackson looked around, but he didn't see Bobby.

"Hey Mr. Willie, where's Bobby?"

"He'll probably be around in a few minutes; he's late a lot."

About 7:45 AM Bobby strolled in while the other guys had already begun their day. Mr. Willie called him into his office and talked to him about being late again, but Bobby gave him another excuse. Mr. Willie told him how important being on time was, but Bobby didn't seem to listen. He was the know-it-all you always seem to find. No matter where you go, there always seems to be at least one. When the door opened, and Bobby came out, Jackson saw the frustrated look on Mr. Willie's face. He shook his head and walked out of his office and headed over to the counter.  He looked at Jackson and smiled and said; "Bobby needs to take a few lessons from you. You know how important it is to be on time don't you?"

Jackson cleared his voice and said, "Yes Sir, my granddad taught me if you can't be on time, be early."

Mr. Willie chuckled, "I think my granddad told me that too. Those are good words to live by."

Jackson looked around the well-lit waiting room and on the wall behind the counter hung a beautiful 8" x 10" picture of a young Mr. Willie, a beautiful woman, and a young boy. They looked to be his family. Even though the picture looked old, the colors were still vibrant. Mr. Willie saw Jackson looking at the picture, and the tone of his voice lowered.

"That's a picture of my family and me on the day we bought the garage."

"How old is your son now?"

Mr. Willie was silent for a few minutes; then he looked at Jackson.

"He was seven in that picture. He would have been 27 this month. They both died in a car accident many years ago. They were coming back home from her sister's house at night in the dark on Riverland Drive, and a deer ran out into the road out of nowhere. She swerved to keep from hitting it and ran into one of those giant oak trees that line the road. We didn't have car seats back then, so my little boy got thrown into the windshield." Jackson's heart melted as Mr. Willie continued his story.

"They always went to her sister's house every week on Tuesday, and they left at the same time, so when they didn't show up back home like I expected them to, I went looking for them. I saw all the red and blue lights, and as I got closer, my heart sank lower than it ever had before when I realized it was her car. I ran over to them, and they were both unconscious. They put them in the ambulance, and I rode with them on the way to the hospital, crying and praying that God would bring them back to me. I sat in the middle of the ambulance holding each of their hands as the paramedics worked on them. My wife opened her eyes and smiled at me and squeezed my hand and quietly said I'll see you again my love. Then she closed her eyes and drifted towards Heaven. My eyes filled up with tears, and I thought my heart would explode. I leaned down to kiss her beautiful face once more. I couldn't believe this was happening. The paramedics tried to console me, but how could I be comforted? I looked over at my son as the paramedics feverishly worked on him. His kind little face; he was going to be such a wonderful boy. They did everything they could, and he was such a strong little fella, but he died before we made it downtown to the hospital. There I was in an ambulance with my whole family gone. Everything was going on around me, but I couldn't hear anything. My heart and head pounded, and I couldn't believe this was really happening. I fell face down on the floor of that ambulance and cried right there. That was the last thing I remember; I guess I passed out, because when I woke up, I was in the hospital and all the boys from the garage were standing around my bed, and they had the most solemn look on all their faces. I thought maybe I had been dreaming, but then the doctor came in and asked me if I remembered what had happened. It all came back again, and I knew I wasn't dreaming, I was living a nightmare. I nodded my head; I didn't say anything. I couldn't bring myself to say their names out loud. My wife's sister and her husband came into the room as well as the pastor of our church, and each one came and held my hand and didn't say a word. William, my old friend, came in with them too. They knew there was nothing they could say that would make any difference. They stayed there by my side along with all the boys from the garage. After a few hours, the hospital people came in and wanted me to sign some papers, so we could prepare their final arrangements. No one had left the room for the last few hours. I sat up in the bed, and I talked with them and signed the papers. I thanked all of them for coming and asked them to go because I wouldn't be staying. They hesitantly did what I asked and then went one by one. My sister finally made it in from out of town right before I was about to leave and came and hugged me as hard as she could. She helped me get my things and get out of there. We made it home, and she stayed with me for the next month. I didn't leave the house for a whole week. After the funeral, I stayed in bed and tried to sleep, hoping it was just a nightmare, but every day I got up, the nightmare was real. Ralphie and all the boys took good care of things down at the garage for me while I was gone. They brought me food every day for a month. There's never a day that goes by that I don't think about my family and what could have been. That picture behind the counter makes me happy every day when I see their faces, and I remember them and that day like it was yesterday."

Jackson cleared his throat. "I'm so sorry that happened to you, Mr. Willie. I couldn't imagine anything like that."

"Jackson, I'm sorry to put that all on you on your first day here."

"It's okay Mr. Willie; I'm glad you told me."

Mr. Willie composed himself and said "at least I got to have them for a short time. That's sure better than never having them at all. I'll see them again in Heaven someday."

Mr. Willie gave Jackson a checklist to use every day when he arrived, so he wouldn't forget anything. Mr. Willie was very organized and wanted things done right the first time. All week long, Jackson arrived early and got everything ready to start the day and stayed late and helped Stephen cleanup. He assisted every mechanic on one kind of job or another. By the end of the week, Jackson knew his way around the garage, so Mr. Willie took him to the tire machine and showed him how to "bust tires."

"Bust tires, what do you mean by that?" Jackson asked.

Mr. Willie laughed, "We just call it busting tires because you're busting them off the rim."

Mr. Willie then taught him everything there was to know about a tire. By the end of the next week, Jackson was "busting tires" with the best of them. Even though Jackson was young, he was turning into a strong, handsome man. He was a slender 6 foot and 180 pounds, and his light sandy brown hair was a little curlier now. His arms were chiseled, and the veins of his biceps bulged each time he picked up a tire or turned a wrench. By the end of the month, he had won over all the mechanics. Each one wanted him to help them out. The mechanics liked how he would listen intently to them and learn as much as he could and work hard.

Mr. Willie told him, "God gave you two ears to listen and one mouth to talk, so you should always listen more than you talk. There are always things that you learn about people just by watching them. These are things that aren't written in a book; intangible things, like how big someone's heart is. These are things you can't measure. Jackson watched and listened carefully to every word. It was getting close to closing time, and Mr. Willie stopped by to talk to Jackson.

"Hey Jackson, do you like to fish?"

"Yes sir, I sure do. I even have my grandpa's old fishing rod and tackle box. He took me fishing a few times before he passed away. We always fished in a pond or by the riverbank. I've never been in a boat and fished."

"Hey, how about calling your mom and asking her if you can go fishing with me this afternoon? Low tide is in a couple of hours, and that's the best time to fish. It's supposed to be calm tonight. No wind. That's perfect for some flounder gigging too. Ask her if you can stay out until about 10 o'clock."

Jackson was excited the rest of the day. There was something about the gentle, quiet life of the salt marsh that he loved. If you looked closely enough, you could see the lonely Great Blue Heron on its silent vigil for its dinner or watch hundreds of fiddler crabs dodging the Sandlapper's quick beak. It was a magical place.

"Mr. Willie, my mom said I could go. Can we stop by my house to pick up my fishing stuff?"

"Sure, let's clean up in here, and we'll head that way. I have the boat ready to go, and it's all packed up. We can stop by D's on the way out and get a "to go" box for dinner."

CHAPTER FIFTEEN

# The Art of Fishing

Jackson was excited about his first boating trip. He lived a few short blocks from the water all his life, but he had never known anyone with a boat. They put the boat in the water and headed out to a special creek along the Stono River where Mr. Willie said some "big ones" lived. Jackson loved the smell of the salt water and the breeze in his face. The sun was heading down, but the sky remained brightly lit. Mr. Willie pulled up to a small little cove and pulled out his cast net to get them some "live bait."

"Ok Jackson, when I pull the net back in, grab the shrimp and put them in the live well. Be careful though, they have sharp points on them, and they'll stick you bad if you're not careful."

Mr. Willie sent the cast net out in a perfect spiral and pulled it back in slowly. As he began, Jackson could see the net teeming with shrimp. Mr. Willie swung the net into the middle of the boat and dumped it. About 50 shrimp bounced all around as Jackson scurried to catch them and put them in the live well. Mr. Willie made another cast and brought in another net full. He continued a few more times, and finally, they had enough to fish. They made their way around another cove to where the rivers came together, and they dropped anchor. Mr. Willie showed Jackson how to rig up his line and what to look for and when to set the hook on the fish. A few peaceful minutes passed, and Jackson had one on his line. Mr. Willie talked him through it and netted him when he got close to the boat. Jackson smiled from ear to ear for the camera as Mr. Willie took his picture.

"That must be an 8-pound Spot tail. That's a great fish." Mr. Willie grinned.

"That was awesome, that's the biggest fish I ever caught."

They sat there for a few more hours, talking about fishing and about life. Mr. Willie told him the story of how he met his wife when he was young. They talked about how important integrity and honesty were. He also said how important it was to make the right decision about the woman he would marry.

"Jackson, you'll meet a lot of women along the way, but there's only one special woman who will steal your heart. That's when you'll know what love is. You won't know what to do without her. I couldn't stand to be away from my wife. She used to work with me at the garage. She kept the books and made appointments. I could grab a kiss from her anytime I wanted. It was wonderful. When we first got married, I was in the Marines. It was tough when I would deploy and have to leave her. My stomach got all twisted up in knots, and it turned upside down every single time I had to tear myself away from her to report for duty. Just make sure you know you have the right woman. It has to be right; otherwise, your life will be miserable. If it's right, life is fantastic. That woman can make you a better man. You'll always want to show her how much you care, and you'll want to work harder in everything you do to make her proud."

Mr. Willie's words resonated in Jackson's heart as the sun sank low in the Western sky.

"I hope I get to find someone as special as your wife, Mr. Willie."

Mr. Willie smiled as he cast his line again for the last time.

"It's getting late. Let's go up there around the bend and gig for some flounder."

The last few glints of sunlight evaporated as the moon began to rise. The water was as smooth as black glass. Mr. Willie lit the fishing lanterns and pulled out the gigging poles.

"The object of gigging is simple, we take these long gig poles, and we move the boat along this shallow cove. When we see a flounder buried in the sand, you gig him and push all the way through; then you bring him into the boat."

Mr. Willie had a nice setup on his boat with marine-grade halogen lanterns angled down over the murky water. You could see the fish and crabs scurrying below.

"It's too shallow in here to run the engine, so I'll have to pull it up. You and I can move along the bank by using the gigging poles."

They got started, and everything was still. The sun was down, but twilight still lit up the sky. Mr. Willie broke the silence with a funny sentiment.

"Tonight, is perfect for gigging. There's no wind. If it's too windy, the water is too cloudy, and you can't see the flounder. It's so quiet right now you could hear a gnat fart."

With that, Jackson laughed so hard he almost fell out of the boat. As they made their way back to the boat landing, Jackson said, "I'm sorry you didn't catch anything today Mr. Willie."

"It's okay Jackson; you don't go fishing just to catch fish. Being out here is good for your soul. It makes you appreciate the beautiful Earth God made for us. It gives you time to think. If you get to catch a fish, that's just an added bonus."

CHAPTER SIXTEEN

# The Unexpected

The sound of a screeching horn rang out through the garage and startled everyone as Bobby flew into an open bay with a customer's car for repairs. Stephen had been mopping that bay and scrambled out of the way just in time to keep from getting hit. Mr. Willie watched the whole thing while he was talking with Ralphie. Bobby jumped out of the car and was quickly met by Mr. Willie.

"What the heck are you doing driving like that in here? I've told you we don't do business like that in here. You could have killed Stephen. Boy, what's wrong with you?"

Bobby looked at him and said, "Sorry man, maybe he should clean up a little faster; I got work to do." Mr. Willie sighed, then gave Bobby the most serious look Jackson had ever seen.

"Come over here, boy."

Bobby sauntered over to where Mr. Willie stood in the corner of the garage. Mr. Willie turned where his back was to everyone. He and Bobby went through a heated exchange back and forth. No one could hear what they were saying, but they could see Mr. Willie was furious. Mr. Willie turned around and headed into the garage to check on Stephen. After he made sure Stephen was alright, he turned again to Bobby.

"Look, Bobby, you're a good mechanic, but I've told you several times that you need to work safer. I know you can do things quickly, and you can move on to the next job, but taking shortcuts and hurrying all the time is gonna get you or someone else hurt or killed. If we have to take an extra fifteen minutes to do it safely, then that's what we're gonna do. If you can't abide by that, then I'll have to let you go."

Bobby rolled his eyes and started to walk past Mr. Willie, and suddenly Mr. Willie stepped in his path and Bobby stopped in his tracks.

"Listen to me boy; you better understand where I'm coming from because I won't have this kind of nonsense around here. Period. I'm responsible for everyone in here. You got that!"

"Yeah, I got it. Now can I go back to work dad...?"

Mr. Willie stepped out of the way and let Bobby go back to work, but he shook his head in disgust as he walked away. Everyone in the garage watched the whole thing. Mr. Willie realized that as he walked back to the office and looked around at everyone staring at him. He glared at each one without saying a word, and they all knew he was deadly serious. Everyone scrambled back to work. Mr. Willie was always a mild-mannered man, and no one had ever seen him that angry. Jackson asked Skeeter if he had ever seen him like that.

"I have worked here for nearly 14 years, and I haven't seen Willie riled up about anything; then again, we never had any guys in here that did things like Bobby does."

Jackson didn't care too much for Bobby either. Bobby chastised Jackson many times about how long it took him to patch a tire. Mr. Willie taught Jackson how to patch a tire, and he always emphasized how important it was to do it right and make sure it was a good patch.

"Someone is counting on this tire to get them home safely. I want you to patch every tire like it was your own mother's tire and make sure it's done well, so it holds."

"Hurry up Jackson, you're as slow as my 90-year-old grandma," Bobby shouted as Jackson was working on a customer's tire. Almost every day, Bobby would find something to mess with Jackson about.

"I'm doing this just like Mr. Willie told me, and you can stick it where the sun don't shine."

The rest of the afternoon went off without incident. About an hour before closing, a girl that Bobby knew pulled in and needed two new front tires and an oil change. Bobby pulled her car into his bay and began jacking it up with the two-ton floor jack. He used the impact wrench and removed her front left tire. Then he slid under the car with the recycling oil pan to get to the drip pan bolt to drain the oil. Mr. Willie came out of the lobby in time to see him under the car and yelled at him to come out.

"What's the fuss old man?"

"Bobby, I told you to never crawl under a car without the jack stands and the floor jack."

"All the jack stands are being used right now," Bobby replied.

"Then you'll just have to wait."

He turned around and walked down to tell JD something and then headed back to the lobby to wait on another customer. Bobby looked around and became impatient, so he made sure Mr. Willie wasn't looking, then he slid back under the car to loosen the drip pan bolt. The bolt was about a foot from the front left tire, and the floor jack had lifted the car under the driver's side fender. As he loosened the bolt, his grip slipped and hit the handle to the floor jack. The floor jack slid sideways under the wheel well and fell on its side, and the weight of the car came crashing down on Bobby's chest.

A blood-curdling scream echoed throughout the busy shop. The scream was so loud; it immediately sent Jackson and the garage on an adrenaline rush. Jackson was the closest to Bobby and ran to help. The jack was caught up underneath the front fender, but it was on its side, so he couldn't use it to lift the car. Jackson screamed for help and kneeled down and turned around to lift up the car using all the strength he could muster. He put his back into it and grabbed onto the vehicle and lifted as hard as he could with everything he had, but he only managed to raise the car a little. He took another deep breath and dug down deep, but he couldn't lift it any further. Suddenly as he was lifting, he could feel the car lift higher and higher. The veins in his neck and arms were bulging out, but he didn't understand what was happening. He looked to his side and saw Stephen with his back against the car and his hands underneath, lifting with him. Blood ran from Stephen's fingers, and he dented the side of the door where he pushed so hard with his legs. Skeeter soon showed up with another floor jack, and Ralphie reached in and slid Bobby out from underneath the car. Jackson and Stephen collapsed on the garage floor, utterly exhausted. Bobby was bloody and having difficulty breathing, but still alive. Mr. Willie called 911, and they could hear the ambulance on its way. The ambulance and police arrived and stabilized Bobby and headed to the hospital for emergency surgery. Bobby escaped with several broken ribs and a punctured lung along with some other cuts and scrapes. After the ambulance left the garage, Deputy Forrest came up and questioned everyone at the scene. When they finally got to Stephen and Jackson, Mr. Willie was standing alongside them.

"Boys, you saved Bobby's life. The paramedics said if he had gone another minute without being able to breathe, he would have died."

Mr. Willie smiled and patted Stephen and Jackson on the back. Stephen didn't have much to say.

"What do you think about that Stephen? Can you believe it? Mr. Willie smiled."

"I just did what I could. It's what anyone would do."

Looking down at his hands, Stephen could see the open wounds that would undoubtedly require stitches. Jackson's hands were in bad shape too. Mr. Willie called Jackson and Stephen's parents and took the boys to the hospital to get stitched up. When they arrived in the ER, they were met by Dr. Karen Long, a beautiful red-haired ER doctor.

She only lived a mile from the garage, and she knew Mr. Willie and several of the mechanics including Jackson and Stephen.

As they all gathered in the room, Dr. Karen said, "Stephen, I hear you and Jackson are heroes."

Stephen smiled and blushed red all over his face; "I was just doing what anyone else would do."

"That was a wonderful thing you did Stephen; Bobby would not have survived if you and Jackson didn't pull the car up enough to let him breathe. We are all so proud of you."

She smiled and leaned over and kissed Stephen on the cheek. As Karen finished talking, Stephen's mom ran in and grabbed him and held him without saying a word.

"Are you okay baby?"

"Yes ma'am, my hands got cut up a little."

She saw his blood-soaked hands and the bandages wrapped around them, then she looked at Jackson's hands and saw the same thing. She reached over and hugged Jackson tight.

"You boys were wonderful today. Everyone's telling me you saved a man's life today."

Jackson sat there and pondered what had happened.

"Dr. Karen, is Bobby gonna be okay?"

"Jackson, he's in surgery right now, but everything looks good for him to make a full recovery thanks to you guys."

Even after all Bobby put him through, Jackson flew to his aid without any thought. Mr. Willie and Jackson's mom came into the room, their faces proud. Leah hugged him and asked how he was doing.

"I'm okay mom; I only needed a few stitches."

Jackson's mom asked, "How is Bobby doing?"

"The doctor said he should be out of surgery soon and that he should make a full recovery."

"That is wonderful. I was so scared when Mr. Willie called me. I didn't know if you were all right."

It was getting close to 7 PM. Mr. Willie stood up and said, "Let's all go grab something to eat; it'll be my treat. How about Buddy's Steakhouse?"

Everyone agreed, and the nurse came in with the release paperwork for the boys.

"Let's say we meet at Buddy's at 8 o'clock."

They each made their way out of the hospital and headed back home. Mr. Willie arrived at Buddy's earlier than everyone else and talked to the manager and asked if he could use the intercom to speak to all the customers.

"Ladies and gentlemen, I'm sorry to interrupt your dinner, but I would like to ask a favor of you. A few hours ago, two boys that work for me down at the garage helped save a man's life when they lifted a car up that had been knocked off its jack stands accidentally. The boy's quick action allowed us to pull our mechanic out from under that car. As a result, he should make a full recovery thanks to these boys. They'll be here in a few minutes, so when I give the signal if you wouldn't mind standing up and clapping for these boys, I would greatly appreciate it."

Mr. Willie reserved a big table for them near the back. He watched out the door as the boys came in with their parents. When they made their way to the glass doors, Mr. Willie gave the signal to all the customers. All at once, the whole place stood up, cheered and clapped. The boys didn't know what to do. They giggled at each other and smiled.

All the cute waitresses came by and gave each one of them hugs and kisses on the cheek, and the boys sure didn't mind that. The clapping went on for a long time as the boys and their parents made their way to their table.

"What was that all about?" Jackson asked Mr. Willie.

"I thought it might be nice for you guys to receive a little recognition for the wonderful thing you did today."

Jackson sat down next to Stephen and hugged him. He leaned down to talk to him.

"Stephen, today you had so much strength it was amazing. I couldn't have lifted that car up without you. If it hadn't been for you, Bobby wouldn't be breathing right now. You are a true hero."

CHAPTER SEVENTEEN

# Christmas Eve

Christmas Eve fell on a Saturday this year, and Mr. Willie's garage would be open until 2:00 PM, to be there in case someone needed them before driving out of town for the Christmas holidays. Mr. Willie was behind the counter taking care of the last few customers. All the mechanics including Jackson were working hard to finish up everything, so they could head home for Christmas Eve too. The waiting room sparkled, and Christmas lights adorned all the windows. In the corner stood a giant ten-foot Christmas tree loaded with candy canes and ornaments. Mr. Willie loved Christmas. He always said it brought out the best in people. The customers seemed friendlier, and all the mechanics wore Santa hats for the day. Everyone was in a good mood. Mr. Willie passed by Jackson doing an oil change and said, "It would sure be nice if we could harness this Christmas spirit all year long and everyone took care of each other like we do at Christmas. We should be thankful all year long for all the blessings we receive and give them back all year long. Tonight is a very special night."

"Everyone sure is in the Christmas spirit. I love Christmas time too. No matter how tight things are for the budget at home, mom always makes Christmas special for me."

"Jackson, how about give your mom a call in a little while and ask her if you can come with me to grab a cup of coffee after we close up the shop this afternoon. Tell her I'll make sure you're back in time for her Christmas Eve dinner, and I won't spoil your appetite too much."

"Where are we going?" He asked.

"You'll see."

Mr. Willie had bought him lunch many times before, and they shared many pizzas late into the evening working on a customer's car. This time was different; he seemed excited, and he had a different look in his eye. Jackson was curious why Mr. Willie was so eager to go. One of the last customers of the day was seventy-four-year-old Mrs. White. She had been a longtime customer and came by for an oil change before she left for her son's house a few hours away. While Jackson was changing her oil, he noticed the poor condition of her tires. All of them were as slick as a bald man's waxed head. He showed Mr. Willie, and he said, "She can't drive to her son's on these

Maypops. Wait just a minute; I'll be back."

"Maypops? What in the world are Maypops Mr. Willie?"

"These tires "may pop" at any time they are so slick. We can't let her drive outta here on those."

Mr. Willie walked out to the waiting area and told Mrs. White it would be about 30 more minutes before her car would be ready. Mr. and Mrs. White had been coming to Mr. Willie's place for years, and just this year, Mr. White had passed away, and this was her first Christmas without him. She didn't have a lot of money, but she always helped people in the community and was always ready to lend a hand to anyone in need. Mr. Willie came back to the garage and talked to three other mechanics. They all came over to her car and just like a NASCAR pit crew, removed all her tires in a flash. Mr. Willie came out of the warehouse pushing the tire dolly with four brand new tires for Mrs. White's vehicle. He told all the guys to hurry because she didn't know about the new tires and she wanted to arrive at her son's home before dark. In record time the guys installed the new tires and Jackson finished her oil change. Mr. Willie handed her the keys and said, "Merry Christmas Mrs. White and have a safe trip."

Mrs. White thanked him and headed out the door, none the wiser. Mr. Willie just smiled as she drove out of sight. Jackson looked at him, and Mr. Willie grinned.

"How are you supposed to make any money if you give tires away?"

"Did you see the look on her face when she talked about seeing her son and her grandkids?"

Jackson answered him back, "I did..."

"Jackson, she lives next door to me, and I ain't seen her smile like that since Mr. White passed away."

"That smile was payment enough."

"You can't make a living on smiles." Jackson exclaimed.

Mr. Willie turned to Jackson and said, "Boy let me tell you something..., my wife and I moved into her neighborhood twenty-five years ago. We moved in next door to them in a cute little house on the corner. We were the only Black couple in the entire neighborhood. Back then, nobody in the area would talk to us much; they would just ride by or walk by and stare at us and talk to each other and act like we didn't even exist. Not Mr. and Mrs. White. They welcomed us on our first day. Mrs. White made dinner for us the first week we arrived in the neighborhood, and Mr. White helped me move our belongings into the house. They were older than us, so they took us under their wing. When my son got sick, Mrs. White would come over and stay with him, so we could work. I owe her way more than the price of some tires. They helped us in ways most people could never dream of. A lot of people say they would like to help, but there are only a few who will do something and make things happen. Those are the kind of people that make a difference in people's lives. They made a difference in our lives. Have you ever had someone tell you I would like to help you, but...? And they just made some excuse why they couldn't help? That excuse doesn't go a long way, does it? That wonderful couple never said I would like to help you, but.... They just helped us any way they could and never made an excuse. Remember, if you tell someone something, and you stick a but... in there, nothing before the but matters. Those new tires were the least I could do for her."

"Okay, okay, I see your point, thanks for putting me in my place. Mrs. White sure had a wonderful smile on her face. Mr. Willie, I called my mom, and she said I could go with you tonight."

Mr. Willie said, "Good, good... I think you'll enjoy it."

Mr. Willie's garage had some of the best Christmas decorations in the whole town. The building was outlined with multi-colored lights, and on the roof, a giant American flag all in red, white and blue lights lit up the sky. All around the garage parking lot, Christmas themed cars and motorcycles, many with moving parts, decorated the landscape. Out by the front entrance was a large Nativity scene including all the animals. One business owner said he protested the Nativity scene being there, but Mr. Willie told him to "Stick it." Only he said it nicely. Mr. Willie kept the lights on all night, and people would even make a special trip just to see them and find out what was new each year. Every year he added something to the display, and he waited for his customers to figure out what was new. This year was a Christmas themed Red Corvette with Santa driving. Jackson and the rest of the mechanics finished up the last customers and closed the shop for the weekend. Before they left, Mr. Willie brought out some Christmas goodies and Eggnog to celebrate a little before sending the guys home to their families. The guys thanked Mr. Willie for his generous Christmas bonuses, and each of them told him how much it helped their family. Not being the one to be in the limelight, Mr. Willie thanked all the mechanics for their work the whole year and how important it was to the citizens of the community. He told them how many compliments he received for their service and he wanted them to know they were appreciated. As they were getting ready to leave, an old Chevy pickup pulled up that no one recognized. The passenger door creaked as it slowly opened and all the eyes in the garage turned to see who it was. Bobby slowly stepped out of the truck with his dad right behind. No one said a word as the two made their way to where everyone was standing. Bobby had been recovering back at a hospital in Tennessee.

"Merry Christmas everyone," Bobby managed to get out, choking a little, still recovering from his third surgery after the accident. He looked much different now, he'd lost a lot of weight and his body was covered with scars from the surgeries. Everyone was a little surprised, then Mr. Willie jumped in. "Merry Christmas Bobby. We're glad to see you and glad to see you're getting better."

Bobby looked around to every guy standing in the garage and cleared his voice as he straightened his posture. "That accident changed me. It changed how I think about everything. Lying in that hospital bed, all I could do was think. That accident was my fault. Nobody else's. I could have died right on that garage floor. The way I treated some of you guys, I wouldn't have blamed you if you would have just left me there." Everyone was silent as Bobby shifted his weight and tried to stand straighter. "You could have left me there, but you didn't. The two guys I treated the worst were the first ones to rescue me and because of them I'm still breathing. I wanted to come back to just say thank you. Thank you for saving my life and giving me a second chance to do things differently. My dad and I hadn't spoken in nearly ten years, but a nurse from the hospital got him to come down and he helped take care of me. He had been sober for five years and he and I reconnected. We're gonna open a garage back in Tennessee. I just wanted to stop by a tell you guys thanks for everything."

All the guys were a little shocked to hear Bobby's story. They stood staring at each other, then Stephen jumped up and gave Bobby a big hug. Bobby cringed in pain as the gentle giant squeezed him. "Merry Christmas Bobby." Mr. Willie and all the guys shook Bobby's hand and waved goodbye as they drove off. Mr. Willie looked at Jackson, "Well, just like I always say, Christmas is the time for miracles. Let's get ready to close up."

It was getting close to 3:00 PM and the guys finally headed home. Mr. Willie was always the last to leave, no matter what. He wished all the guys a Merry Christmas and told them to be safe. Jackson helped him lock up, and then Mr. Willie said, "I'll pick you up about 4:30 PM okay."

Mr. Willie pulled up in Jackson's driveway about 4:23 PM in his shiny white Silverado 4x4 pickup truck. "Merry Christmas Mr. Willie! Come on in." Leah greeted him.

Mr. Willie smiled and gave Jackson's mom Leah a great big bear hug. Leah called down the hall to Jackson's room.

"Jackson, Mr. Willie is here."

Jackson checked his watch... 4:25 PM. Mr. Willie always said, "If you can't be on time... be early."

He said that to Jackson and all the guys every day hoping it might finally sink in. Jackson came down the hallway, grabbed his jacket and was ready to go. Mr. Willie promised Leah that Jackson would be back by 7:00 PM, in time for dinner. They piled into the truck and Jackson said, "I have something for you when we get back."

Mr. Willie asked, "What is it?"

Jackson replied, "You'll see."

Mr. Willie and young Jackson drove for about 10 minutes and stopped at a little diner down the road. The place was packed, but they came just in time to be seated in a booth next to a roaring fireplace. Decorations adorned every table, and a giant Christmas tree stood proudly in the corner. The smell of fresh bacon, eggs, and biscuits filled the air, and the warm glow of the fireplace and the candles in the window made them feel right at home. A beautiful young waitress named Diane stopped by the table to take their order. She was in her middle twenties and married about five years with a young daughter named Sarah who was at home with her daddy. Mr. Willie liked this place, and he ate dinner here a lot.

"Merry Christmas Diane!"

Mr. Willie smiled as Diane hugged him and welcomed them to the diner on Christmas Eve.

"What time do you close tonight Diane?"

"We're closing at 7:00 PM," Diane said as she had a puzzled look on her face.

"How many people you got working tonight?"

"Well, let me think, three cooks, seven waitresses, and one hostess. Eleven people altogether. Why do you ask?"

"I was just wondering how many people it took to run this place on Christmas Eve. I'm sorry you have to work on Christmas Eve."

"It's okay Mr. Willie. Every little bit helps pay the bills. What can I get you, gentlemen?"

"How about a cup of coffee for me, a Coke for my friend Jackson and two slices of your famous Apple pie?"

"Coming right up," Diane turned and walked into the kitchen.

Jackson shrugged his shoulders and asked, "Mr. Willie why are we here?"

"Let me see... Jackson, how long has it been since you came to work at the garage... I guess it's been over two years now and you'll be 18 soon and graduating high school. Ever since you started at the garage, I saw a lot of potential in you as a young man. Do you remember how I always told you that it was so important to help people?"

"Yes sir," Jackson nodded.

Mr. Willie went on, "There are a lot of things in life that happen to people that they didn't ask for or plan on happening to them. Those events just happened, and they had to make the best of it and keep moving on. Many people struggle day in and day out. They work hard. Just look around here. Look at the waitresses and cooks in here on Christmas Eve. Why are they here? They're here because they have to be here to support their families. While most people are at home enjoying a Christmas Eve party or dinner, these folks are here taking care of other people and thinking about their family. They wish they could be home with them and not working today."

Jackson listened intently as Mr. Willie was talking.

"Two warm pieces of our best apple pie for your Christmas Eve snack," Diane smiled as she carefully set the plates down.

"Thanks, Diane, they look great."

Mr. Willie continued, "Over the years, we always treated our customers at the garage with honesty and respect. In return, they kept coming back year after year and telling their friends about us. That honesty and respect we paid them has paid us all back as the garage has become more successful. When that happens to you, you can't keep it to yourself. You have to be generous and spread it around. The blessings you receive in return, far outweighs anything you give."

Jackson sat there taking in all that Mr. Willie had said, but he still didn't quite understand.

"Tonight, we have a chance to do just a little to help brighten the day of some of these hard-working people on Christmas Eve. Take a bite of your pie, we need to go."

Jackson exclaimed, "We just got our pie."

"We didn't come here for the pie; we came here for this."

As Jackson watched, Mr. Willie pulled out a large stack of envelopes with small Christmas cards in them. Inside each envelope, he had placed five crisp one hundred-dollar bills. On the outside of the envelope were the words, please don't open until closing time. When Diane came back to check on Jackson and Mr. Willie, they had already left, but next to their check and a one hundred-dollar bill, she found a note with instructions to take one envelope and pass one to each of her fellow employees at closing time. The note also said to make sure she didn't tell anyone who had left the money.

Mr. Willie and Jackson walked around to the side entrance door where there was a small window. Through it, they could see the waitress's station and the kitchen. They watched through the window as Diane couldn't wait and opened her envelope. Her face glowed with amazement as she slowly pulled out the hundred-dollar bills. She jumped up and down and ran around handing them to each of the other waitresses until everyone who was working had an envelope. Jackson and Mr. Willie laughed as they watched the scene unfold before their eyes. Inside the diner, Diane was causing quite a commotion in the dining area, so she ran into the kitchen with the other waitresses following close behind.

"Can you believe this? I didn't know how we could buy Christmas presents for the kids this year and we didn't have a lot for Christmas dinner tomorrow either. I can do it now. We can take care of it all before the store closes."

Diane went on as tears rolled down her face. All the waitresses asked who left the money, but Diane kept the promise on the envelope not to tell. The other waitresses cried, and a few of the cooks had a few tears forming in the corner of their eyes as well. Johnny, one of the cooks in the back said, "I can make it to the store before they close and pickup that bicycle that my daughter has been wanting all year. My wife isn't going to believe this."

Everyone who had received an envelope had a different story, but all of them really needed it at just this moment in time. Jackson and Mr. Willie climbed into the truck and pulled out of the parking lot. Jackson was smiling and thinking about what he had seen and what that would mean to all the diner employees. Mr. Willie was smiling too.

"Let's do that again," replied Mr. Willie.

Jackson shouted, "What??"

"Yeah, let's do that again." Mr. Willie laughed.

They stopped at two more diners and carried out the same routine; envelopes for every employee and a note to wait until closing time to open them. Each time reminding the recipient not to tell who left the money. The last stop before Jackson had to be home was at a little restaurant called "The Seaside Grille," out on Folly Beach. It was a beautiful restaurant with a million-dollar view of the beach. Right outside the door was the Folly Beach fishing pier that extended out about a quarter of a mile into the ocean. At the end of the pier was a large covered platform where you could see for miles into the Atlantic and around Folly Island. On top of the platform was a giant Christmas wreath with bright white lights. It was a beacon, welcoming anyone who wished to enjoy the views. The pier was mostly empty except for the few lonely souls testing their luck with the fish. The sun was sinking low behind the Seaside Grille, but the sky was full of amber and red colors. Jackson and Mr. Willie just stared out over the ocean and took it in without saying a word. The two walked into the cozy restaurant, and the co-owner, Becky Jones, greeted them.

"Hey Mr. Willie, hey Jackson. Merry Christmas to you guys. I've got a great booth for you two."

A few customers remained, enjoying their dinner and coffee before heading home for Christmas Eve. As they walked into the restaurant, Jackson ran into a large basket labeled "suggestion box." He moved the basket back, and Mr. Willie asked Becky about the suggestion box. Becky told Mr. Willie that her husband John had just put it out, hoping to improve the restaurant and make it more popular with as many people as he could. Business had dropped off some, and he was doing everything possible to turn that around. Becky handed Mr. Willie and Jackson each a little suggestion card and asked if they wouldn't mind writing something they might like to see improved or changed.

Mr. Willie asked, "Have the customers been filling these out today?"

"The response has been pretty good. I checked it after lunch, and we had quite a few. I re-checked it a couple of hours ago, and the basket was filling up. We haven't read any yet, but we will."

Mr. Willie and Jackson sat down in a large comfortable booth next to a plate glass window that gave an unobstructed view of the ocean and the beautiful sky. It was the best seat in the house. Jackson and Mr. Willie had been to the Seaside Grille many times before, and Jackson liked to come here especially in the summer when he hung out with Red and his other friends on the beach. It became a great meeting place for all the local high school and college kids. John and Becky bought the restaurant many years back and wanted to cater to the locals as well as the many tourists who flocked to Folly Beach for a long, laid-back vacation. John and Becky also wanted a safe place for the local kids to hang out and do homework. A separate wing underneath the main restaurant had been built to house all the booths and tables just for the kids. On top of the restaurant was a big loft where Becky and John lived. It had huge windows that wrapped around the loft on all sides displaying beautiful views of both the ocean and the Folly River. As the sun had already begun to set, the warm glow of the multi-colored lights that outlined every window and the little Christmas trees on every table made for an inviting scene.

While Jackson and Mr. Willie talked about how cozy the place was, the most beautiful young girl Jackson had ever seen stopped by to take their order.

"Merry Christmas, I'm Hannah, what can I get for you tonight?"

She had long sandy blonde hair and a genuine smile that lit up the whole restaurant. Jackson had never seen her before, and his tongue got all twisted up, trying to order.

Mr. Willie helped him out; "He'll take a cup of warm cocoa and a piece of that famous chocolate cake and I would like a cup of coffee and a piece of that cake as well."

Hannah smiled and said, "It'll be ready in just a few minutes."

That beautiful smile melted Jackson's heart, and he felt it beating faster and faster. Hannah turned and walked down a few booths to check on the last few customers as they finished dinner.

"Who is that?" Jackson asked in astonishment.

Mr. Willie laughed. "I don't know; I've never seen her in here before."

Jackson couldn't help but stare at her. He had never seen a girl quite like her before. Her skin was a sun-kissed golden brown even though it was December. Her soft eyes sparkled, and she had a way about her that made everyone feel welcome. If there ever was a "girl next door," she was it. In a minute, she returned with their order and Jackson couldn't keep his eyes off her.

"Can I bring you anything else?" Hannah smiled.

Jackson couldn't speak again; he just stared.

Mr. Willie jumped in, "I think that will be good for us Hannah, thank you."

Mr. Willie laughed, "Boy what are you doing? You couldn't even say thank you. It's like you've never talked to a girl before."

"I didn't know what to say," exclaimed Jackson.

"She is so beautiful; I was trying to find some words, but they wouldn't come out. I wanted to talk to her, but I was so nervous."

"Well eat your cake and work up your nerve before we leave."

As Jackson sat and stared at Hannah, he tried not to let her see, but several times their eyes met, and she gave him the sweetest most genuine smile he had ever received from any girl.

"I have to talk to her. I've only known her for five minutes, and I can't stop thinking about her."

With every bite, Jackson's eyes followed her around the restaurant. He even missed his mouth once with a bite because he was so mesmerized.

"Well, are you going to talk to her or what?" Mr. Willie laughed.

"I will; I will. What can I ask her to start the conversation?"

"Just ask her when she started working here and maybe where she's from."

"Okay."

Becky stopped by the table, "How is the cake you two?"

Mr. Willie replied, "The cake is fantastic Becky; how are you feeling?"

Becky had been recovering from her first bout of chemotherapy. She was diagnosed with breast cancer right after Thanksgiving.

"I have my good days and bad days. Today is a good day. Thank you for asking Willie. Can I get you anything else?"

Jackson asked Becky, "Who's that girl Hannah?"

"She's my niece. She is staying with us for a while here at the beach before she decides where she's going to college."

"Where's she from? I've never seen her before."

"Hannah's from Michigan. Her mother, my sister, died last year from breast cancer. John, myself and her grandmother, my mom, are the only family she has left. My mom still lives up there in Traverse City, Michigan. She has a beautiful place up on Lake Michigan where Hannah's mother and I grew up. Hannah called me a few weeks ago and asked if she could stay with me for a while. She didn't want to spend Christmas in that house without her mother and her grandmother insisted that she go. Since I couldn't have children, she was like the daughter I never had. We went up there all the time, and they came to stay with us down here when they visited. She's only been here a few weeks, but she says she loves it. Hannah's still sorting out her mom's death, and now she's worried about me."

A small tear glistened the corner of Becky's eye as she walked away. Hannah looked out across the tables and smiled that beautiful smile to Jackson. Jackson didn't know what to do or what to say, but his heart was on fire. He had to get to know her.

"I sure like this place Mr. Willie, and now that Hannah is here, I like it even more. I wonder if she would let me call her."

"There's only one way to find out."

Hannah came by to check on them, and Jackson finally got up the nerve to ask her for a pen. As she handed it to him, their hands touched, and it felt like a spark shot through his body. Every square inch of him tingled inside. He muffled the words thank you for the pen as she smiled back.

"Would you like anything else?"

Mr. Willie leaned over his coffee smiling at Jackson, then he whispered to him. "Boy, you better work up your nerve soon. We got to go."

Mr. Willie turned to Hannah, "I think we are good here Hannah, thank you."

"You know Becky, and her husband have been going through some rough times. They haven't raised the prices in a long time, but their expenses and property taxes keep going up. I guess that suggestion box might give them some ideas about changing some things to bring more people in here and pick up the business."

Mr. Willie stared outside to the end of the pier looking at the beautiful Christmas wreath on top, and he put his hand to his chin and thought for a while.

"That suggestion box gives me a great idea. Jackson, these people need a little bright spot tonight with all that they've gone through."

Mr. Willie and Jackson finished their cake and Hannah came back to check on them one more time.

"This is your last chance," Mr. Willie motioned to Jackson.

"I hope you guys have a wonderful Christmas and I hope you come back soon." Hannah stood there for a few seconds and smiled at Jackson. It was like she looked right through him into his heart. Jackson smiled back but didn't say a word. She turned and headed towards another table to clear it.

"Okay buddy, we have to go, but I need you to distract everyone while I put something in the suggestion box. Just go over there towards the restrooms and make some kind of commotion that will draw their attention away while I do what I need to do."

Jackson got up and headed towards the restrooms, but he didn't know what to do to get their attention, so suddenly, he tripped over a chair and fell to the floor. He played it well because the first person to reach him was Hannah. She kneeled beside him and grabbed his hand and asked if he was all right. He squeezed her hand, and that spark ran through his body again.

"Well, I am a little hurt right here as he pointed to his cheek. Is there any way you could make that feel better?"

"Well, what did you have in mind?" Hannah laughed.

"I guess that would be up to you."

She grabbed his hand and pulled him up to his feet. Her hands were so warm and soft. He laughed as he shook off the fall.

"Are you sure you're okay?"

"Yeah. I'm sorry I startled you."

They stared deep into each other's eyes for what seemed like an eternity. Jackson didn't want to go.

"Hey Jackson, are you ready to go, buddy?"

"Yes sir, I'll be right there."

"I hope I get to see you again soon Hannah."

"Me too."

Jackson and Mr. Willie said their goodbyes and headed out the door. They walked around to the side window staying out of sight and waited for the last customers to leave. Becky locked the door and turned the welcome sign around. She picked up the suggestion box and headed to the big table where her husband John and Hannah were sitting. John's face was weathered with worry about the love of his life and possibly losing the restaurant if business didn't pick up. Over the years, they had fed many teenagers who didn't know where their next meal was coming from. They gave a lot of the kids jobs that they really couldn't afford, but they wanted to teach the kids about work and the importance of working hard. Now they gathered around the table on Christmas Eve worried about the $75,000 balloon payment that was due by the end of March, 15 months from now, on the major renovations they had just finished. They didn't have any idea how they would be able to save that much money by next year.

Becky pulled out the first suggestion card and read what it said.

"I wouldn't change anything. You guys are the best."

John and Becky smiled together, and John hugged her and pulled her close and kissed her forehead. She pulled out another one, and they gave some suggestions about music and other things. On reaching the bottom, she pulled out a manila envelope. Becky glanced at John with a look of unknowing and then she opened it up. She reached inside and pulled out several small envelopes with each person's name on them. Becky called to the boys in the back to come out and see what was inside. Earl and Floyd came out and asked what the commotion was about. Becky handed each person their envelope. She handed Hannah her envelope and smiled at her. Each person opened them up and pulled out five crisp $100 bills. As they fanned them out, they all gasped in astonishment at each other, and they just sat there in silence.

"Who gave us this?" Earl asked.

"I don't know; the envelopes were in the suggestion box."

"You did Aunt Becky didn't you...?" Hannah grinned.

"No, I promise I didn't. I don't know who put them in here. We've had a lot of customers in and out of here all day."

Hannah looked over into the bottom of the basket and pulled out another thick envelope that Becky had missed. It said, "Merry Christmas Becky and John."

Hannah handed it to Becky, and she passed it over to John. He opened it up and inside was a cashier's check for $10,000 from an anonymous donor. Inside was a little note. "Thanks for all you do for the community." Becky and John just looked at each other with tears in their eyes. John held Becky close, and she looked up as she was crying.

“This will sure help on paying off our renovation loan,” Becky smiled through her tears.

By this time, everyone was wiping their tears away. Mr. Willie and Jackson enjoyed the view looking through the side window being careful not to be seen.

"Let's go Jackson."

They pulled out of the parking lot and headed towards Jackson's house. The first few miles they were just silent, and Jackson stared out the window looking at all the Christmas lights along the way. It was his favorite time of the year, and he had just witnessed one of the greatest displays of generosity he had ever seen.

Mr. Willie broke the silence, "Jackson, do me a favor, don't tell anyone at the restaurant what we did tonight. I don't need any thanks. Those expressions in the window were more than enough."

"Okay, Mr. Willie, whatever you say. What about my mom? I just have to tell her."

"Ok, just her. Make sure she doesn't tell anyone else. It's Santa's secret."

CHAPTER EIGHTEEN

# Merry Christmas

Mr. Willie's truck pulled into Jackson's driveway 20 minutes before dinner.

"Thanks for taking me tonight, Mr. Willie, I had the most fun I've ever had on Christmas Eve. You sure did make a lot of people happy tonight."

"That's what it's all about Jackson. God has blessed me over the years, and I do my best to pass those blessings along to other people. I had a wonderful time too. We sure did enjoy looking through the windows and seeing the smiles on their faces. Times are hard for a lot of folks around here."

"Why don't you come inside and have dinner with us?" Jackson said as he opened the door.

"Thanks, Jackson, but Ralphie and his family invited me for dinner a few weeks ago."

Jackson smiled and said, "Mr. Willie, wait a minute, I have something I want to give you. Can you come in for a minute?"

Mr. Willie turned off the truck and headed into the house with Jackson. Jackson ran inside to get his mom and the special gift he made for Mr. Willie.

"Close your eyes, Jackson called from the back room."

Mr. Willie said, "Okay, they're closed."

Jackson came closer, "Okay, you can open your eyes now."

Mr. Willie opened his eyes, and a large colorful package met his gaze. He opened the package and pulled out a painting of the old worn picture that stood behind the counter of the garage for the last 20 years of his family when the garage opened. Mr. Willie stood silent. The colors were so vibrant; the painting looked so real, it was like they were at the garage. He slowly ran his fingers over the canvas and touched each one of his family member's faces. They stood together quietly as Mr. Willie explored every inch of the painting. Tracing their faces, led him back to them. In the corner of Mr. Willie's eyes, a tear formed and trickled down the side of his weathered face.

"This is unbelievable. How did you do it?"

"Well, when you went to the doctor in November, I took it off the wall and made a copy. I worked on it every night until yesterday when

I finished. I hope you like it."

Mr. Willie wiped his eyes, trying to compose himself.

"Like it? I've never received a gift as nice as this. It looks so real. When I touched the painting, I felt like I was right back at the garage on that beautiful day in April when we bought it. I smelled my wife's perfume, and I could feel my son's hand move around and him step on my toes as he was fidgeting for the camera. This is just great Jackson. It'll take the place of that old picture behind the counter at the garage."

As Mr. Willie got a tissue out of his pocket and wiped his eyes, he made his way to the front door and gave Jackson and his mom a hug goodbye and told them Merry Christmas. Jackson walked Mr. Willie out to the truck, and even in the brief time Mr. Willie had been there, the temperature had dropped a few more degrees. Jackson put his hands in his pockets to keep them warm, and he felt something. He reached further down and pulled out a pen. It was the pen Hannah had let him borrow at the Seaside Grille. Jackson showed it to Mr. Willie.

"I guess you've got your reason to go back now huh?" Mr. Willie laughed.

They both looked up at the sky without saying a word. The wind was blowing, but the night was clear. Millions of stars lit up the heavens, and they both stared at the Majesty above them.

"Jackson, I better be getting on. Ralphie and his wife are waiting for me. Thanks again for the beautiful painting. I couldn't ask for a better Christmas gift."

Mr. Willie pulled the last two envelopes out of his coat pocket and handed them to Jackson.

"Merry Christmas buddy."

"What's this Mr. Willie?"

"Don't open them until I'm gone okay."

"Ok, Merry Christmas Mr. Willie."

As Jackson watched Mr. Willie place the painting in his backseat, his heart swelled with emotion, and he felt the hairs on the back of his neck stand up. He knew he was a good artist, but this was the first time that someone was moved by what he had painted. That feeling was wonderful. Jackson waved goodbye as Mr. Willie drove away and he headed back inside to the warm house. All the wonderful smells of Christmas goodies danced throughout his house. He was starving. All he had was one or two bites at each place they went. Jackson walked into the kitchen, and his mom hugged him. She held him in that warm embrace for a long time without saying a word.

"What was that for?" Jackson asked.

"What you did for Mr. Willie was something special. Didn't you see the look on his face? It touched him down deep in his heart. You have a very special gift. There are a lot of good painters in the world that paint beautiful pictures, but very few painters can evoke such emotion in people. The tears were flowing in my eyes too. I knew you were working on something, but I didn't know what, so instead of peeking, I decided I would wait until you finished. The wait was worth it because I wouldn't have wanted to miss seeing Mr. Willie's face."

"Thanks, mom. Down at the garage, Mr. Willie talks to that picture every day. Not a day goes by that he doesn't tell me a story about them. He really misses them. It must be tough being all alone during the Christmas holidays. He's so good to all the customers and everyone that works for him. I just wanted to do something to give a little back to him."

"I think you succeeded. Come on and wash up Jackson. Let's get ready to eat. Shirley and Frank should be here any minute."

Jackson walked into the bathroom, and as he was washing his hands, he took a long look in the mirror and smiled at himself. He saw the face of a young man now. No longer a boy, he was different now, he felt good. His shoulders were broad and muscular. A few scars covered his hands from work down at the garage. The feeling he received tonight was one of the best feelings he had ever had. He wanted to keep that feeling going. Just then, the doorbell rang, and Shirley and Frank came in to share dinner.

"I'm sorry we're late," said Shirley as she took her coat off. Shirley and Frank had been friends of Leah's for a long time. They came over on every holiday and a lot during the summer. Leah had grown up with Shirley, and they were dear friends ever since. Frank was a kind man who tried to do as much as possible with Jackson. Frank and Shirley didn't have kids of their own, and they loved having Jackson over. He would even spend the night sometimes and stay up late with them watching scary movies after the 11:00 PM news signed off.

"Merry Christmas Jackson," Frank said as he came in.

"Merry Christmas Mr. Frank," Jackson smiled as he shook his hand.

"Wow, that's quite a grip you got Jackson. I guess those last couple of years down at the garage have made you a strong young man?"

"Yes sir, I guess so."

Jackson got his plate and was amazed at all the food that his mother had made. They all made their way to the dining room table.

Jackson's mom asked him to say the blessing. He hesitated at first, then he began.

"Thank you, Lord, for a wonderful day and the wonderful friendship I have with Mr. Willie. Please help my painting to comfort him when he misses his family and bless my mom for all she does for me and thank you for great friends. In Jesus' name, Amen."

They all sat in the candlelight enjoying the meal with the familiar sounds of Christmas music playing in the background. After dinner, they exchanged gifts and talked a while over coffee. Jackson still had the envelopes in his pocket but didn't want to say anything since he had promised to only tell his mother about the extraordinary things he'd experienced earlier that evening. Frank and Shirley said their goodbyes and Jackson and his mother were in the house alone.

"Hey mom, we haven't even talked about what happened tonight with me and Mr. Willie."

"What do you mean? I thought he took you to get a little bite to eat before dinner."

"You will not believe this mom," Jackson said with uncontrollable excitement.

"What is it, what is it?"

"You have to make a promise first mom. Mr. Willie asked me to promise not to tell anyone except you, and he asked for me to keep it a secret. Will you please do that?"

"Why, what happened?"

"Mom, please promise."

"Ok Jackson, I promise. Now what gives?"

"Mr. Willie took me to four different restaurants, and we had a little dessert and something to drink in all four of them. He had a bunch of envelopes in his jacket pocket. As we were leaving, he pulled them out at the table, and when we left, he left enough envelopes for every one that was working in each restaurant tonight. Mr. Willie left instructions to the waitresses to give each person who was working one of the envelopes. In each one was $500."

"What... $500?" His mom exclaimed.

"It's for the people who were working. He said that people who were working on Christmas Eve, and nights and weekends really had to work. While most people were home with their families, these people are out working to support their families. Just like you when you work on the weekends to support us. Mr. Willie said he had been blessed, and he wanted to give back. After we walked out of the first restaurant, we went around to the side window and peered inside to watch what happened. When the first waitress came back to the table to pick up the check, she almost fainted. She had to sit down in the booth for a minute before she regained her composure. We stood outside for a few more minutes and watched her hand the envelopes to each one of the workers. We couldn't hear what they were saying, but we sure saw the look on their faces. Mr. Willie grinned that classic smile and then he told me we had to go. We did that at three more places. The last restaurant was the Seaside Grille, and that was the best one."

"Why was that?" His mom asked.

"There was a beautiful girl at the restaurant. She's Mrs. Becky's niece. She is the most beautiful girl I've ever seen. And when you look into her eyes and see how she interacts with other people, you can tell she's just as beautiful on the inside too. She wasn't just beautiful; she was genuine. I couldn't even talk to her, I was so nervous. Mr. Willie laughed at me while I was struggling to say something to her. She looked at me and smiled, and I guess she understood that I was a little nervous. She kept looking back at me while she was talking to the other customers. Mr. Willie had to be careful about the envelopes at the Seaside Grille, since we go there so much. He didn't know the people in two of the other restaurants quite as well, and he didn't want Becky and the others at the Seaside Grille to know who gave them the money. It turns out that they had just put up a suggestion box that day and there were a lot of suggestions already in the box. Mr. Willie slipped the envelopes into the suggestion box when no one was looking. I made a little distraction on the other side of the restaurant, so no one would see him. Business is always a little bit slow in the winter months at the Seaside Grille, and Mr. Willie loves that place. He wanted to make their Christmas special. I've got to go back on Monday to see her."

"Maybe you can catch a ride with someone up to the office and then you can take my car and come back and get me when I get off work."

"I can't wait till I have enough money to buy my own car. All the other kids my age already have cars."

His mom looked over at him and said, "Jackson, be patient, keep working hard and soon you will have enough money for a nice car or truck. Until then, we're a one car family. Plenty of people get along like that."

Jackson sat and stared into space, thinking about the beautiful girl that now consumed his every thought. As Jackson pondered what had happened earlier, he couldn't get Hannah off his mind. It was like he never left the Seaside Grille. Jackson's mom rattling plates in the kitchen sink jolted him back home to the dinner table.

"Hey mom, I almost forgot, Mr. Willie gave me and you an envelope. He said we couldn't open them until he was gone."

Jackson reached in and pulled out the envelopes from his jacket pocket and slid the envelope addressed to his mom across the table. She took a long look at it, and then slowly opened it. As she looked inside, her eyes filled with tears. In the envelope was $5000 and a small handwritten note from Mr. Willie. It read, "Thank you for letting Jackson be a part of my life. My son was taken from me so early. For so many years after they died, I just went through the motions. I worked all the time to take my mind off things. When Jackson came along, I wasn't just doing him a favor by giving him a job; he was doing me a favor. He was helping me live again. I got to teach him a few things that I didn't get to teach my son and pass some things on to him, to help him out along the way too. He's always been a good listener and eager to learn new things, and he's not one of those know it all kids who don't want to learn from the older generation. Jackson listens to me and all the guys around the shop, and he takes it all in. I know it must be tough being a single mom and I know that it's expensive raising a child nowadays. Please take this money and don't give it back. Use it as you see fit to help you and Jackson out."

Jackson's mom sat holding the note, as the tears kept rolling down her face.

"What's wrong mom, what is it?"

She sat there for a while longer until she could talk. "He gave us $5000!"

"Wow! Tonight, keeps getting better and better."

"He said he wanted me to use the money to help take care of us and he didn't want me to give it back."

They both looked at each other not saying a word. In front of Jackson was the envelope Mr. Willie had given him. His mom looked down at it and said go ahead and open it. Jackson ran his fingers over the outside of the envelope and felt something hard on the inside. He opened it up and pulled out twenty-five $100 bills and an old key taped to a note. It said, "This key is to a very special car. It needs a lot of work, but anything worth having is worth working hard for, and I promise you she'll be worth it. The boys and I will help you along, but you'll have to do most of the work yourself. Just remember to learn everything you can and enjoy the experience. You won't forget it. You can see her tomorrow afternoon. Give me a call, and I'll come pick you up. Until then, take a look at this picture of how she is now and how she can be again when you bring her back to life."

Jackson pulled two pictures out of the envelope of a shiny Red 1966 Chevy Corvette and held them side-by-side.

"Her name is Betsy," the note went on. "She's a little worse for wear right now, but underneath, she's got a heart of gold, and she can fly once more."

Jackson looked at both pictures of Betsy again and imagined her years ago. In her prime, she had a beautiful candy apple red paint job and shiny chrome that lined her body from front to back. Right now, Betsy didn't look so good. Jackson had seen Mr. Willie, and the boys restore many cars since he worked at the garage, and each one looked unrecoverable, but when they were done, they had breathed new life into each one of those old classics. Jackson's mind raced, dreaming of how he would go step-by-step and piece by piece through restoring Betsy until that day when he could sit behind the wheel and fire her up for the first time.

"Mom, he gave me a Corvette to fix up and $2500 to do it! He said he would help me, but I would have to do most of the work. I can't wait to show Red."

Jackson's mom jumped up from the table and ran over to hug him. They held onto each other and thought about everything that happened that evening.

"That is unbelievable. What a blessing this is, and on such a special night." Leah said as she wiped a few tears of her own away.

After everything that happened, Jackson's mind was spinning in circles. Now Jackson had two girls on his mind, Hannah, and Betsy.

CHAPTER NINETEEN

# Dreams of the Future

Even though Jackson was maturing into a strong young man, his love for Christmas and especially Christmas morning never waned. As a young boy growing up, he couldn't even sleep just knowing that Santa was on his way. Even though they didn't have a lot, Jackson's mom made Christmas wonderful every year. She worked two jobs most of the year to make ends meet, but during Christmas, she went all out. Leah made neat crafts and lots of homemade goodies. They would go Christmas caroling with folks from the church, and they would even help provide food for neighbors in need, even though they were in the same boat.

This morning, Jackson opened his eyes and looked out the corner of one of the two windows that covered the East wall of his small room. The curtains blew quietly back and forth from the heater vent as it worked hard to keep their sparsely insulated home warm. The forty-year-old glass was cloudy with condensation from the warm air inside. A lone brilliant Red cardinal stood on a branch on the giant Magnolia tree outside his room and beckoned him to look. The sun was bright, and the sky was a clear diamond Blue. What a perfect day he thought. He had always wished for a "White Christmas," but this far south, snow only happens every few decades.

Stretching his arms above his head, he tried to work out the soreness in his arms and shoulders; a regular routine after a long day at the garage. Sitting there for a moment alone, he replayed in his mind his first glimpse of Hannah. Illusions of walking with her down the beach and getting to know her ran quickly through his mind. So many images ran through his mind, he couldn't think of anything else.

"I just have to get to know her," he said to himself as he stretched one more time.

His mom greeted him from the kitchen with a loud, "Good morning Jackson, Merry Christmas. It's time to get up."

He jumped out of bed and donned his robe and slippers. Usually, his robe stood silently in his closet, right beside his slippers. Today was a special occasion. It was Christmas after all. His mom was already making breakfast. The coffee was on, and the smell of fresh buttermilk pancakes and scrambled eggs awoke his senses. As he stepped into the living room, he saw his presents from "Santa" along with a few that were wrapped from his mom carefully laid out on the couch. Different size canvases and a new large easel were in one corner. A little farther down lay a brand-new brush set with many shapes and sizes. His eyes brightened, and he thought of the many things he could paint, and he couldn't wait to get started. As he continued to look around, he came across a large package wrapped in bright red and green wrapping. He yanked off the wrapping and discovered his first mechanic's toolset. It had wrenches and sockets of every size. His mom smiled, "Now you have the proper tools to work on that new car."

Jackson looked a little puzzled.

"Mr. Willie just gave me the car last night. How did you know I needed a toolset?" His mom answered, "Well, you've been working at Mr. Willie's garage for several years, and I thought it was time you had some tools of your own."

"Thanks, mom. Everything is wonderful. It's time for you to open your presents."

She sat down in her chair, and Jackson handed her two small boxes. The wrapping was a little shabby, but Leah didn't care. She opened the boxes and inside were a beautiful pair of gold earrings and a necklace to match.

"Jackson, this is too much. I told you not to buy me anything this year."

"How could I not give you something when all you do is give?" Leah's eyes welled up with tears again in less than 12 hours.

"Wow, this has been quite a wonderful weekend. Are you hungry? Everything is warm. Let's go eat and get ready for church."

Jackson and his mom enjoyed a fantastic breakfast and talked about the future and fixing up Old Betsy. They got ready and headed out to church. Running just a few minutes late to church, they slipped in the back door. The place was packed.

"Wow, there's a lot of Christmas Poinsettias here today."

Jackson looked up to the altar, and he saw only five beautiful pots.

"What do you mean a lot?" Jackson asked, "I only see a few up there."

His mom laughed.

"No, no, I'm not talking about the real Poinsettia's, I'm talking about all the people that are here that we don't normally see. You know, we only see Poinsettias once a year. That's the way it is with some of these folks. It's just a little joke. Let's get a seat."

They enjoyed the Christmas carols and listened carefully to the message, and when it was over, Jackson was met by several of the old men who had kept an eye out for him over the years as he grew up without his father around. Some took him hunting and camping; some took him fishing. They all tried to help in some way to give him a little "fatherly attention."

Jackson was fond of all of them but was a little scared of "Big Russ." He was a mountain of a man that made sure all the kids behaved in church. If you acted up, he would let you know right after the service. If you really acted up, he would come sit down next to you in the service. He seemed scary, but he had a heart of gold. Jackson and his mom had been invited to Shirley and Frank's home for Christmas dinner. Leah brought some of her famous desserts and Jackson helped her load the car. All day long he couldn't stop thinking about Hannah.

Christmas dinner was amazing. He couldn't remember the last time he ate so much. After he helped clear the table, he found his way to the den while Frank, Shirley and his mom talked in the kitchen. Jackson sat by the fireplace in a charming well-cushioned rocking chair. The chair was wide, and the fabric was soft and smooth. It was spacious enough to fit two people. He sat there staring into the fire and drifted off to sleep. The fire was so warm and inviting, he dreamed about Hannah again. He dreamed of taking her driving down the beach in his beautifully restored 66 Corvette. He dreamed of getting close to her. Jackson had a few girlfriends along the way, but never anyone really serious. No girl had ever made him feel like she did. Jackson's mom gently nudged him awake, and he slowly opened his eyes, not wanting to leave his dreams.

"It's time to go Jackson. That must have been some dream. You had such a smile on your face, and you were saying some pretty funny things."

He blushed and didn't say a word as he helped her load the car.

"Mom, Mr. Willie said to give him a call when we got home, and he would take me to meet Betsy."

"Give him a call; I bet you can't wait to see her," his mom smiled.

"Hey mom, can I ride down to the beach after I see Betsy?"

"What for?"

"Well, I accidentally put the waitress's pen in my pocket, and I wanted to return it."

"They're not open today Jackson."

"I know, but Hannah was having dinner with her aunt and uncle at the Seaside Grille and a few family members. I overheard her talking about it. You know the owners live in a loft above the restaurant don't you."

Jackson's mom laughed and said, "I'll take you down there to return it."

"No that's okay mom, I can ride my bike to Mr. Willie's place, and he can take me and my bike to see Betsy and then I'll ask him to drop me off at the beach. I can ride my bike back home."

Leah gave a funny smile and just shook her head and told him to be careful.

"Don't forget your jacket."

CHAPTER TWENTY

# Betsy

"Hey, Mr. Willie, Merry Christmas," Jackson spoke into the phone.

"Merry Christmas buddy. I guess you're ready to meet Betsy from the sound of your voice?"

"Yes sir, I sure am."

"I'll pick you up at 5 o'clock, see you in a little while."

"Okay, I'll see you then Mr. Willie."

Jackson hung up the phone and went to the bathroom to get ready. He stared in the mirror and practiced what he would say to Hannah. Nothing made sense or sounded cool. He looked down at his watch and realized he didn't have much time left to get ready. He took a quick shower and put some new cologne on he just got for Christmas. Being almost 18, he was becoming a strong young man. Those years of working in the garage and doing landscaping continued to keep him lean and fit. He looked in the mirror one more time to find the words, but he just kept stumbling over the introduction.

Mr. Willie pulled up in the driveway and tapped his horn. Jackson kissed his mom goodbye and headed out the door.

"Be careful Jackson."

"I will mom, don't worry."

Jackson waved to Mr. Willie and said Merry Christmas as he grabbed his bike from the side of the house.

"Would you mind dropping me off at the Seaside Grille on Folly after we meet Betsy?"

"What do you need to go there for? They're closed for Christmas."

"I know, but since I accidentally put Hannah's pen in my pocket, I wanted to return it to her."

Mr. Willie just laughed and said "She won't miss that pen, man. I guess you planned that all along, huh?"

"No, no. It was an accident. Honest. Maybe it has some sentimental value to her," Jackson grinned.

"Ok, ok. I'll take you there. I'll come back and pick you up too. It's getting cold out, and that's a long way back at night on a bike. Just call me when you're ready, and I'll come back and pick you up."

"Thanks, Mr. Willie."

"Hop in and let's go meet your other girl Betsy."

Jackson jumped in, and they were off towards the garage. Mr. Willie pulled around the back and stopped in front of a car with an old Army tarp on it.

"Are you ready to see her? Just remember, she's been through a lot, but we can make her good as new again."

Jackson jumped out, and his heart pounded with anticipation. Mr. Willie walked over and with one swift motion, pulled the tarp off, and there stood a 66 Chevy Corvette Stingray fastback. Under what was left of the hood was a 427-cubic Inch Big Block engine with a huge 4 Barrel Holley carburetor. Mr. Willie was right; she looked like she had been through the war herself. There was only one quarter panel left that didn't have any damage. Even though most of the body would need a lot of work, most of the engine and frame were intact. The steering wheel was missing, and all the seats were damaged. The interior and exterior would take a long time to make new again. Underneath the years of dirt, Jackson saw that famous Rally Red color from the original paint job.

"I know she looks tough, but we can fix her. Skeeter is one of the best body repairmen I know. He's restored over ten cars in the last five years. He told me he would be glad to help you."

"I saw the old tarp last week, but I didn't know what it was," smiled Jackson.

"I bought it at the auction. All the boys said they would help, but you had to do most of the work yourself. If we don't have any customers, you can work on it any chance you get, and I'll stay with you anytime you want to work on it after we close, or you can come up here and work on it by yourself. I'll give you the key."

"Mr. Willie, I don't know what to say." Jackson's eyes welled up with a few tears. "This is great. I know we can make her new again. I can get my buddy Red to help too. He loves cars. His dad has an old 68 Mustang that looks great, and Red helped him restore it."

He reached over and gave Mr. Willie a great big bear hug.

"Okay, okay, you're welcome. We can get started Monday after work."

"That sounds great."

"You ready to go visit your other girl?"

"Yes, sir."

Mr. Willie pulled his Silverado into the parking lot of the Seaside Grille.

"Just call me when you're ready, and I'll come back to pick you up."

"Thanks, Mr. Willie."

Jackson looked around, and the sun was almost a faded memory for this Christmas day. There wasn't a soul in sight. Jackson crept up to the small side window he and Mr. Willie had looked through the night before. A giant fire was roaring in the fireplace, and everyone was talking. He saw Becky walking around, trying to take care of everyone, but he didn't see Hannah.

"Hey, can I help you?"

Jackson was startled and jumped and spun around trying to compose himself. There he stood, only a few feet from Hannah. Instantly his palms started sweating, and his heart was pounding.

"We're closed today. Sorry."

A few awkward seconds elapsed and then Hannah spoke up again.

"Oh, hey. You were here last night, weren't you?"

Trying not to look so nervous, Jackson said, "Yeah we were, I just came back to return the pen, I accidentally borrowed from you last night."

Jackson pulled the pen out of his pocket and handed it to her. Hannah looked at the pen and smiled.

"We have a lot of these. Uncle John just got a box of a thousand in. You could have just kept it."

Smiling, he went on, "I didn't know if it had any sentimental value, so I thought it would be good if I brought it back to you in person."

They stared at one another and exchanged deep warm smiles without saying a word. Becky looked out the window and saw Jackson talking to Hannah. She motioned for John to look and they both grinned. They knew Jackson from the times he spent there in the summer and when he and Willie would stop in. They even bought one of his paintings the year before. Becky hugged John and patted him on his chest.

"How long have you been here Hannah? Mrs. Becky said you used to live in Michigan."

"I've been here a few weeks. My mother and I lived up on Lake Michigan in a place called Traverse City. She died not so long ago, and I didn't want to spend a gloomy Christmas in that house this year."

"I'm sorry about your mom." Jackson cringed because he realized Hannah was getting upset.

"Thanks. She had a lengthy battle with breast cancer, and now she's at peace in Heaven. You didn't have to come down here to bring me that pen."

Changing the subject, Jackson asked, "Would you like to take a walk down the pier? We can look back across the river and watch the sun go down."

"Sure, I'd like that. I'll be right back."

Hannah stopped back inside and told Becky she was going to take a walk down the pier with Jackson. As each moment passed, it began to get colder, but the sky was a brilliant shade of dark blue, amber and red. They both strolled side by side stopping at a few benches along the way to stop and talk.

Hannah stopped. "I love this pier. I could stay out here all day, and since no one else is here, I'll just call it my pier for the day. When I first got here, I walked up and down this pier several times a day. In the early morning, on my breaks, whenever I got the chance, I would walk out here. This pier is the closest thing I have that reminds me of home. Being out here when all I can hear are the sounds of the ocean and the seagulls, is comforting to me. There's no hustle and bustle out here. Everything is relaxed. As I walked down its long-worn boards to the end, I saw women older than my mom fishing with their husbands and children and grandchildren, and I kept saying to myself, why can't my mom still be alive to be here with me. Why did she have to go so young? I feel so lost without her. The grief is unbearable sometimes."

Jackson just nodded in agreement. He didn't have any words to say. He wanted to hold her, but since he'd only met her yesterday, he didn't think he should.

"Wow, it's getting colder out here." Hannah shivered.

Jackson quickly pulled off his new fleece jacket and wrapped it around Hannah.

"You don't have to do that; now you'll be cold."

"I'll be okay; I'm a little warm anyway."

"This jacket sure is warm and soft and it smells great too. What cologne is that?"

Jackson smiled and told her what it was and asked if she was warm.

"I am now."

Finally, reaching the end of the pier, they sat down on one of the big fishing benches. It was worn and weathered, but the sun, the wind, and the rain had made it smooth as she ran her hands along it. The sun had at last gone to bed for the night, and the moon had taken over. Stars shined brightly on this chilly, crisp night. The new Christmas wreath the county had put up on the pavilion at the end of the pier sparkled against the backdrop of the dark blue sky. All the lanterns were lit, lighting the way down the pier. This was the first time Jackson had been on the pier when there was no one else around. Usually a few natives always walked along the beach, but not tonight. The pier and the beach were all theirs, not a soul in sight.

"Do you live around here Jackson?"

"I live about 8 miles from here. I work for the man I was with last night. He gave me a job when I was 15 and really too young to work, but it's been great. I've learned a lot. He's been more like a father to me than a boss. We do a lot of things together, and he has taught me so many things about life."

"What kind of work is it?"

"Mr. Willie owns the Island Garage down on Folly Road. We can fix anything on a car. He taught me how to do most everything on a car from putting new tires on to overhauling an engine. My parents got divorced when I was little, and my dad lives in Washington State. I see him once or twice a year maybe. Mr. Willie is the best man I know. He knows pretty much everything, and he's the nicest person you would ever want to meet. He gave me a really special Christmas present earlier today."

"Oh yeah, what was that?"

"It was an old 66 Chevy Corvette that we're going to fix up. It'll be my first car. He gave me some money too to help fix it up. I've had my license for a couple of years now, but my mom and I only have one car. When Betsy is finished..."

"Who's Betsy?"

"She's the Corvette. That's what we named her. I'm not sure why people call their cars female names, but maybe it's because they can be so beautiful on the outside, and hot on the inside, and all you want to do is be with them."

"Oh really?" Hannah smiled.

"Yeah, when Betsy is finished, I'll be taking her on drives everywhere along the beach. Hopefully, you can come with me..."

"That's an awesome gift. He must really think a lot about you."

Jackson told Hannah the story of Mr. Willie losing his family, and how everyone at the garage helped him through it.

"He has taken me under his wing and taught me things he didn't get a chance to teach his son. It's helped me a lot since my dad hasn't been around. Mr. Willie is someone I can look up to. He's showing me how to be a man."

After a while, the two just sat there in silence for a few short minutes then Hannah broke the silence and began to talk about her life back in Michigan. The two talked for almost 2 hours. She told him about her grandmother and how she had helped raise her. Her father had been killed in an auto accident when she was seven. Hannah and her mom had moved in with her. Her dad was headed home on a Friday afternoon, and Hannah and her mom had their car packed and ready to go on a weekend camping trip when a drunk driver crossed the middle line and hit him head-on. The policeman at the scene said he died instantly. The drunk driver in the other car didn't have a scratch on him. He was convicted of felony DUI and sent to prison. Twelve years later she was still feeling the pain and the loss of her father. Now, she didn't have her mother either. She had been dealt a terrible blow to be so young and lose both parents.

Jackson pondered what he might say, but all he could do was lean over a little, and he slowly reached for her hand. When his fingers touched her hand, he could feel his body tense up. Jackson didn't know if he should, but Hannah grabbed his hand tightly and leaned into him. He put his arm around her, and she leaned her head against his chest.

"Your heart sure is beating fast, are you okay?"

"Sure; I guess I'm just a little nervous."

Hannah smiled that beautiful genuine smile and leaned into him again.

"It's getting late; I guess I better get back to my Aunt and Uncle. It has been great meeting you Jackson. I feel like I've known you for a long time."

"I feel the same way about you Hannah."

The two strolled their way back to the restaurant and Hannah invited him inside. Becky and John got up and invited him in for some cake and to sit by the fire. Jackson thanked them and came inside for a few minutes. Hannah brought him a piece of chocolate cake, and they sat down in the big rocking chairs next to the fire. They talked some more, and Jackson looked at his watch. It was getting close to ten o'clock. "I better give Mr. Willie a call, he was going to give me a ride home."

"I can give you a ride home. Uncle John is letting me use his old VW Bug. Do you want to leave now?"

"Are you sure it's not too much trouble?"

"It's no trouble."

"Do you mind if I use your phone to call him?"

"Go ahead, its right behind the counter."

Jackson called Mr. Willie and let him know he didn't need a ride.

"I can stay a while longer if I'm not intruding on your family."

"They don't mind. We've been here all day."

They sat by the fire for another hour and talked all about Folly Beach and the lifestyle there and around Charleston. Jackson looked at the clock again and said, "I guess I better go. It's getting late."

Hannah jumped up, "I'll get my keys."

Jackson said his goodbyes and thanked Becky and John for their hospitality, and then they were on their way. Hannah pulled up in Jackson's driveway and turned off the old VW.

"I had a wonderful time talking to you tonight Jackson. I'm glad you thought the pen was important to me to bring it back or else we might not have gotten to talk."

Jackson smiled and said, "To be honest, I just had to see you again. I've never met anyone like you before, and I just needed to see you again. Thanks so much for the ride home. Can I see you again?"

"How about tomorrow afternoon after work?"

"That sounds great."

In an instant, Hannah leaned over and gave Jackson a big kiss on the cheek. Jackson didn't know what to say, he just reached down and touched her soft hand again and thanked her for the ride. He jumped out and waved goodbye. Jackson walked to the edge of the road and watched her disappear into the night. Jackson's mom had seen the last few minutes of what transpired in the car as she looked out the window. Busting into the house, Jackson yelled, "Mom, I had the most wonderful night ever."

"What's all the fuss about? Why are you coming in so late?"

"I went to look at Betsy, and she was great, and then Mr. Willie took me back to see Hannah, and I talked to her for hours. She's wonderful. I'm going back to see her tomorrow."

"Wait a minute, who's Hannah and how did you get her to bring you home?"

"Remember, I told you she was Mrs. Becky's niece."

"Ok, now I remember."

They sat and talked until after midnight.

"You better get a shower and get to bed young man; 5:30 AM comes early."

"I will mom. I love you. Good night."

Jackson showered and got in bed. His curtains were still moving just like on Christmas morning, and he looked out and saw the beautiful moon that he and Hannah had talked under. He went over the evening repeatedly in his mind. Across town back at the loft above the Grill, Hannah stepped out of the shower and got ready for bed herself. As she slipped on her nightgown, she felt the softness of it and wrapped her arms together and remembered how good it felt to be hugged by Jackson. Hannah laid her beautiful head on her pillow and looked out her window and gazed at the bright, inviting moonlight. She wondered if Jackson saw it too.

CHAPTER TWENTY-ONE

# Getting Closer

Monday morning came, and Jackson's alarm went off promptly at 5:30 AM. Jackson's mom Leah was up with the coffee on and making breakfast. Jackson made his way to the kitchen, poured himself a fresh cup, grabbed a quick bite and they both headed off to work.

"Have a great day at work and be careful Jackson."

"I will mom; you too. I love you."

Jackson pedaled his bike at top speed and pulled into the garage just as Mr. Willie pulled up. They opened the garage and began their morning routine. Mr. Willie got the cash register and the office ready while Jackson got the garage ready for the guys. Mr. Willie didn't say a word about last night. Jackson was dying to tell him, so after he got everything started up, he poured himself and Mr. Willie a cup of coffee and rushed in to tell him what happened last night. Mr. Willie smiled and laughed as he listened to every word.

"Well, what are you going to do with two girls on your mind?"

"What two girls? It's just Hannah."

"What about ol' Betsy the Corvette?"

"Oh, sorry, I didn't forget about her. I can't wait to get started. Maybe I can start today if it's not too busy?"

"Skeeter will be in later; he's doing something for me this morning. He said he would look at it when he gets back. The first thing we need to do though is get her up on the lift and do a good check on the frame, and then we need to get her running. After that, we can work on the body and the interior."

They only had a few customers all morning. A lot of people had gone out of town for the holidays, but Mr. Willie wanted to be open to help anyone who needed them. He would say that people that came to visit might need some help getting back. Right after 10 o'clock, Skeeter pulled up in an old Ford F100. It was a little beat up, but overall it was in good condition.

"What's this truck for?" Jackson asked.

"It's the parts truck. If we need a part, Willie wants us to be able to go get it instead of waiting for them to deliver it. He said it would save our customers time waiting for a part to arrive."

Mr. Willie came out smiling, "She looks real good Skeeter. Hey

Jackson, I was thinking that maybe you could take care of this old parts truck until you get Betsy ready to go. What do you think?"

"You mean I can drive it until I get Betsy going?"

"Sure, you can take it home with you and drive it around. You can use it for whatever you want but take good care of my truck. We will need it to pick up parts for us during the day. Since you're a senior this year and you get out around 11:30 AM that should be okay for us. We can use another vehicle to pick up anything if we need to before you get here. It will be a company truck, so the garage will pay for the insurance. You'll just have to pay for the gas on the weekends."

"Thanks, Mr. Willie, I don't know what to say."

"Say you'll take care of her and not wreck my truck."

"I will take good care of her, don't worry."

As they turned around, Jackson and Mr. Willie heard the most terrible grinding noise coming from an old Chevy pickup as a young man pulled up.

Mr. Willie met him at the truck.

"Young man, your brakes don't sound too good."

The young man hopped out of the pickup wearing an Army uniform. He was Private First Class Will Hanan that had graduated from James Island High a couple of years before. He was home on Christmas leave but needed to be back at Fort Jackson outside of Columbia by Midnight.

"Let's get the wheels off and take a look."

Mr. Willie smiled as he got the keys from Will. Skeeter guided him into the bay, and they got it up and took the front wheels off. Both sets of drums were in bad shape.

"Your drums need to be replaced. I can't believe they've lasted you this long. We don't have them here, but the parts store down the street stocks them."

The young private started looking worried.

"How much is this going to cost?"

"Let's see, Mr. Willie smiled as he added the figures. With new rotors and pads and all the labor, it will be about... Oh wait a minute, I forgot to include your military discount. It will be about $100.00. Is that okay with you?"

Will took a deep breath.

"Yes, sir that'll be just fine. Thank you."

Mr. Willie watched as the young soldier breathed a sigh of relief.

"It's the least I could do for my fellow veteran."

Jackson went and picked up the new rotors, and Skeeter and JD put them on for Will and thanked him for his service. They waved goodbye as he headed back to Fort Jackson.

Near closing time, Jackson was finishing up a customer's invoice and looked out the front window as Hannah's VW bug pulled up. Jackson's heart sped up as he dropped the invoice on the counter and stepped outside to meet her.

"Hey," she smiled as she got out of the old VW bug.

"Hey. I didn't know you were going to stop by. It's great to see you. You sure look beautiful today."

Hannah smiled and stared at him.

"I was just finishing up some paperwork. Is there something wrong with your car Hannah?"

"No, I just wanted to see you again. You are the first person I have really talked to outside of my family about my mom, and I had a great time getting to know you. You listened to me, and the best part is, you didn't just try to fix it. It will take a long time for that. I thought we could talk some more."

"Sure, I get off in a few minutes, and I could go home and take a shower and meet you somewhere."

"Can't you go like that?"

Jackson looked down at his dirty uniform and said, "How about I at least go wash up a little and change clothes?"

"Ok, I'll wait for you."

By this time, Mr. Willie had finished up in the garage and was heading into the office when he got a glimpse of what was going on outside. Jackson walked in, and Mr. Willie smiled at him.

"So, that's why you didn't need a ride home last night."

"Why didn't you ask me about her this morning?" Jackson asked with a perplexing tone.

"I figured when you were ready, you'd tell me."

"She's so wonderful Mr. Willie. She came here just to see me, so we could talk again. Do you mind if I leave a little early?"

"Go ahead buddy, have fun."

Jackson went into the locker room and washed up the best he could without a full shower. He put on his old jeans; they were the softest and the best fitting. He pulled on his dark blue sweatshirt, put on a little cologne and out the door he went saying his goodbyes to Mr. Willie and the boys. They all looked and laughed.

"Would you like to see Betsy?"

"She's here?"

"Yeah, she's in the back. I'll take you around and introduce you to her."

They walked around to the back and Jackson unveiled the old beauty. Hannah looked a little apprehensive.

"She's had a pretty hard life; do you think you can fix her up again?"

Jackson opened the passenger door and reached into the glove box revealing an old Polaroid picture of Betsy the day her original owner bought her. He was smiling with his wife standing in front of the shiny new Rally Red Corvette. Hannah looked at the picture and then looked at Betsy; then she looked again.

"You sure you can do this?"

"The guys in the garage say they can. I already have a lot of parts, courtesy of Mr. Willie. We're getting started tomorrow."

Jackson threw the old tarp back on Betsy and wished her good night. They walked back up to leave as Hannah took him by the hand.

"I have a feeling you will be driving her real soon. I can't wait to go for a ride."

"We will go for that ride sooner than you think. I'll work on it every chance I get. Would you like to go get something to eat?"

"Sure, I heard about this great barbecue place down on Folly Road. Martin's or something like that."

"You mean Melvin's; it's the best barbecue place around. I'd love to take you there."

They arrived at Melvin's, and Jackson got her up to speed on all the best food on the menu and what to expect. Melvin's has been a staple on James Island for years. They sat down in a corner booth that afforded them some privacy. They talked for hours after their meal over lots of iced tea and banana pudding.

"This banana pudding is the best dessert I've ever had." Hannah smiled.

She put her spoon down and reached over and grabbed his hand.

"I had a wonderful time tonight Jackson. Thanks for listening."

While they talked, a server named Lily stopped by their table after wiping down all the others around them.

"Jackson, it's almost 9 o'clock, and we'll be closing soon. Do you mind if we said goodnight and saw you again real soon?"

Hannah and Jackson looked over at the pig-shaped clock on the wall and apologized to Lilly for staying so long. They jumped up and helped clear the table and headed back towards the beach.

"Hannah, could you pull into the garage for a minute? Mr. Willie is letting me use this work truck until I get Betsy finished. I'll follow you back to the beach."

When the young couple arrived back at the Seaside Grille, it was a little past closing time and John and Becky were cleaning up.

"Hi Jackson," Becky smiled as she finished the last table. They sat down in front of the roaring fire again to talk. Today, John had bought a new leather love seat and it got delivered earlier. It was the softest leather they had ever felt. Becky and John said their goodnight's and headed upstairs to the loft above the restaurant. All the lights were off except for a few Christmas lights that still twinkled in the windows. The warm glow of the fire made Hannah's eyes sparkle.

"I thought about you all day," Hannah smiled. "It took me a long time to go to sleep last night."

"Me too, I kept replaying our conversation in my mind, and I kept thinking about how good it felt to hold you. I know we haven't known each other but just a few hours, but I feel like I already know you and I want to get to know you more."

Hannah leaned into him and kissed him on his cheek. "Maybe you will get to. I have to go to the ladies' room; I'll be right back."

Hannah made her way down the weathered hardwood floors and into the corridor by the restrooms when she glanced at the beautiful painting hanging on the wall separating the two. She looked down at the corner of the painting and saw the artist's signature. She could barely make it out, Jackson Henderson. Her heart skipped a few beats. She stood there and studied it over and over. Hannah had admired that painting every time she passed by, but she never paid attention to who painted it until tonight. It was a nighttime portrait of the pier and the ocean with a Harvest Moon shining on the waves. In the distance, she could see the light at the end of the pier on top of the pavilion. She looked out the window, and the same display was going on outside. It was the biggest moon she had ever seen. Jackson watched her all the way to the restroom and saw her stop. He saw her look outside and then back to the painting and then back again. Then she turned and looked at him. She came running back full speed.

"You painted that?"

Jackson smiled. "Yeah, I did, a few years ago."

"When you were 15?"

"I was almost 16. Do you like it? Becky and John bought it one day when I was selling them in the park."

"What do you mean them? Are there more? And yes, I love it. It's so realistic. It almost looks like a picture instead of a painting."

"I started painting one day at the end of Fifth grade, and I have ever since. I have sold a few paintings over the years, but I haven't made a lot of money."

Jackson told her the story of how he got started, and the paintings he sold. Before they knew it, the clock over the fire was chiming Midnight.

"I better go; it's getting late."

Hannah walked him to the door and hugged him goodnight and kissed him on the cheek again. This time, she held it there much longer than last night. This time, he didn't turn to go, he turned in to her and gently kissed her lips. Instantly every nerve in his body was pulsed, and she kissed him again. They held their warm embrace and finally kissed again for the third time.

"Your heart's beating so fast again. Mine is too. Be careful driving home."

"I'll see you tomorrow," Jackson smiled as he stumbled down the steps looking back at her.

Mr. Willie's old Ford Pickup truck was on auto-pilot as Jackson cruised through the green lights on Folly Road. He kept picturing himself back in Hannah's arms, and he didn't want to leave. Jackson had never felt this way about anyone. Every ounce of his being was on heightened alert, and he couldn't stop thinking about her. He pulled in the driveway, got a shower and dressed for bed. He looked out the window facing east toward Hannah and whispered,

"Here goes another sleepless night."

CHAPTER TWENTY-TWO

# New Year's Eve

December 31st; one day before the New Year and Jackson and Hannah had been inseparable since they met. Jackson spent every moment he could with her. As soon as work was over, he would head straight for the beach and the Seaside Grille. While Hannah worked, he sat in a corner booth and read or drew out a sketch for his next project. She was the subject of most of his sketches. He helped her clean the tables and carry out the food; anything to be close to her. Becky and John offered to pay him, but he wouldn't take it. They kept him fed, and that was enough for him.

Tonight, was New Year's Eve and the Seaside Grille was having its annual New Year's Eve Party. It was a tradition at the beach. Everyone would enjoy the party and dancing, and then they would shoot fireworks off the end of the pier. A huge crowd would gather as they counted down the minutes. Not only were the adults at the party, John and Becky decorated the big room downstairs for the teenagers to have fun too. No alcohol for the teenagers, but a lot of food, fun, and dancing. It was a safe place for them to go and it kept them out of trouble. Becky always outdid herself every year, and the kids kept wondering what she would come up with next.

Tonight, was very special; all the rooms sparkled with silver decorations. Lights hung everywhere, and the place looked like a Winter Wonderland. Jackson helped put up the decorations, and now he was helping in the kitchen with all the orders. It was getting close to Midnight, and the partyers were getting ready to watch the ball drop in Times Square. All the TV's tuned in, and the countdown began. 10, 9, 8... 3, 2, 1, the ball dropped, and everyone around was celebrating the New Year. Jackson grabbed Hannah by the hand and motioned for the door. They made their way through the crowds and out into the chilly night. Jackson stopped at the railing and looked out at the fireworks exploding in all their splendor; then he turned to Hannah.

"I know I've only known you less than a week, but I'm in love with you. I've never felt like this before, so I know it must be love because I can't stop thinking about you, and I want to spend every moment with you."

Hannah smiled, then lowered her head to his chest, shielding herself from the midnight breeze. Her perfume smelled so incredible; it was intoxicating. She looked up into his eyes... "I feel the same way too; I was nervous because I didn't know if you felt the same way I did. Aunt Becky noticed it in me on Christmas night. Can you believe that? She told me tonight that she watched me every day with you since Christmas night and she said each day I got happier and happier. I knew I was happy, but I didn't know anyone else could tell, except you of course."

They hugged in the most caring embrace. "Jackson, did you make a New Year's resolution?"

"Sure, I did, I resolve to spend every waking moment I can with you."

Hannah pondered his words in her heart; "Well, I'll make sure you keep that resolution."

Jackson leaned down to kiss her and as their tongues entwined for the first time, both their hearts exploded with fiery passion, and they knew at that moment that they were meant for each other.

Jackson smiled at her as they came up for air.

"Some people say that at our age, we can't tell what love is and that it's just a fantasy. I've had a few girlfriends before, but I haven't ever felt like this. You're the most genuine girl I've ever met. What you see is what you get. I wish I didn't have to sleep; I wish I could lie next to you and just quietly watch you sleep. I wish I could trace the outline of your beautiful face and the beautiful curves of your body."

They walked down the pier, closer to the fireworks. The percussion sound of the fireworks made it hard to hear.

"You see and feel those fireworks up there? That's how I feel every time I kiss you and hold you."

They both held each other for the rest of the Midnight spectacular, then made their way back to the Grille to help close. It was almost 2:00 AM and everyone finally headed home. John had a taxi service that took anyone home who needed a ride, so they wouldn't get behind the wheel after having a drink. Jackson had finished sweeping up downstairs, and he took the final bag of trash out. Hannah finished cleaning the tables upstairs, and she and Becky finished mopping the floors. John and the other cooks finished cleaning the kitchen and were ready to head home. Hannah walked Jackson to his truck to say good night.

"I've never had a better New Year's Eve Hannah. It was the most special evening ever. The fireworks were brighter, and everything was so clear and so real; I can't explain it. One thing I do know is that I have fallen in love with you. I mean completely in love."

"Well, that makes two of us. I love you too. Be careful driving home; I'll see you tomorrow."

Jackson cranked the truck up but couldn't bring himself to get inside. He didn't want to leave. He began to get a groaning pain down deep in his core.

"I wish I didn't have to leave."

"I wish you didn't have to go either, but you have to. Your mom is probably worried sick about you."

"I told her I'd be home around 2:30 AM; she normally sleeps on the couch until I get home."

"Well, hurry home so I can see you again tomorrow. I had the most wonderful night."

Jackson wrapped Hannah in a big hug and stared down into her beautiful sapphire blue eyes. She loved feeling his warmth against her.

"I won't get much sleep again tonight thinking about you, but I guess I should try. I love you, Hannah. I've never said that to a girl before... other than my mom of course. I just can't explain how my heart feels. Every time I see you, my heart starts pounding like it's gonna come out of my chest."

Hannah stared at him, lost in thought.

"What made you come to the Grille on Christmas Eve?"

"It was Mr. Willie's idea," as he started to "let the cat out of the bag" about the money Mr. Willie had left but quickly stopped himself just in time and recovered.

"He likes to go out on Christmas Eve to see all the people; especially the people that have to work. He asked me to go along. It was the best thing I could have ever done... coming with him."

"I think so too."

Hannah leaned in and lowered her head into his firm, beating chest, and she was aroused by the scent of his body and his cologne. She held on tighter and breathed in deep, drinking him in.

"I'm so glad you came with Mr. Willie. You've started my New Year's off with great hope for the future. A few weeks ago, I couldn't tell you what the future would hold for me. Maybe Christmas Eve and the nights we've shared since have started to paint me a new picture."

Jackson smiled and leaned down and kissed her, then slowly started kissing her down her neck. Her rapid breath and gentle sigh told him she approved. He moved back over to her iced pink glossed lips and stayed there a while. They both were trembling with passion when he returned to her neck, then he ever so gently began kissing and moving along her ears and then behind them. As his lips and tongue gently kissed her, she breathed in deeply, trying to catch her breath. They stood there loving each other for what seemed like hours.

Finally, Hannah pulled away slightly, gasping for air.

"Wow..."

Jackson looked at her and just stared, taking in all her beauty.

"You gotta go Jackson. It's getting so late."

"I don't want to go." Jackson frowned.

Hannah grabbed him and kissed him quickly once more and said.

"You have to go; the sun will be up soon."

Jackson disappointingly got into the truck and cranked it up while staring at Hannah. He turned it towards home and waved to her and blew another kiss to her good night. Jackson was driving on instinct again on the way home with his thoughts pouring through his mind. What would he do? He didn't want to be anywhere without her.

CHAPTER TWENTY-THREE

# Love

A few hours' sleep had been the routine for Jackson the last week. His mom Leah sat down on his bed to wake him up.

"Wow Jackson, 4:00 AM! That's later than you've ever stayed out. This girl must be something special?"

Jackson bounded up in his bed.

"She is mom. She's wonderful."

Jackson fumbled for the right words as he scratched his head and stretched his strong arms above his head.

"It's unexplainable how great she is. We've only known each other a week, but we've talked for hours and hours about everything. I feel like I've known her my whole life. Mom... I love her."

Leah had a puzzled look on her face.

"Love."

"I told her I loved her because I do. I've never said it to any girl before, and I've never felt this way before. I've dated a few girls, but nothing ever felt like this. She’s beautiful and kind, but most of all she’s genuine. She's the real thing. What you see is what you get, and what you see is something else."

"But love Jackson? That's a serious word."

"I know it is, and I'm not using it lightly. I've liked a lot of girls before, but there has never been a time when I thought or said that I loved them. It just wasn't there. This is more real to me than anything I've ever felt."

"You better be careful son and not get your heart broken. Love is a wonderful thing if you are both committed and it's terrible if you're not. It can ruin your life and sour you as a person if you're not careful. I want you to really think about that as time goes by with you and Hannah. Life or love is not always easy."

"I will mom. I promise."

"Let's get something to eat; I have to get to work."

CHAPTER TWENTY-FOUR

# 53

School began again after Christmas break, and Jackson hardly slept between January and Valentine's Day. Between schoolwork, the garage, fixing ol' Betsy the Corvette and Hannah, there was scarce little time for sleep. He usually laid his head down on his pillow to dream about Hannah around 12:30 AM and was greeted by his mom at 5:30 AM for school.

"Hey mom, did Mr. Steve say I could bring Hannah to the "River Room" for our Valentine's dinner tonight?"

"He said if you came at 5:00 PM, you and Hannah could have the "River Room" to yourself before all the other customers started arriving."

"That's great."

Jackson had asked Mr. Willie if he could be off two weeks ago, so he could take Hannah out for Valentine's. Jackson gulped down a little breakfast and flew out the door for school. Later that afternoon, Jackson pulled Mr. Willie's truck into the local florist, eager to pick up his special order. Kate, the florist, smiled and said to Jackson, "I've never got an order for 53 roses before. Why 53 roses?"

"It's just a really special number," Jackson replied, not wanting to start a conversation. He was out the door and over to his other favorite restaurant early to set up the "River Room."

The "River Room" was at the Sand Dunes Club restaurant that Leah worked at on the weekends. The "River Room" faced west looking out over the tranquil flowing Folly River. The large table in the center of the room was arranged so that the guests on both sides of the table could look through the giant picture window out into the marsh landscape and watch the sun sink low in the sky. Jackson met three of the waitresses who were friends with his mom, and they set up the room with roses placed strategically throughout the room.

"This sure is a lot of roses Jackson," Barbara replied. "Why do you have so many?"

"It's just a special number to Hannah and me."

Barbara laughed and checked the rest of the room. Everything was beautiful and ready for Jackson and Hannah. The owner, Steve, stopped by to check on Jackson and see if the room was up to his expectations.

"Thanks so much for letting us use this room, Mr. Steve. It means a lot."

"You're welcome, Jackson. Do you think you will be done by 6:30 PM? We have a large group that would like to use it then."

"Yes, sir that will be plenty of time. Thanks again."

Jackson finished looking around the room and headed out to pick up Hannah back at the Seaside Grille. He arrived at the beach within a few minutes, and Hannah was waiting in the back-corner booth by the fireplace. The day had been clear with ocean blue skies, but it was cold. The lights gently lit the pier as the sun began its descent for the day. Jackson said hello to Becky and John, and then they were on their way to the "River Room," a few miles away.

"Where are we going?" Hannah asked with a smile.

"Someplace very special. I know you'll love it."

They made their way up the crushed oyster shell driveway that meandered through a line of live oak trees swaying in the wind. A few pesky pelicans guarded the entrance but reluctantly moved as they walked up. As they entered the lobby, Mr. Steve and Lily, the hostess, were waiting on them and greeted them with a smile. While they waited in the lobby, Hannah's eyes noticed a large portrait of the restaurant at sundown. She walked over to it and stood there admiring the radiant colors and sharp detail of the painting and then she saw the small plaque with the picture and citation of the much younger Jackson. She raised her hand to her mouth trying to catch her breath in amazement and then turned to see Jackson smiling.

"This is unbelievable! It's so beautiful."

"So, you like it then?" Jackson grinned. "Really, I've never seen anything like this and especially to have done it when you were so young. Could you paint something for me someday?"

“I’ll be glad to paint you anything you wish Hannah.”

Just as they were talking, Lily came back and said their room was ready. They followed her around the quaint restaurant filled with nautical novelties and pictures of Charleston and Folly Beach adorning the walls. Lily opened the double glass doors into the "River Room," and Jackson and Hannah were greeted with the most beautiful auburn sundown, reflecting a smile across the river.

"This place is beautiful Jackson, what a view!"

She leaned over and kissed Jackson with a warm, wet passionate kiss, and she held it there, not wanting to stop.

"The roses are so beautiful! I love them."

Hannah walked around to every vase and touched each one and then turned and looked lovingly back to Jackson. After she had made her rounds of the room, she stopped and looked out the giant picture window and asked him, "How many roses are here?"

"53 roses; one for every day I've known you. They've been the best 53 days of my life."

Hannah didn't know what to say. She ran to Jackson and jumped into his strong arms and kissed him passionately. After they both came up for breath, Jackson laughed.

"So, I guess that means you like the room and the roses?"

They sat down at the old long Teak table, and Hannah ran her fingers along it feeling the smoothness that came with its age. She wondered how many meals and parties this old table had been a part of, and now with them together in the room alone, she thought about how they would become part of its history. All the memories shared there; mostly good she thought, but probably a few heart breaks.

"This place is perfect Jackson; it's just so perfect."

Jackson wrapped his right arm around her and kissed her neck. Instantly he felt her rapid breath, and he could feel her heart pick up pace. He continued around the back of her neck along her ear, and he was taking his time, and he lingered in those spots that seemed to excite her the most. Her body language and gentle sighs guided his lips. He caressed her left hand as he continued in a southerly direction down her back. After she couldn't take it any longer, she turned and pulled him to her, their hearts beating in unison.

"Good evening ya'll." They were startled by a sweet southern accent, they both quickly looked up trying to compose themselves. Standing in front of their table was Rita, Jackson's mom's best friend at the restaurant.

"Hey Rita," Jackson smiled.

"Hey Jackson; I guess this must be the beautiful Hannah?"

"Yes, ma'am it is."

"Hey Hannah, I'm Rita. Leah has told me a lot about you, and I'm glad to finally meet you. She said Jackson hasn't been the same young man since he met you."

Jackson's face turned a bright shade of red, and he tried to move the conversation along as he told Hannah about Rita and his mom's friendship with her.

"It's great to meet you, Rita, this room is fantastic."

"What can I get for you two lovebirds?" Rita laughed.

"Would you like the steak and lobster dinner?" Jackson smiled and kissed her cheek.

"No, that's too expensive." "

It's alright Hannah; tonight, is a special night. Please get what you want."

After several minutes of gentle discussion, they ordered and were once again alone. For the last 53 days, Jackson's world had been turned upside down. Before, he enjoyed life and had fun; but now everything was brighter, happier and more real. He couldn't believe how much energy he had. Even though he got a lot less sleep in the last 53 days, he sprang from the bed every morning to get going so he could see Hannah. He would call her before school and drop by the Seaside Grille after school just to steal a kiss before he went to work. Love had taken over him completely. Concentrating in school was hard because she was in his every thought.

"Well, I haven't asked you this lately, but how are you coming on Betsy the Corvette? You haven't spent a lot of time on her that I can tell."

"She's coming along slowly but surely. Mr. Willie and I removed all the old body parts and stripped her down to the frame. He and Skeeter looked her over, and he said she looked good underneath all that old junk. I took out all the seats, and the dashboard and Ralphie helped me take out the engine. We have it on a stand in the back corner of the garage. Red is supposed to come by tomorrow afternoon, and Mr. Willie is going to show us how to put in the new pistons. He said the block was in decent shape and we shouldn't have to do any special machining to it. Mr. Willie lets me work on it anytime it's slow, and we don't have a lot of customers. The other guys help me with it too. They seem just as anxious as I am to see her restored to her original beauty. I can't wait to drive you around Folly Beach and downtown around the Battery."

"Me too. I can picture it now in my head. Are you going to let me drive it?"

"Do you think you can handle her?" Jackson laughed.

Hannah elbowed him in the stomach.

"My best friend Laura's dad in Michigan restored a lot of old Mustangs, and he always let me, and her test drive them after he was finished. I can put any car through its paces. I'm sure I can handle Old Betsy. One of the first ones he restored was an old 67 Mustang Fastback that he gave to Laura for her first car. I bought it from her this past year. It's still back home at my grandmother's house in her old barn. I didn't want to drive down here when I came, and Uncle

John had the VW Bug and all."

"Why didn't you tell me that before? I didn't know you knew anything about cars."

"There's a lot you don't know about me..."

"Well, I guess I'll have to remedy that situation, then won't I?"

"I guess so," Hannah smiled.

They talked and enjoyed their dinner together. They both felt so comfortable together, and they were beginning to head down that unknown road of love. The sun was almost gone, but some stray sparkles danced off the river. The Palmetto trees swayed in the wind, and a few stars were beginning to come out of hiding. Jackson and Hannah finished enjoying their candlelight dinner and stood and walked to the window hand in hand.

Jackson twirled her around and kissed her.

"We have to go soon; do you have any special requests?"

Hannah quietly looked out over the water; the sun had made its way over the horizon, and the moon was beginning to peek its head out.

"These last 53 days have been wonderful for me and more than I ever dreamed. When I came here, I was just trying to get away from the pain of losing my mom. I just couldn't walk by her bedroom and see her things on her dresser and know that she was never coming back. I thought if I wasn't there, some of the pain wouldn't be so strong. You've helped me cope with a lot of things I didn't think I could get over. Here I am, so young, and both parents are gone. It's been a rough year but coming here has been the best decision I could have ever made. Aunt Becky and Uncle John have helped me a lot too. I feel more stable now. My life was turning upside down, and I felt I was out of control. I didn't know what to do or where to turn. My grandmother kept pushing me to come here. She told me I needed to find happiness again. I'm so glad she did."

She turned and kissed Jackson as deeply and as passionately as she ever had.

"Be with me forever..."

Jackson kissed her again and held her tight for a long time.

"I will always be with you, Hannah. No matter what happens. I promise you that. I won't let anything come between us. He looked into her eyes and was as serious as he had ever been. Whatever happens, I'll find a way to always be with you."

They held each other for a long time in silence and then Jackson broke the silence.

"I just have one question for you Hannah... What took you so long to kiss me?"

Hannah smiled and elbowed him again and hugged him tightly.

"What took me so long? Oh, I see how it is huh?"

She buried her head into his chest then looked up at him.

"Tonight, has been perfect Jackson. Let's go for a walk on the beach when we get back if it's not too cold."

Jackson and Hannah gathered their coats and Rita met them at the truck with two vases filled with the 53 roses. "Thanks for everything Rita."

"You're welcome honey," Rita smiled as she kissed Jackson on the cheek.

Steve came out just as they were leaving, and Jackson thanked him again for letting him use the room and how special it was for them.

"I'm so glad you had a good time Jackson, it was our pleasure to have you."

They made their way over the Folly River bridge and along Center Street. The Town of Folly Beach was crowded, and all the local restaurants were full. Even though it was Valentine's Day and one of the busiest for the Seaside Grille, Becky wanted Hannah to be off entirely for the night, so she could be with Jackson. Most nights, Jackson would come by after work and finish his homework and stay with Hannah to help until closing. They spent as much time as they could together, but Becky knew how special Valentine's Day was and she wanted her to enjoy it.

"Let's take a walk down my pier," Hannah laughed.

"It looks like some other people are on your pier tonight, not like Christmas Eve when we had it to ourselves." Jackson laughed.

They strolled along the pier. The frigid winter wind blew off the ocean with a slightly northwesterly direction, and they could feel the crispness of the air. The moon shined brightly along the waves as they huddled together. It was a clear night, and the stars were out by the millions. They stopped to take in the beauty written on the sky, and they were quiet. Hannah reached around and slipped her arm under Jackson's coat and squeezed him. She could feel his smooth flat mid-section, and she thought how much she longed to see him shirtless on the beach. She couldn't wait for summer.

"Let's take a walk down the beach."

Jackson smiled, "Whatever you wish, my dear."

They made their way to the beach, and the moonlight lit their path. The wind seemed to be calming down a bit, and it didn't feel as cold as it did on the pier. Maybe the passion between them made it feel warmer. As they walked, they talked about the future and what it might hold for them.

Jackson stopped.

"I know we haven't talked about this, but where do you think you want to go to college? Have you thought about going to college downtown?"

Jackson's heart began to beat faster anticipating Hannah's answer.

"When I first got here, Aunt Becky showed me around downtown, and the college was beautiful. I wasn't sure at first, but now I think it would be a good place for me. Aunt Becky said I could stay with her as long as I needed. And now that I met you; this feels even more right."

Jackson's body relaxed in a great sigh of relief. The fear that had gripped his face when he first asked her the question, faded away. He was all smiles.

"What was all that about? Are you okay?"

"Yeah, I'm okay. I've been dreading asking you that question since New Year's Eve. I fell so hard in love with you that I couldn't stand to be away from you if you went to college somewhere else out of town. I thought about it every day since then, but I tried to just block it out of my thoughts. You don't know how happy I am to hear you say that you would like to go to college downtown. I've been looking for you all my life Hannah. I know I'm only 18, but my feelings for you are real and deeper than I ever thought possible. I just kept praying that you would want to go to college here."

Jackson pulled his hands from the warmth of his pockets and gently held Hannah's face and kissed her again. As they stood there together, the wind began to blow a little harder, and they decided it would be better to head back to the Seaside Grille. As they made their way up the worn steps of the pier, they could see the welcoming glow of all the candle lights in the windows of the Seaside Grille. It was almost 9 o'clock, and the place was still packed. Becky greeted them at the hostess stand and asked Hannah how her night was with Jackson.

"It was awesome Aunt Becky. I'll put my purse up, and Jackson and I will help you until we close, then I'll tell you all about it."

"That's okay Hannah, enjoy the rest of your evening with Jackson."

"Aunt Becky, we've had a wonderful night together, and now we want to help you."

"Okay then, I just seated a party of four at table 12. Could you take care of those folks, please? Red and Gina are in the back table if you wanted to stop by and say hi."

Hannah took care of Table 12 then sat down next to Gina and hugged her and Red.

"Happy Valentine's Day Hannah! Where's Jackson?" Red asked.

"He's in the kitchen. I'll let him know you guys are here."

Jackson came out and sat with Red and Gina for a while, talking a little about their wonderful evening.

"Well I better get back to the kitchen, this place is crazy tonight. I'll see you guys later."

Jackson headed back into the kitchen and asked John what he could do to help. The whole kitchen was a frenzy of activity. It was one of the busiest nights they had ever had. They had implemented some of the suggestions from customer feedback in their suggestion box. Tonight, it seemed to be paying off. Jackson picked up supplies from the walk-in cooler, helped bring customers their food and even cleaned up the tables for their customers to sit down. It didn't stop slowing down until around 11 PM. The last couple to leave headed out the door around 12:15 AM. As Becky turned the sign around, they all sat down and breathed a sigh of relief. They finished cleaning up everything and Becky totaled up the receipts for the night. They had served 276 customers. It was the best night they'd ever had since they bought the place.

It was getting late, and Jackson had to take the same dreaded walk he had made for the last 53 days. He didn't want to spend one minute away from her. Even though they had been working for the last few hours, it was still okay with him. Whether it was touching her hand as he handed her a plate, stealing a kiss in the kitchen or smelling the scent of her perfume as he passed by her was more than enough to make him happy. And now was that time of the night that he hated most. It was time for him to climb in that old truck and make his way down the quiet highway as he replayed the events of the evening in his mind.

As Jackson made his way down Folly Road, he rubbed the back of his neck trying to relieve some of the tension that had built up when he talked to Hannah earlier about college. Jackson smiled and took a quick glance in the mirror, happy with what had transpired. Hannah's heart had felt like his. She was going to start a new life right here with him.

CHAPTER TWENTY-FIVE

# Springtime

Spring had sprung in Charleston. The beautiful myriad of colors of all the flowers in bloom made this a mystical time of year. There's not a more beautiful display than the gathering of Azaleas, Dogwoods, and Wisteria that line the whole city in the spring. This was Jackson's second favorite time of the year next to Christmas. Hannah and Jackson's relationship had continued to blossom into a deep and abiding love.

Since Jackson met her on Christmas Eve, not a day had gone by that he didn't see her. Some days it would only be for an hour or so; others it would be for the whole day. No matter how tired or how long he worked, nothing was stopping him from seeing her.

It was Sunday afternoon, and Jackson would be showing Hannah an extraordinary place. The sky was a beautiful blue with a few cotton ball clouds drifting by. Hannah wore a gorgeous yellow sundress that cut just above the knees. She had the body of a swimmer and a dancer combined. Her long blonde hair was let down, and she wore matching sandals with her cute toes painted pink. Her legs were long and lean, and her skin was a beautiful sun-kissed brown.

The same story played out every day. Jackson's anticipation of seeing Hannah and being with her was overwhelming. She would open the door to the loft or the restaurant, and Jackson felt lighthearted when he caught his first glimpse of her. Sometimes he would just look at her in amazement at how beautiful she was, and that outer beauty was even overshadowed by her inner beauty. She was the kindest, most caring girl he'd ever met. He was totally captivated by her.

"Where are we going?" Hannah asked.

"I have a place I want to show you. I think you'll love it," Jackson's smiled.

They made their way across town and headed down Highway 61 towards Middleton gardens. Miles of stately oaks lined the meandering road. Beautiful Yellow Jasmine grew everywhere along the route. Hannah admired the landscape as they made their way down the road. They reached the gravel driveway of the famed gardens and made their way up to the entrance and Hannah was enchanted by its beauty.

Middleton gardens was established in the early 1700's and throughout the years, various members of the Middleton family owned it. It was designed to have something in bloom every month of the year, but the absolute best show was put on in March and April when most of the flowers were in full bloom.

Jackson had made a picnic lunch, and they found a secluded area near a row of old Camellias and beautiful Azaleas to lay down the blanket. They had walked deep into the gardens, and it was getting late into the afternoon, so Jackson was sure that they were alone. They enjoyed their lunch then Hannah laid down beside Jackson. He was laying on his right side, and she made herself comfortable and rested her head on his chest and stared up at the sky.

"This place is beautiful Jackson; I can see why you love it so much."

Jackson's body tensed as he lay there holding her. He leaned his head down and kissed her forehead.

"I love you, Hannah."

Hannah quickly turned, and in a moment, she was laying on top of him. His heart beating faster and faster.

"Will it always be like this?" Hannah asked him.

"What do you mean?"

"This is such a special place, and I feel so special when I'm with you. Every day when I get up, I can't wait to see you. I feel like your name is written on my heart. I sleep with that brown sweatshirt you gave me, and I smell your cologne and I drink you in. I hold it against my chest close to my heart, and I feel you. I don't want this feeling to end. Do you think we could always feel like this?"

"I could feel like this forever Hannah. My every waking and dreaming thought for that matter is of you. Even when I just get to see you for a little while at the Grille helping customers and I come close and smell your perfume, it drives my senses crazy. Sneaking a kiss in the walk-in cooler isn't so bad either. I wish I could spend every minute of the rest of my life with you."

With that, Jackson rolled her over on the blanket, and she was staring up at him in anticipation now. Both of their feelings on overload... both of their hearts were beating in melodic rhythm. They began kissing slowly and then grew more and more passionate. Their chests were rising higher and higher, breathing faster and faster. Their tongues entangled in rhythmic poetry. He began kissing down her neck and made his way to just above her yellow sundress. She was quietly moaning as each kiss caressed her body. They were both excited and deeply in love. The wanting inside them was overpowering, and they wanted so much to give in to their feelings. Suddenly, they heard a rustle of the leaves. Jackson crawled around a large Azalea mound and looked to see where the sound was coming from. All in a neat row was a group of local Boy Scouts coming up the road. They were on an outing to the gardens in search of insects for a Merit Badge.

Hannah and Jackson quickly gathered their composure and their picnic lunch and escaped out of sight, laughing as they ran through the giant bouquets on display. They made it to the signature terraced gardens, looking out over the Ashley River. They looked out over the vast expanse and enjoyed nature's show. The young couple held each other close and Jackson looked into her eyes.

"I love you Hannah, and someday I'll make you my wife."

She smiled and kissed him.

"You promise?"

"I promise. I love you more than anything, and I will do everything I can to always make you happy."

"Jackson, I had such a great time today, this place is magical. I love all the varieties of flowers and trees. I could spend all day out here."

"We'll come back again soon."

CHAPTER TWENTY-SIX

# The Test Drive

Spring gave way to summer, and the thermometer headed north towards triple digits. The beach was packed every weekend, and the Seaside Grille had been busier than ever. Jackson and Hannah's love continued to grow stronger with every day they spent together. Hannah didn't work on Sunday evenings, so she would hop in her little VW Bug and spend the evening with Jackson at his house.

Sometimes Jackson would finish homework, other nights he would fix things around the house. Mostly, he would paint, and Hannah would sit behind him reading a book and checking on his progress. Tonight, she planned on helping him fix up ol' Betsy the Corvette. The new seats for ol' Betsy came in on Friday and Jackson was eager to put them in. Most of the body panels on ol' Betsy were damaged so badly, they had to be replaced.

Mr. Willie had found an old Corvette dealer up in Summerville that had a few Corvette wrecks and they salvaged the body parts they needed from four different cars. The only thing they had to order was a new hood and windshield, which had still not arrived yet.

Red had been helping Jackson put old Betsy together for months, and he was ready to see her run too. Red and his girlfriend Gina met Jackson and Hannah up at the garage and brought pizza to share before they started. They all sat around a makeshift table in the back of the Island Garage swapping stories over dinner. After they finished eating, Jackson and Red got to work on Betsy while the girls chatted.

The boys began on the side quarter panels and the new seats. The transmission rebuild was completed last week, and the old Corvette had brand-new tires and rims. The engine got lowered into place two days ago, and Jackson had been itching to fire her up and take the old girl out for a spin.

Over the last six months, Jackson was involved in every aspect of restoring the old classic. All the mechanics from Willie's garage helped him and showed him a different part of the rebuild. Young Jackson had grown in his knowledge and wisdom of cars, and life along the way. Each one of the mechanics taught him something about life while they were bringing ol' Betsy back from the brink. They told stories of success and failures, perseverance and hard work. And smart, some of these guys knew so much, Jackson felt like he might not be able to absorb everything. He was patient, and he tried to do everything right, just like they told him.

Last week, when they put the carburetors in, Mr. Willie let Jackson crank it up. The first time he cranked the engine, fire flew out of both carburetors like the afterburner of a jet getting ready to take off. Jackson almost jumped out of the car it startled him so bad. After that initial surprise, ol' Betsy calmed down and purred like a kitten, only missing every once in a while.

They hadn't got the throttle adjusted just yet. It kept sticking, and Mr. Willie wanted to make sure it got fixed before Jackson took it out on the back roads. The boys worked for several hours. Jackson installed the front seat on the driver's side, but he could only put in the two back bolts. The front holes in the floorboard wouldn't line up with the ones in the seat. Red put all four new quarter panels in and was ready to help install the new dashboard.

"Hey Red, you wanna take her out for a spin?"

Red looked at Jackson and shrugged his shoulders.

"Do you think we should? Is she even safe to drive? We don't even have a hood or a windshield."

"We can take old Betsy the back way down Riverland Drive. It's Sunday night; there's hardly anyone on the road."

"Well let's go then."

Jackson learned how to drive a stick shift a week after he started working at the garage. Ralphie and Skeeter took him under their wing to make sure he handled a car like a NASCAR racer. Skeeter even loaned Jackson his old Trans Am when he took his mom out for her birthday dinner.

"Hey Hannah, me and Red are going to take Betsy for a little spin down Riverland drive."

"Are you sure it's safe? Look at this thing; it's not ready for the highway."

"It's okay; we're just gonna go down a couple of miles and turn around. I want to see how she feels on the road."

Jackson could tell Hannah was nervous. He smiled at her, and that gave her a little reassurance.

"Please be safe."

"We will. We'll be right back."

Hannah and Gina kissed their boyfriend's goodbye and waved as ol' Betsy sputtered out of the garage with new life in her.

They drove slow for a few blocks, then made their way on to the straightest section of the road. "You ready to find out what she's got Red?"

"Let's do it."

With that, Jackson put the gas pedal to the floor and popped the clutch. Betsy sprung to life and squealed the back tires and threw them back in their seats. Since the front bolts weren't in, the seats rocked back and almost threw them out. The seat belts hadn't been installed yet either, so it made for quite a ride with the front seats feeling like rocking chairs. He gave it some more gas and changed gears, and when he hit 50 mph, he shifted into third gear. He popped the clutch again and floored it. The speedometer raced past 75 mph, and he let off the gas, but this time, the throttle stuck wide open. He squeezed the pedal over and over trying to unstick it, but it wouldn't break free. They passed 85 mph as they came to a fork in the road near old man Smith's cornfield. He tried to downshift, but with the throttle stuck, it redlined the tachometer. Jackson slammed on the brakes but felt a mushy pedal. He kept pumping and pumping and at last, the front brakes built up enough pressure to slow down the car, but by that time, they passed the fork and were headed to a dead-end road and on the other side was old man Smith's cornfield. Jackson slammed on the brakes as hard as he could, but the brakes didn't have enough to stop the car in time. He tried to swerve to avoid the dead-end barrier, and when the brakes finally grabbed, the car went into a spin, and they hit the neat rows of corn going 75 mph. Red and Jackson both were screaming for dear life, and Red said everything in the book cussing Jackson. Red protected his head from the flying ears of corn, and Jackson did his best to do the same while steering the car to safety.

After tearing up over 200 yards of old man Smith's prize crop, the car ran out of gas and came to a stop. For about a whole minute, neither of them said a word, and then Red broke the smoky silence.

"What the heck happened? You could have got us both killed you idiot."

"The throttle stuck, and I couldn't get it unstuck, no matter what I tried."

Red gave him a few more choice words, and then Jackson stopped him.

"I know, I know...I don't know what happened, but it sure was fun wasn't it?"

Red just looked at Jackson in pure amazement and then busted out laughing.

"It was the most fun I've ever had, and the most scared I've ever been."

Back at the garage, the girls were wondering why it was taking so long for them to get back.

"I'm getting a little worried."

Hannah raised her eyebrows, gesturing towards Gina.

"I'm sure they're okay. Maybe they just went a little further to see how the car ran."

Another half hour went by and the boys had not returned.

"Let's go see if they broke down." Hannah motioned to Gina.

They piled in her VW and headed after them. As they turned down Riverland Drive, they saw the skid marks and they followed them around to the fork in the road. Hannah saw something that made her heart stand still. Smoke poured up in the distance. She sped towards the smoke, and as each moment passed, her chest got fuller and fuller, pounding heavier with every beat. They made it to the end and saw ol' Betsy resting at the edge of the long path of destruction she left behind. She and Gina jumped out and ran towards the car as the two boys surveyed the damage. Hannah saw Jackson and leaped into his arms and kissed him.

"Are you okay baby? What happened?"

Jackson and Red were still pulling corn tassels out of their hair, clothes, and ears as they retold the story to the girls.

"Thank God you guys are alright."

"God sure was with us. That throttle stuck all the way open. It was a good thing Mr. Smith's cornfield was here, and we didn't have that much gas."

He knelt down and ran his fingers through his hair.

"Mr. Willie is gonna kill me. He didn't want me to take it out until the throttle got adjusted. Now I can see why."

The girls took them back to the garage, and he called Mr. Willie. He was definitely not happy with Jackson but was thankful that no one got hurt. Mr. Willie had bought an old wrecker that he used occasionally to transport vehicles. He told Jackson where to find the keys and said he would be up there in a few minutes.

Jackson had learned how to use the wrecker about a year earlier and even made a few pickups with Skeeter. He and Mr. Willie drove back down to the cornfield with Red. Mr. Willie didn't say a word on the trip until he got to the cornfield. He slowly made his way out of the truck and shook his head.

"You boys must've been hauling butt when you came through here.

Look at all this corn. Old man Smith is going to have a heart attack when he sees this. Just as they were talking, old man Smith pulled up in his old Ford pickup.

Old man Smith had farmed this area for years and knew Mr. Willie very well. He stepped out of his truck in his overalls and his straw hat. He shook Mr. Willie's hand and then looked around at all the damage. In his calmest tone, he said, "Well what do we have here?"

Jackson told Mr. Smith the story, and he promised that he would work for him to pay back what he had damaged. Mr. Smith made arrangements with him to come and work until he paid off his debt. Then Jackson hooked up Old Betsy to the wrecker and brought her back to the garage.

When they made it back to the shop, Mr. Willie had a heart to heart talk with Jackson in private.

"Jackson, what you did tonight was not a wise thing. I told you that throttle still needed to be adjusted. You're lucky that you and Red didn't get killed. God sure was looking out for you. He must really have something special in mind he wants you to do. You can't do things like this. What if that cornfield wouldn't have been there and you guys couldn't stop?"

Mr. Willie let a few minutes pass while Jackson thought about what he'd said.

"I am proud of you for taking responsibility for your mistakes and working to pay off Old man Smith. He's a good man and is fair. He will teach you a few things too; just be sure to listen."

"I'm really sorry Mr. Willie. Thanks for coming up here to help me."

"I'll always be here for you Jackson. You're just like a son to me."

They got ol' Betsy settled in for the night in the back of the garage... her engine compartment still full of corn.

"Let's all get some rest tonight."

Mr. Willie laughed as they all headed their separate ways back home. Hannah drove Jackson back to his house, and his mom pulled up in her car after waitressing at the Sand Dunes Club restaurant. She saw the cuts and bruises on Jackson and ran to find out what happened. She and Hannah helped clean him up, and then he walked Hannah out to her car to say goodnight.

"Jackson, you could have left me today. I've been thinking about this over and over in my head since I saw the smoke and the car in the cornfield. You have brought me so much joy and a reason for living again after all that's happened. I don't want to lose you. I love you so much. Please don't take that car out again until everything else is fixed completely and done right and Mr. Willie says it's okay. Promise me, Jackson."

"I promise. I was scared to death when it wouldn't slow down, but it was fun after it was over, when I knew we were okay. No more joy rides until she's one hundred percent ready."

CHAPTER TWENTY-SEVEN

# Half Rubber

"Half rubber? That sounds weird. What in the world are you talking about?" Red asked Jackson with a dazed look.

Jackson laughed. "Get your head out of the gutter man. It's a beach game. Or an anywhere game. Didn't you play stickball back in Michigan?"

"Sure. All the time."

"This game is kind of like stickball, except it's harder. We take a baseball-sized solid rubber ball, and we cut it in half with a hacksaw, and then you have a half rubber ball to play half rubber with. You play with two or three-person teams. On defense, there is one pitcher and one catcher and maybe a fielder if you have that many people. The other team is up to bat. A lot of the time, we only played with two-person teams. Since the ball is cut in half, it's a lot harder to throw. It's also a lot harder to hit and catch since it's only half a ball and its rubber. You play the game just like baseball, except for a few differences. When the pitcher pitches the ball, if the batter swings and misses and the catcher catches the ball, the batter is out. If the batter swings and misses it, the batter can continue until he either hits the ball or the catcher catches it. There are no strikes. If the batter hits it on the ground past the pitcher, that's a single. If he hits it in the air past the pitcher, that's a double, and then you make a marker out a certain distance for a triple and a home run. You understand?"

Red nodded in agreement.

"It's a lot of fun and all you need to play is a rubber ball or two and oh yeah, I forgot to mention about the bat. You use an old broom handle or a shovel handle or something like that. It's much thinner than a regular bat. We need to go over to C&J's store and get a couple of balls, so we can cut them up and get a game going."

They bought a few rubber balls and Jackson cut them precisely in half. C&J's even provided a hacksaw the customers could use to cut the balls in half. Jackson cut the end off an old mop at the Grille that John said they could have and went out to a quiet part of the beach where the beach was empty. Jackson practiced pitching to Red as the catcher. It was hard for him at first, but then Jackson showed him a technique to trap the ball, then Red caught on fast. Once he got the hang of it, those gigantic hands wrapped around that little half of a ball and he even started catching one handed.

"Hey Red, let's find a place with a backstop so we can practice hitting. It's just like baseball practice except this ball curves a lot more, and the bat is much thinner, so it's much harder to hit. I even heard that a long time ago, when the kids played stickball there were so many of them, they came up with an idea to cut the ball in half so as many people as possible could play. I guess that's how half-rubber got started."

They went down the beach a few blocks to an old two-story beach house that belonged to a friend of Hannah's uncle John. It had a nice flat wall that they used to pitch against as a backstop.

"Just follow the little ball in old man and see if you can make contact. I'll make it easy on you for the first few." Jackson laughed as he pitched to Red for the first time.

The way you held your fingers and the angle of the pitcher's arm as you side-armed the ball determined how much or how little curve the ball made.

Jackson threw a pitch in there nice and straight, and Red took him downtown. He hit the ball all the way back into the retreating ocean at low tide. Red was a natural. They found a couple of other buddies to play and in three weeks' time; Red was playing like a pro. They even taught Hannah and Gina how to play.

In July, a big Half-Rubber tournament is always held out on Folly Beach out near the fishing pier.  Hundreds of people would gather to watch and cheer the teams on. Jackson convinced Red they should enter. The boys had beat everyone they played in the last few weeks, and the boys thought they might have a chance to win.

"I don't know Jackson." Red shrugged his shoulders in doubt. "I've talked to a few people, and they said that the guys that come to this tournament are the best around. Do you think we even have a chance?"

"We don't have any chance if we don't enter. I've been playing a long time, and you have picked this game up faster than anyone I've ever met. You can pretty much hit any pitch that I have thrown to you; even the hardest curve balls. We'll be fine. Quit worrying you, big baby."

"Well, you better not embarrass me. Gina says a lot of people come to watch these games."

"Don't worry. Let's just play our own game and do the best we can."

Game day came, and Jackson and Red picked up the fourth game of the day. They stood on the beach with Hannah and Gina and watched the first game. Jackson had never seen the first team that stepped up to bat. Good friends, Jeff Lyle and Chris Sullivan from Savannah had traveled up the coast this morning for the tournament. The other team featured Doug and Dave Robinson, two brothers from James Island. Red and Jackson played them last week and barely beat them. Dave started out pitching as the game began. Jeff Lyle was up to bat and let the first pitch go by without even moving. Dave moved over a little and sent a rocket of a curveball flying in only to have Jeff hit the ball way past the home run mark. It was 1-0 on the second pitch. Chris Sullivan got up to bat and hit a single on the first pitch. The barrage of hits just continued until Dave and Doug finally got them out and got their chance to bat. By that time, it was 8-0.

"Wow, those guys are awesome," shouted Red. "They made Doug and Dave look like little league players."

The game finished up after about 20 more minutes when the score reached 15-1. Doug and Dave left the beach shell-shocked. They were some of the best players on Folly Beach but were reduced to mere young boys by the crew from Savannah.

Red and Jackson got their turn, and they won their first game 10-7 and moved on to the second round. They hadn't seen all the players yet but were anxious to find out who their next opponent was. The tournament was double elimination, so Doug and Dave had another chance. They won their second game against a duo from Myrtle Beach. Now, Doug and Dave had to battle Jackson and Red.

The game began, and quickly became a slugfest. Each player hit at least two home runs during the game and time was running out. Jackson and Red were down by two runs. Jackson hit a quick double over Dave's head and Red followed him up with a triple. Only a few minutes remained in the game and Dave threw a lightning fast curve and Jackson got just a piece of it. Doug dropped it, so Jackson was still alive at bat. Dave followed up the curve with a rocket fastball and Jackson caught it just perfectly. The rubber ball sailed far past the last marker for the home run and the crowd went wild. The game official sounded the air horn ending the game with Jackson and Red on top. Doug and Dave were eliminated.

The boys shook hands and Doug said, "I hope you guys get a chance to get some revenge on the boys from Savannah and give a little pride back to Folly Beach after that beating we took."

"I hope we do too. Thanks, guys, it was a tough game." Jackson nodded.

The boys walked over to the girls. "You guys did great." Hannah smiled as she jumped into Jackson's arms and kissed him. "I was nervous at the end. I didn't know if you guys would be able to pull it out."

Jackson laughed. "Me too. I didn't know if we could either."

Jackson and Red made it to the semi-final round but still didn't know who they would play next. The semi-final game would be tomorrow at 9 AM with the final the next day. Tournament organizers stretched the games out over the weekend. It helped Folly Beach tourism and made for a fun weekend.

It was getting late in the afternoon, and they headed to the grille for a bite to eat. The boys had been out there all day and were covered with sand. Their skin was red and stinging from the sun. Becky seated them in their favorite corner booth. She always tried to keep it open for them. The girls went to wash up, and Jackson and Red talked about their upcoming game. As Hannah walked back to the table, Jackson stared at her and just took in her beauty. He watched her watching him during the game. She was so strikingly beautiful and unique, and he said a prayer every day thanking God for her. Hannah made her way back to their seat and leaned in and gave Jackson a warm wet kiss.

"You were wonderful today. I had so much fun watching you guys. I guess everyone around here loves half rubber as much as you do."

Jackson and Red took their turn and headed to the restroom. Red stopped and stared at the painting that Jackson finished so many years ago, and he looked at Jackson and smiled.

"I would have never guessed you for an artist when I first met you. This is really good man. I've seen this painting a million times, but I never get tired of looking at it. I've never seen anything like it. The only painting I do is with my fingers or maybe with a roller when my dad says it's time to paint the house."

"Thanks, Red. It's a special painting to me too and this is such a special place."

They made their way back to the table and discussed their strategy for tomorrow over some of John's signature fried chicken. The place was packed with customers from the tournament and Becky and all the staff did everything they could to keep all the customers happy. Hannah and Jackson promised to help as soon as they finished eating and Red and Gina said they would help too. It was one of the best nights they remembered in the last few months. The sun headed off to bed and it was almost midnight before they finally got the last customers out the door.

"Whatever happens tomorrow, I'm proud of you and I love you. Don't forget that Jackson." Hannah hugged Jackson tightly.

"It really means a lot to me for you to be with me tomorrow Hannah. You give me great strength and energy. Every time I touch you I can feel it. This has been the best summer of my life and I will never forget it. Every day I'm with you, I fall deeper and deeper in love with you. You are so special to me. I never want this to end."

"It doesn't have to. Don't forget what you said to me at Middleton gardens."

"I think about that every day. If I were able to support you, I would marry you right now. Mr. Willie pays me pretty good, but it's not enough. I'm still figuring out what I'm going to be majoring in at college this fall. I can do a lot of things, but I have to be able to put food on the table and a roof over our heads."

Hannah looked up at Jackson, "We'll both be at school together this fall. We can figure things out together. We can study together and share lunch in between classes. You and I were meant to be together; I have no doubt about that. Everything has been so much better since I met you. I finally feel like my life is headed somewhere good."

Jackson smiled and kissed Hannah.

"I still don't know how my mom and I are going to pay for college. It's expensive and we still need about $10,000 for this year. I'm still waiting on word from a couple of scholarships and the final amount of my financial aid. I know things will work out though."

By 9 o'clock the next morning, the sun was already high in the sky without a cloud in sight. The sky was a beautiful deep blue and when you looked across the ocean, you couldn't tell where the sky stopped, and the water began. The sand blazed on their feet at 97F, and the crowds gathered for the semi-final round. Jackson hadn't seen who they were playing yet. He only saw the name, the Outlaws, on the leader board. He had never heard of them before, but their entry said they came from Charleston.

Jackson was talking to Hannah and then he turned and saw a face that was familiar to him but not a pleasant one. The team they were playing was Billy Barbatt, the bully from ninth grade and one of his henchmen, Lou Jones, who looked worse than Billy. Jackson had a few more interactions with him throughout the last four years of high school. Each one was different, but for some reason, Jackson knew Billy was jealous of him. The last altercation with Billy, Jackson had defended a young freshman Billy tried to shakedown.

Billy had been arrested for underage drinking again, extortion and shoplifting last year and had recently finished his community service. He still bullied anyone who wouldn't fight back. Billy never forgot that day at the bus stop. Whenever he saw Red in the hallway, he would look the other way and do anything he could not to look at him face-to-face. Billy had gotten much bigger over the summer; so had Red and Jackson. Jackson worked out before school or before work and his 6 foot one-inch 195-pound frame was chiseled and strong. Red was 6'4" and a formidable 240 pounds. They acknowledged each other before the game with a cursory nod. The officials gave the final rules, and the game began.

Jackson and Red batted first. Billy started off pitching. Red got the first chance at Billy. The first pitch came in high and inside and almost hit Red in the head. He looked at Billy and gave him a dirty look. The next one was low and outside a little bit, but Red took one step over and blasted the tiny ball farther than Jackson had ever seen him hit a half rubber ball.

As Billy watched it land in almost another zip code, he was furious. The crowd went wild again. They loved watching Red get up to bat. He looked like a lumberjack half rubber player. Jackson was next and ready for whatever Billy could bring. The first pitch flew straight down the middle and Jackson swung as hard as he could, but he missed it completely and Billy's catcher dropped it, so he had another chance. Billy wound up again and fired another fastball right down the middle. This time, Jackson connected with it and it rocketed back towards Billy faster than he'd thrown it. Billy couldn't react fast enough, and the ball hit him square in the mouth. The ball came off the bat with such force that it pushed his top lip down hard on his teeth and busted his lip wide open. It poured blood. The paramedics came out to help him and after about 10 minutes they got the bleeding to stop. The paramedics recommended that he not finish the game, but he refused. If Billy was mad after Red's home run, you can't describe how mad he was now. Since Jackson's hit didn't make it past the pitcher, he didn't get on base, so he was still at bat.

Billy tried to compose himself and get his head back in the game. He threw four more pitches and Jackson reached out and hit a double. Red came to bat again and he tipped one and Lou the catcher got him out. Jackson was up and went down just like Red. They changed sides, and they battled back and forth for over an hour. Only a few minutes remained, and Billy and Lou were up to bat. Jackson and Red led the contest by one run. Lou hit a triple and Billy stepped up to the batter's box. Jackson fired in a fastball with all his might. Billy swung so hard he looked like he pulled a muscle in his back. He didn't touch anything, but the ball hit Red in the hands and he bobbled it. He dove into the sand to try to catch it, but it fell to the ground, just out of his reach. The next pitch was even harder, but this time, Billy got a piece of it and popped it up high above Jackson's head. The bright red ball hung up like a kite floating in the breeze and Jackson ran after it as fast as he could. It began its descent toward Earth and just before it hit the sandy beach, Jackson dove and stretched out as far as he could. He looked like a wide receiver trying to catch the winning touchdown in the Super Bowl. In his outstretched hands landed the ball, and he closed his grip around it while he was still in mid-air. He fell to the ground, and they won the game. The crowd went crazy. Red ran up to Jackson and hoisted him up on his shoulders with one arm. Billy and Lou walked off disgusted. They didn't even shake hands with Red and Jackson. The crowd booed them as they made their exit to the parking lot.

Once the celebration died down a bit, Jackson ran over to where Hannah was patiently waiting. She wore a chocolate brown bikini and Jackson just blocked out every sound around and ignored everyone else. To him, it felt like the two of them were all alone, staring at each other.

"Well, what do you think about the game?" Jackson smiled as he leaned down to kiss Hannah.

She didn't say a word but grabbed him and kissed him like never before. "How about that for appreciation?"

Hannah grinned back at him, as she handed him a towel to wrap around his waist to avoid a little embarrassment from what her kiss incited.

"Wow, can we do that every day?" Jackson smiled.

"I think that could be arranged. Let's go celebrate. Aunt Becky is making something special for you guys."

As they walked inside the Grille, the crowd broke out into rousing applause for Red and Jackson. Many of their friends already made it up to the Grille and were seated. Red and Jackson made the rounds along the tables like heroes.

When they got to their table in the back corner, Becky brought out a giant pot roast with carrots and potatoes for the whole group. Jackson jumped up and hugged and thanked her.

"This is great Aunt Becky."

He had started calling her Aunt Becky a few months ago, and she even encouraged him. The two couples enjoyed their meal and talked until the sun began to go down.

"I guess we better get some good sleep tonight Jackson. We play the boys from Savannah for the Championship tomorrow."

"I guess you're right Red. We can head out in a few minutes. Hey, when I went to go to the restroom, the tournament official stopped me and told me the Savannah boys shut out everyone they played except the first game against Doug and Dave. He said the pitcher was unbelievable and the catcher hardly ever drops anything. He wished us "good luck" in a not so convincing manner."

"I know it's gonna to be tough, but we have been playing well and all we can do is "play our game." Red laughed.

They all turned in for a good night's rest.

Jackson couldn't sleep. He was so nervous.

"What if we get crushed tomorrow? How embarrassing will that be? Those people are coming out here to see us win for Folly Beach. We can't let them down. What will Hannah think of me if we get embarrassed?"

Jackson kept playing these same questions over and over until he finally drifted off around 2:00 AM. His mom made breakfast, and he awoke to the sound of a conversation in the kitchen. He jumped up and put his shorts on and wandered back to find out what was going on. Sitting at the table with his mom was Hannah. She came early and helped Leah make breakfast. She wore a white string bikini wrapped in a turquoise sarong. Her sandals matched her sarong and showed off the glow of her beautiful tan bare feet with a perfect French manicure.

Jackson stopped and stared. His tan body and washboard abs were a sight for Hannah as well. Jackson ran his hands through his hair trying to calm down his bed head.

"Good morning ladies. Hannah, this is a wonderful surprise."

"Your mom called me last night and asked me to come this morning for breakfast. She's coming today with me to the finals."

"You are? I thought you had to work?" Jackson looked at Leah.

"Yes, I'm coming today. I'll work a different shift next week. I wouldn't miss this for the world. We used to play half-rubber when I was your age. A few guys I used to know started the tournament at Folly Beach that you're playing in."

They finished breakfast and headed out to a packed Folly Beach. The local TV news crews assembled in several tents along the field marked off on the beach. Red and Gina walked up hand in hand and they hugged everyone, and the girls wished them the best for the day ahead.

The game officials assembled the young men and discussed the final rules for the Championship. The boys from Savannah had a distinctive look to them. They were all business. They laughed occasionally, but you knew they took this game seriously.

Red and Jackson got the first chance to bat. Red always batted first. The first pitch came in lightning fast and inside. Red swung hard, and in a second, he was out. Jackson stepped up and stared down the pitcher. He felt his stomach turn upside down, over and over. His first pitch was a fastball outside. Jackson didn't move a muscle. The next pitch was an inside curve and again Jackson didn't move. The pitcher started complaining.

"Are you looking for me to give it to you on a silver platter?"

Jackson remained quiet, and this angered the pitcher a little. His next pitch was a fastball again, but this time, Jackson connected with it and hit a triple. The pitcher, a little shocked and confused, sheepishly told him "good hit."

Red came up again and was ready to improve on his earlier appearance at the plate. He opened his stance a little, and the pitcher threw a hanging curve ball and Red made perfect contact with it. The crowd watched as the ball sailed past the Homerun marker and they erupted with great applause.

Jackson was up next and hit a line drive straight to the pitcher and in an instant, Jackson was out. Now it was the Savannah boy's turn to see what they would do. Jackson threw as hard and fast as he could with every pitch, but these guys were great players and hit a lot of his best pitches. Mostly singles, but enough to be winning the game 3 to 2 by the time they switched sides for Jackson and Red's last bat. Jackson hit a quick double and Red followed up with a single. Jackson was up again and changed his stance a little. This time, the pitch came inside fast and tight and Jackson connected with it in the middle of the bat. It sounded almost hollow, but still had enough force to sail past the home run mark, changing the game to their advantage. The score stood at 4 to 3 in favor of Jackson and Red. This was it. The last half of an inning for the South Carolina Beach Half Rubber Championship.

Red and Jackson had their final conversation and looked at Hannah and Gina as they cheered them on. Their bronze skin and string bikinis made it difficult for the guys to concentrate. It had been a long grueling tournament and Jackson wanted to spend some alone time with Hannah. The Savannah boys were up, and they had been playing great all tournament. Red and Jackson still couldn't believe that they were ahead. No other team ever had the lead against these guys for any game.

Jackson threw the first pitch in as a sliding curve. One of the Savannah boys changed his stance and hit a double. Red and Jackson could feel their stomachs in knots as they knew the game hung in the balance. The next batter took his place in the batter's box and Jackson sailed the fastest pitch he had thrown all day past him. Jackson could almost feel the wind from the force of his swing as he swung with all his might not touching a thing. The ball flew right through into the awaiting hands of Red. They had their first out and only one to go to be the Champs.

Up to bat after his double, Jeff was ready to go. Jackson sent another rocket fastball past him and he tipped it and sailed over Red's head. He looked at a few more pitches as Jackson gave him everything he had. All day he swung at Jackson's fastballs, but the curves he waited on. Jackson decided he would try an inside slider. The pitch was lightning fast but finished with a quick twist at the end. He fired it in there and Mr. Savannah swung and tipped it. It flew high and Red chased after it. He reached as far as he could with his outstretched hands and the ball landed in his right hand and bounced out, landing on the sand. Red slammed his fists down in frustration. That could have been it he thought. They would have won it all if only he would have caught it.

The batter had new life. Jackson wound up for another rocket fastball and as he released it, slow motion reality took over. He couldn't hear anything. He just watched the ball spinning, ever nearing the batter. Jackson saw people screaming and cheering, but no sound. He followed the bright red half rubber ball into the batter's box. He could see the batter tighten up his massive arms as the descent of his swing reached the center of the batter's box. Immediately, Jackson heard the distinct pop of the best hit ball anyone had made all game. He watched in agony as the ball sailed high above his head, hanging gracefully above the sand and coming to rest way out in the surf. Well past the home run mark. It was over. Red and Jackson had fought hard, but the boys from Savannah had triumphed. They were great sports and gave gracious congratulations to Red and Jackson. "You guys are the best we have ever played. We got lucky today."

Jackson smiled, "Well, we can say the same thing. You guys are awesome. It was great playing you. It won't be so easy for you guys next year."

They exchanged handshakes and parted their ways. The girls made it through the crowds to Jackson and Red. Everyone had congratulated the boys on their hard-fought game and how they represented Folly Beach so well.

Jackson grabbed Hannah and spun her around as he kissed her. "You made this last game hard on me."

"What are you talking about? I didn't say anything to you."

"You slipped out of those shorts and all I thought about was that bikini. It drove me crazy looking at you and trying to focus."

Hannah grabbed him and pulled him close. "I hope I can always make you feel like that."

Red cut in, "Hey let's go get something to eat. I'm starving."

CHAPTER TWENTY-EIGHT

# The Call

The summer had just begun, and Jackson and Hannah wanted to make the very best of it before they had to trade the fun-filled days of the season for the new beginnings of the fall semester at college a few short miles away at the College of Charleston. They enjoyed every minute they could together as Jackson showed her around the historic city and all the places of his childhood on James Island. He borrowed Mr. Willie's boat a couple of times and had taken her fishing and just riding around the creeks.

Each time they went in the boat, the last leg of their journey was always up Coburg Creek to where a giant rope swing hung over the water from one of the branches of a stately oak. It was such a warm, familiar place. They would always bring a picnic lunch and swim and talk the whole afternoon away. He coaxed her to climb up to the highest point in the tree to ride the thick rope out into the middle of the creek. That little cove was one of their favorite places where their love grew, and memories were made. In the evenings before the sun went down, they walked to the end of Folly beach and all the way around to the river on the other side. They found sand dollars and every type of shell that washed up from the Atlantic.

He taught her how to catch fiddler crabs and use them for bait to bring in a fish called Sheepshead. In the eight months they'd been together, the young couple made each day special. Over their short lives, they had witnessed great heartache, and they didn't want that to happen to them. They understood that when they were together, they would appreciate each other and not take the other for granted.

One afternoon, Red stopped by the Seaside Grille to see Jackson and Hannah. Jackson was coming out of the kitchen while Hannah was finishing up taking an order.

"I need to talk to you guys." Red motioned to the couple as he sat down at a table in the back. The gentle giant wore a great big smile on his face as they all gathered around.

"Hey, guess what Y'all?"

"What's going on man? What's got you so excited?" Jackson laughed.

"I got hired on the shrimp boat down at Crosby's on the River.

They've been looking for somebody to help out and learn the ropes of the job. And they picked me."

"But what about college, I thought you were going with us?"

Red stared down at the weathered table and ran his hand along its surface before looking up.

"Let's face it man, my grades aren't that good, and I'm not really the college type. My dad was a fisherman on Lake Michigan and I spent all summer with him on the lake and almost every weekend. I miss being out on the water. The owner's down at Crosby's told me the South Carolina Marine biologists said that since this year had been so hot, that it should make for a lot of big shrimp to harvest. That means a ton of money."

"But what about your plans for the future? What about Gina? What does she think about this?" Jackson replied.

"She wanted me to go to college with her and you guys, but I'm not sure yet if college is for me. Gina understands that. I asked her to give me a year to see how it goes and how much money I can make. The Crosby's said if the harvest is good, it can be very lucrative. Their family has been in the shrimping business for several generations, and they are all doing well. I want a little piece of the pie too. I told them I could handle anything."

As they were sitting and talking, Becky came up to the table with a look of terrible grief on her face. "Hannah dear, could I talk to you for a minute?"

Hannah's heart sank as she slid across the seat and followed Becky to the back office. She didn't know what to think.

"Hannah, your grandmother has had a stroke and she's partially paralyzed and can't speak right now."

Suddenly, the agonizing feeling that haunted Hannah for so long crept back into her soul. They stood facing each other, as silent tears meandered their way down her cheeks. Hannah wiped the tears away and broke the long silence.

"What happened? She was in such great shape. She walked 3 miles every morning. I don't get it."

"Her neighbor Debbie found her in the garden when she stopped by to return a book she had borrowed. It's a good thing she did because the doctor said if she would've been there any longer she would've died. John and I are leaving at three to go up to Traverse City."

"I'm coming with you."

"Are you sure Hannah? That house has so many painful memories for you."

"Grandma needs us. She's always been there for me. It's my turn now. I'll tell Jackson, and then I'll get my stuff."

Hannah returned to the table trying to keep calm.

"Hey, what's going on Hannah? Is your Aunt Becky okay?"

"Jackson, come outside. I need to talk to you."

Jackson felt his heart beat faster and he had no idea what was going on. From the looks of things, it wasn't going to be good. They found a quiet spot on the pier and Hannah told him the news.

"Jackson, my grandmother, has had a stroke, and she's partially paralyzed. She can't talk either. Uncle John and Aunt Becky are going up to Traverse City at 3 o'clock, and I told them I would go with them."

She was standing in front of him holding both hands and looking at him with that beautiful but sad face.

"Is she going to be okay? She doesn't have any other family up there does she?"

"No, she doesn't. Aunt Becky, Uncle John and I are the only ones she has left. She has some great friends that look in on her, and they are with her now. It'll take about 16 hours for us to drive up, so we are going to drive straight through, and each of us will take turns while at least one person sleeps."

He stood silent for a while trying to comprehend what all this meant for him and Hannah.

"What does the recovery period look like?" Jackson asked.

"I'm not sure. Sometimes a few months, maybe a year or more. Other times, people never recover. They become permanently disabled and they never make it back to their normal self."

She looked out into the ocean, searching for words. The comfort she usually experienced from the beach seemed to elude her.

"I'm not sure what we're dealing with. When we get to the hospital tomorrow and talk to the doctors, I'll call you and tell you everything."

Not trying to let on that his world was crumbling around him, Jackson hugged Hannah tightly and reassured her that everything would be okay.

"I've got to go pack my bags. I'll come back and tell you goodbye."

When she walked inside, he didn't know what to do. He was sweating, and his heart was beating fast, and he felt like he had just been kicked in the gut. All that was certain was the love of his life was going to be over 1000 miles from him, and he wouldn't be able to see her beautiful face for the first time since he had met her. He walked back inside, and there was a somber tone throughout the kitchen.

Nicole would handle running the restaurant, and the boys in the kitchen would take care of everything else until they figured out what to do next. Nicole was a long-time friend of Becky's and was recently divorced. She moved to Charleston for a fresh start and had been working at the restaurant for a few months. She was great with all the customers, and she had a kind heart for all the people that worked in the kitchen. Nicole and Becky almost finished each other's sentences.

They loaded the car, and Jackson and Hannah took a walk down the pier to say goodbye. As they walked hand-in-hand, the knot in both of their stomachs grew tighter and tighter. They reached the end of the pier and found a spot to sit.

"I don't know what all this is going to entail, but I know I love you and I want to be with you. Just give me some time to find out what we need to do, and I'll call you and tell you everything. Jackson, these last few months have been unbelievable. I feel whole again. When I got here, my spirit was in such a low place that I didn't know if I could ever get out. It's going to be hard not seeing you tomorrow. You've been the bright spot in my life. Every day it's the same. I can't wait to see you."

She stood up and sat on his lap and gave him her most passionate kiss and then... she gave him another. She felt his heart pound as she caressed his lips.

"I'm glad I still have that effect on you."

He smiled and held her close, trying to hide that sick feeling deep in his gut.

"It's almost time to go. Promise me you won't forget me while I'm gone..."

"Not a chance."

They began their long stroll back to the restaurant and Jackson took every step as slow as he could, trying his best to prolong the inevitable. The young couple stopped in "their" corner of the deck where they first kissed on New Year's Eve.

"Remember this place? I'll be seeing you back here soon."

They kissed again for the last time before she left. John and Becky were in the car waiting for her and Jackson helped her with the rest of her bags. As he stood in the parking lot waving goodbye, he felt like his heart was being ripped out. Just an hour before, they had been talking about college. Now, he didn't know what was ahead.

⍰

CHAPTER TWENTY-NINE

# New Life

"She's gone, Mr. Willie..."

Mr. Willie looked up from his desk with a puzzled look on his face.

"What are you talking about Jackson?" Mr. Willie had never seen Jackson so dejected.

"Hannah's headed up to Michigan right now. Her grandmother had a stroke, and Hannah, Becky and John left for Traverse City a few minutes ago."

"Now hold on Jackson, everything's gonna be okay. Do they know how bad it is?"

"Well, she's paralyzed on one side, and she can't talk. I'd say that's pretty bad."

Mr. Willie stood there in silence for a little while looking down, trying to think of something to say that would help. In situations like this, no one knows what words they should choose. News like this makes people feel helpless. Mr. Willie wanted to help his young friend. Jackson had worked most of the summer, but he and Mr. Willie had only been fishing a few times, and they had worked on old Betsy the Corvette just a few more. Mr. Willie remembered what it was like to be in love. He didn't hold it against Jackson, but he missed him. Those talks where he would share his wisdom became fewer than before.

"How long does it take for someone to recover from something like this Mr. Willie?"

"It can take some time Jackson. It depends on how much damage was done to the brain and how long it was before she got treatment. Each person is different. I've seen people get better in just a few months. I've also seen it take several years and even then, they were never quite the same. All you can do is pray for healing and let the good Lord take care of it."

Jackson sat there, his head down, trying to figure out what to do next.

"Hey Jackson, I've got an idea I think might help. Ol' Betsy's been missing you, and we haven't worked on her in a while. Since Hannah is gone, how about we work on her in the evenings as much as you can before you start college and all. When Hannah gets back, you can have

Betsy all fixed up and take her for a spin around town."

Jackson half-heartedly agreed, and they walked around to the back of the garage and Jackson pulled off the tarp and studied her once again.

"She's coming along real good Jackson. I'd say we can get her running, cleaned up and painted within about a month. It'll be a big surprise for Hannah when she comes back."

Jackson had missed working on her. There were never enough hours in the day to do everything he needed to. The memory of his first wild ride came back when he jumped in the hot seat. Jackson loved 99% of that trip, except for that last little part at the end. The raw power under the hood and the way the wind felt on his face gave him a renewed hope to breathe "new life" into old Betsy. With Mr. Willie's encouragement and help from the rest of the boys, Jackson rekindled the passion he had to restore her to her original beauty.

Mr. Willie said, "Once we get all the body put together, Skeeter said he would show you how to tape it up and paint it. The paint arrived yesterday. How about you and I go down to Melvin's and grab some dinner?"

Jackson barely slept that night. He tossed and turned wondering where she might be. It wasn't until late in the afternoon when he got the call.

"Hey, Jackson. How are you, baby? I miss you so much already, and I love you even more," her voice crackled as she began.

"She's in really bad shape Jackson. I broke down when I first came into the room. The eerie sound of the ventilator made me so nervous. The doctor said she had the stroke in her garden and laid there for a long time before her neighbor found her. They don't have any answers for us. They said it's just going to take some time."

As he listened to her sweet voice, his hands trembled. He wanted to be there to hold her and comfort her, but he was 1000 miles away and it felt like a million.

"I was so worried Hannah. I'm so sorry about your grandmother. How was the trip up there?"

"It was a long ride. We all switched off driving but driving at night is hard. All I could think about was her lying in the garden all alone. The doctors are running all kinds of tests to find out how extensive the damage was to her brain. Her initial brain scans showed some damage to the left side of her brain. That's why she can't talk or remember who we are. She's also paralyzed on the right side of her body. I guess I didn't remember that the left side of the brain controls the right side of the body and vice versa. The doctors here are giving us a new education on brain function."

They talked for half an hour and as each minute passed he longed to be with her.

"I guess I better go; we're going back to grandma's house and try to get a little sleep before tomorrow. They should have the results of the rest of the tests, and we'll be able to decide where we go from here. I love you Jackson. I'll talk to you tomorrow."

Day one of not seeing her was miserable. Jackson suffered through most of the day in a fog. After work, Mr. Willie asked him to do a little restoration work on Betsy. He reluctantly agreed and managed to get the front headlights and the front grill installed. Mr. Willie tried to make small talk with him, but Jackson was quiet.

"I guess I'll see you tomorrow Mr. Willie. Thanks for your help."

"Okay buddy, see you tomorrow. Everything's gonna be okay. Keep the faith."

That night, Jackson had the most vivid dream of picking Hannah up on a crisp fall afternoon and driving the winding roads along the mountains of North Carolina with the top down. Once destined for the junk heap and now restored back to its original glory, ol' Betsy began her "new life" with Jackson at the reins. The wind was blowing through Hannah's beautiful hair and the way the sun shined on her melted his heart. It's the kind of feeling that comes from being with someone you can't live without. Stealing the last memory of his dream, the incessant beeping of Jackson's alarm clock jolted him back to reality as he reached across the bedside table to silence its wailing. He didn't want any part of reality. Back in that dream with her was the only place he wanted to be. He laid there a few minutes longer, thinking, his mind replaying as much of the dream as he could remember. He didn't want it to be a dream; he wanted it to come true. Then it occurred to him, his mission in life; for now. Jumping out of bed and swallowing some breakfast, he headed to the garage. He bid the usual greetings to Mr. Willie and the rest of the guys, but he had a renewed focus. That dream would be realized. He worked all day and through lunch. Around seven he washed up and got ready for Hannah to call the garage. Tuesday and Wednesday, the garage stayed open until 7 PM. Mr. Willie was in the office finishing the work orders from today. As Jackson was sliding his shirt on, the ringer on the locker room phone broke the silence and Jackson picked up.

"Hey Jackson, it's good to hear your voice. It's been a long day here, but we still don't have any answers. My grandmother still hasn't made any visual progress that we could tell, but the brain scans the doctors performed seem to show some improvement. We're optimistic the doctors will have more information for us tonight."

"I dreamed about you again... I wish I could hold you right now."

"I wish you could too; I could use those big strong arms about now." She paused for a while and then began... her voice trembling.

"Jackson, I don't have many answers right now, but the recovery of my grandmother may take a long time. I've been talking with Aunt Becky and Uncle John about who would stay with her while she recovers. We're the only family she's got left. Becky and John have to get back to run the Seaside Grille, and Becky is scheduled to undergo another round of chemotherapy next week. I'm her only family that can stay. A lot of her friends are here, but we can't expect them to take care of her 24/7."

Not wanting to sound unsupportive, Jackson gingerly asked, "How long do you think the recovery might take?"

"No one knows right now. We don't even know how extensive the stroke was. The doctor is supposed to talk to us with some of that information tonight. When I find out more details, I'll let you know."

Except for the day his grandfather passed away, Jackson had never felt lower. Jackson slowly hung the phone up, and the dull pain in his stomach began to get worse. One hand still held on to the receiver, still trying to touch her. For the next half hour, Jackson sat staring at the phone. He imagined her on the other end. Just then, Mr. Willie stepped into the locker room and asked how Hannah was doing.

"Mr. Willie, she's gonna have to stay there for her grandmother's recovery. Who knows how long that could take?"

Mr. Willie sat down on the bench next to Jackson.

"Well now Jackson, you can't worry about this son. Hannah's in a tough spot. Becky and John can't stay there. She's the only one left. Remember, her grandmother took care of her after her mother died. I know you miss her, but I promise you everything will work out okay. I know you can't see what that is right now, but it'll work out; just wait and see. Are you gonna see what you can get done on ol' Betsy tonight?"

"No, sir. I'm gonna head on home. I don't feel much like working on her tonight."

CHAPTER THIRTY

# A Different Tone

Late August arrived, and Jackson was scheduled to start college alone. Several weeks had passed, and Hannah remained in Traverse City providing around the clock care for her grandmother. Her grandmother had been released from the hospital and was recovering at home, but progress in regaining her mobility and mental awareness was slow. Hannah and Jackson talked on the phone every day and continued to talk about their future, longing to be together again.

"I'm sorry I won't be there to begin classes with you, Jackson."

"Me too. I feel so alone without you. Maybe I should wait to start until you come back. Mr. Willie would let me work full time in the garage until we can go together."

"No. Absolutely not. You can't spend your life waiting for me. You have so much ahead of you and so much to offer the world. You can't wait for me."

"I'll wait on you for as long as it takes Hannah."

"I don't know how long that will be Jackson. My grandmother can't do anything for herself right now. She is getting better; I can see small changes every day. It's just taking a long, long time."

"It doesn't matter how long it is. I will be here waiting for you."

Jackson couldn't be sure, but something in her voice was different. She seemed distant. Was he imagining it? He knew she must be tired, but she didn't sound the same. No, it wasn't the same, she definitely sounded distant.

"What's wrong Hannah? You seem different tonight."

"Nothing Jackson, everything is fine."

In Jackson's short number of years on the earth, he at least learned that when a woman says she is "fine," she is definitely not fine.

"I know these last several weeks have been tough on you the most. Every other time we talked on the phone, your tone was upbeat and positive. Tonight, it feels like there's something wrong."

"It's nothing Jackson, can you just please stop asking me? Just shut up about it okay?"

Jackson held the phone, imagining her on the other end. He was stunned. She had never told him to shut up before. Come to think of it, she had never said anything to him that even came remotely close to that.

"Maybe I should let you go, and I'll talk to you tomorrow?" Jackson offered.

"Okay Jackson, goodnight."

Click... Then silence...

She didn't tell him I love you or I'll talk to you tomorrow; she just said goodnight. His heart pounded with an ache so deep, he had difficulty catching his breath.

A thousand miles away on the other end in Traverse City, the tears began to flow profusely. Hannah still held the phone close to her heart as she laid down on the floor, her legs curled up in the fetal position. Her crying, silent at first, became louder and louder as each wave of pain echoed through her body.

Her mind raced. "I can't do this to him. He can’t wait on me. I love him too much for this."

CHAPTER THIRTY-ONE

# The News

The next evening's phone call began with the normal small talk they had become accustomed to. After a long pause, Hannah broke the silence.

"Jackson, you have to move on without me. You can't wait for me anymore. My grandmother's recovery could take years, or she might never get better. It has to be over between us Jackson. Please don't call again."

With those two sentences, Jackson's world fell apart. Never in his life had he experienced such gut-wrenching pain.

"What are you talking about? Why are you saying such a thing?"

"That's how it has to be. I can't see you anymore. I can't expect you to wait on me. The doctors said Grandma's recovery would be extensive. It could take years, if ever. There's nothing left to say."

Her voice sounded much different than ever before.

"Don't call me again, please. It's better this way. Goodbye Jackson."

"Wait!! Don't hang up. How can you just turn off what we have together like a light switch? Don't you love me?"

Click. The phone was silent.

Jackson dropped the phone and collapsed on his bed. Tears flowed like a stream down the side of his face. He turned over and buried his face in his pillow. Right beside it, he saw the pink nightgown Hannah gave him to sleep with that was covered with the scent of her favorite perfume. He screamed as loud and as hard as he ever had. He felt like his heart would explode and he would die right there.

His mother Leah heard the commotion from her room and ran in to find out what was going on. Jackson mumbled some incoherent words to her at first, but then she managed to salvage an explanation from him.

"I'm so sorry Jackson. I'm sure she didn't mean it. She's under a lot of stress with her grandmother. She'll come around."

Her heart sank as she tried to comfort Jackson rubbing his back. She sat there for over an hour while Jackson stared at the ceiling.

"I don't know what to do mom. I don't know what to feel. How could she do something like this? We talked about getting married and spending the rest of our lives together and tonight out of the blue she tells me it's over, and she doesn't want to talk to me again. How can that be?"

"Why don't you go take a shower and try to get some rest. I'm sure things will be better tomorrow."

Jackson didn't say a word as he stumbled to the bathroom to try to wash off some of the pain. That night, he barely slept. After his body had enough, he drifted off around 4:00 AM.

CHAPTER THIRTY-TWO

# Is this it...?

A strange voice answered the phone up in Traverse City.

"Hi, this is Jackson, can I speak to Hannah please?"

"I'm sorry Jackson, this is a friend of Hannah's grandmother, Hannah isn't feeling too well. I'm afraid she isn't accepting any calls."

"Could you please tell her it's me? I'm sure she'll reconsider."

"Jackson, she specifically asked me to tell you to please not call again. I'm sorry son."

The dial tone at the end of the line told him that this wasn't a bad dream. How could this be happening? How could he have been so wrong about her?

Didn't he understand her completely? He would have waited for her forever. Now, nothing seemed right. The compass of his life was spinning in circles, out of control. He was dizzy and had to sit down. In the corner of his room on his easel sat a painting he had been working on of them together at the Sand Dunes Club restaurant on their special Valentine's Day. It was almost complete.

He stared at the canvas and slowly rubbed his finger over Hannah's face as the tears began to fall again. He gently picked it up off the easel, then violently smashed it on the ground, ripping it to shreds. The pain overwhelmed him. He had totally given her his heart, and now it was being ripped out.

In an instant, he bolted out of the house and headed down the street and towards the fire station and the river. He ran as fast as he could down to where the waves pounded the shoreline. Standing there all alone, he screamed with all his might again, trying to gain some relief from the pain.

"Why God? Why is this happening to me? What did I do wrong?" He fell to his knees, struggling for air.

"Hey, buddy."

Jackson turned around to see his lifelong friend, Red, out of breath. "Your mom told me what happened. I saw you run past my street, but I couldn't keep up with you. I finally did just now. It's gonna be alright man. I can promise you that."

"She said it's over. Just like that. No warning, no nothing."

"She's going through a real tough time now. Hey Jackson, let's go talk to Mr. Willie."

"What's he gonna do? There's nothing to do. I just don't get it."

"Come on Jackson. I'll drive."

The boys walked back to Red's house, and Jackson reluctantly piled into Red's old beater truck, and the boys met Mr. Willie at his house.

"Come on in guys. How about some dinner while we talk?"

"No thanks, Mr. Willie." Jackson replied.

"You gotta eat Jackson. I just picked up a bucket of chicken, and I can't eat it by myself. Come on in fellas; we'll figure this out."

CHAPTER THIRTY-THREE

# The Talk

"Just like that, she said it was over Mr. Willie!"

"What do you think is going through her mind? You didn't say or do anything to make her feel that way did you?" Mr. Willie gently asked.

"No! One day she tells me how much she misses me, and the next day she says it's over. She told me I couldn't wait for her. I told her I would wait as long as it took. I even told her I would wait to start college. She got all mad when I said that. I feel like I'm dying inside Mr. Willie. She's the only girl I've ever loved. We even talked about getting married. The last time I called up there, some lady answered the phone and told me to never call back again. She was polite at first, but then she turned as cold as ice. I don't get it!"

"Man Jackson, I'm sorry as I can be to hear that. It just doesn't seem like her. I knew she was in love with you. She told me so herself. She said she was scared to death when she saw the smoke coming from the cornfield when you and Red had your accident. I could see the way she looked at you. I knew she was serious. Maybe she just needs some time to work through some things. Her grandmother helped raise her; she spent her whole life there. A big part of who she is still remains there. Just give her a little time, she'll come around."

Mr. Willie, Red and Jackson talked well past midnight. Mr. Willie told stories of when he and his wife first started dating. He told them how she played hard to get and all the things he did to win her heart.

"Wow Mr. Willie, you were quite a romantic guy. Your wife sure did play hard to get." Red laughed.

"Boys, a good woman will make you a better man. God made us totally different in pretty much every area. When I wanted to win the heart of my wife to be, I had to figure out a way to show her that I really loved her for her and not just because of her beauty, and man was she beautiful. You can't just say you love someone. That sounds good, but you have to back it up with deeds. Little things do mean a lot. A compliment here, holding the door there, whispering in her ear how much you love her and kissing her neck while you're doing it. Just being kind. When she sees that you care for other people, she will love you even more. Just listening to them and being someone they can count on and trust is so important. You have to be that rock that she can cling to. And when she knows she can cling to you, you'll be able to draw strength from her love. It will become your purpose and what keeps driving you to be a better man."

It was past 2:00 AM and the boys finally headed out the door. Jackson hugged Mr. Willie on the way out and thanked him for his advice.

"Hang in there Jackson. Everything will work out. I promise you."

CHAPTER THIRTY-FOUR

# Mr. Reynolds

Shortly after the breakfast rush at the Seaside Grille had ended, a slender gentleman in a blue suit came in and asked to speak to Becky and John. His dark brown hair was greased back, and his leathery skin matched his hair color. Nina, the hostess, greeted him and showed him to a table, then went to get Becky and John. Sarah, one of the waitresses, was watching him when he came in and wondered what he wanted. Becky and John came from the kitchen and sat down at the back booth with the mysterious gentleman.

"Who's the guy over there in the slick suit and the slicked back hair with Becky and John?" Sarah asked Nina as they both looked on.

"I don't know. I've never seen him before. He just came in and asked to see Becky and John. Why don't you go over to their table and find out what he wants?"

Sarah headed over, determined to see what was up.

"Hey good morning sir, what can I get for you this morning?"

The man looked a little perturbed that she would interrupt them. Becky offered him a menu, but he just said coffee.

"Well, if you need anything, please let me know." Sara smiled in the most insincere way.

"Well? Did you find anything out?" Nina asked.

"Not yet. I'm working on it. This guy gives me a bad feeling. I can read people like a book and he looks like trouble."

Sarah made it back to their table and leaned over to pour his coffee and caught a glimpse of the paperwork he pulled out of his briefcase. The letterhead was from the bank where Becky and John had taken out a loan for the renovations.

She made her way back over toward the counter and looked back towards their table and tried to figure out what was going on back there. Whatever he was saying, was not sitting well with Becky and John. Becky had recently finished another round of chemo and proudly wore the knitted hat that one of the nurses gave her at the cancer center. She had been so brave, she never complained once, always wearing a smile on her face even when everyone knew she felt terrible. Becky wasn't smiling right now though; she was mad.

"Last month, you were two days late on your installment payment for the renovations. According to the contract, we can elect to accelerate your loan payments to ensure our interests are protected if a customer is one day late. I'm the new commercial loan Vice President, and I am here to inform you that we elect to accelerate your loan. The full balance of $68,500 will be due by Friday December 24th. If that amount isn't paid in full by the due date, the property which was held as collateral will be foreclosed on by the bank and subsequently sold to the highest bidder."

"We mailed that payment in plenty of time to be posted to our account before the due date, Mr. Reynolds. There has to be a mistake." John calmly talked to him, even though he was about to explode on the inside.

"John, I assure you there is no mistake."

The slick Mr. Reynolds pulled a copy of their statement out and it showed what he had said.

"Mr. Reynolds, where are you from?" Becky asked, holding back tears.

"I'm not sure of the relevance?" Reynolds replied.

"You must not be from around here. Because if you were, you would know what a special place this is to so many people. We have customers who have been coming here year after year celebrating the anniversary or birthday or any number of special occasions. This restaurant is part of Folly Beach and so are we. We can't come up with that much money by that time. It's just too soon. We have been making significant progress paying down that loan. How could you think about accelerating our loan? We can't lose this restaurant. This is also our home. We live right upstairs."

"Becky, I'm sure you understand my position. I have to do what is in the best interest of the bank."

"We are good customers and have been for over two decades. How could you think about doing something like this to loyal customers?"

"The policies have changed, and I am merely following it," Reynolds smugly replied.

"Please leave Mr. Reynolds," Becky managed as she wiped the corners of her eyes.

Becky and John slid out of the back booth, and John hugged her and kissed her head then watched her as she turned to go into the kitchen to help get ready for lunch.

"Who was that guy?" Nina asked.

John looked very concerned. "He was a man from the bank. They are accelerating our loan to be paid back before Christmas."

"What?" Nina shouted.

John talked to all the girls and told them not to worry about anything, and then he headed into the kitchen to help get ready for lunch too.

"Where's Becky?" John asked when he entered the kitchen and didn't see her.

Sarah said, "I saw her heading back to the office."

When John got to the back, his heart stopped as he found Becky lying on the floor.

"Oh God no! Becky! Becky!" Her eyes slowly opened and looked up at him.

"I don't know what happened. I felt a little dizzy and then I don't remember anything else."

He held her close as tears of joy streamed down his cheeks. "I'm so glad you're okay."

John helped her to the chair, and after a while, he took her upstairs to the loft to lay down.

"I'll be okay John. The lunch crowd will be here soon. They need you in the kitchen."

John unwillingly went back downstairs to help out.

CHAPTER THIRY-FIVE

# College

Three months had passed since Hannah's grandmother's stroke. Jackson reluctantly started the fall semester at college. He hadn't decided on a major, and he was just going through the motions.

Jackson called Hannah every single day precisely at 7 PM, and every day he heard the same voice of the digital answering machine. Every day he left the same message.

"Hannah, I can only imagine how you feel. I know you're probably scared and confused. If I were in your situation, I would feel the same way. I would be doing just what you are doing. I would be taking care of my family too. Just know that I love you and I'll wait for you as long as it takes. I will be here. I promise I'll be waiting for you."

The first class of Jackson's college life started quickly. It was a modern art class taught by a beautiful, petite professor that moved from Florida only five years earlier. She introduced herself to the students and began discussing their first assignment.

"This first project is your chance to show me your talent and how well you understand all the aspects of the transition from a subject to the canvas. Once I receive them all back, we will direct our paths to improve the areas that are needed the most."

"Everyone, you will have two weeks to complete a painting of "The Cistern" that sits at the front of the college on a 20" x 30" canvas. Here's a picture I took last spring before classes were out. I would like to see each of you do your best to bring this picture to life. I want to feel just like I felt that morning when I took it. Well, that's about it for today. I'll see you all on Friday. You can start right away. For those of you who may not know the history of the cistern, please take some time and do a little research."

The famed "Cistern" on the College of Charleston campus was a familiar landmark of Charleston that was quietly guarded by towering oaks and framed with the backdrop of the college's oldest building; Randolph Hall. It was a beautiful gathering place for students to study. This historic location was the site of the commencement ceremony every year. The original cistern had been built in the 1850's to aid in flooding control and to act as a reservoir of firefighting water in those days. Years later, it was filled in, and grass planted around the area.

Today it serves as an all-around meeting place. It is the most iconic place on campus. It has even shared the "big screen" with some celebrities as the backdrop for several Hollywood movies.

A few quiet remarks about their future assignment came from a few of the wary students. Several of them complained that it wasn't fair and how could they be expected to complete such a big assignment so soon. Jackson slid the photograph into his backpack and headed out the door.

Greg Sawyer, a student Jackson met at the beginning of class asked Jackson to join him and his girlfriend Rachel for a bite to eat.

"Sure, I guess I have some time before work."

They made it down to a small café on King Street. Jackson and Greg arrived first, followed by Rachel and her friend Jan a few minutes later. Both boys stood up like fine Southern gentleman and helped the girls get seated.

"Hey girls, this is my friend Jackson. He's in my art class."

The girls in their cute sundresses and sandals greeted him with a smile. They sat and talked for over an hour. Nearing the end of lunch, Jackson found himself laughing just a little. It had been over three months since he remembered laughing. Greg seemed to be a natural born comedian. He could make anyone laugh. Still, Jackson felt guilty about it. Jan was a beautiful girl, and she seemed quite interested, but every thought he had was of Hannah.

"Well guys, I really must be going. I have to head to work." Jackson stood up.

"Come on and stay for a little while longer Jackson, we're just starting to get to know you." Jan smiled.

"I'm sorry, but I have to go. I can't be late for work. I enjoyed meeting you both. I'll see you guys around."

CHAPTER THIRTY-SIX

# A Difficult Struggle

Jackson walked through the door of the Island Garage about 3:30 PM while Mr. Willie was hard at work behind the counter.

"Hey there Mr. College boy. How was your first day of classes?"

"They were okay Mr. Willie. I made a few new friends and I already got an assignment in one of my classes."

"Oh yeah? What's your first assignment?"

"One of my art teachers wants us to paint a picture of the College of Charleston Cistern."

"Well, that should be right up your alley huh?"

"Yeah, I guess so."

Jackson got dressed and headed out to the garage. Sarah from the Seaside Grille pulled up for an oil change on her old Honda Accord. She was a good friend of Jackson and Hannah's, and she missed him down at the Grille.

"Hey, Jackson, how have you been? We haven't seen you since Hannah went up to be with her grandmother."

Jackson tried not to look at her and show his expression.

"I've been better." He paused before continuing.

"Sarah, have you heard anything from Hannah? I call her every single day and get the same answer on the answering machine. She won't talk to me, and I don't know why. It is killing me."

"No, I haven't heard a lot. Becky and John are kind of tight-lipped about that stuff. They did say she was doing okay though. Not much else. I'm sorry Jackson.

You guys were so great together."

She sat down in the waiting room as Jackson finished up her car.

In a short time, Jackson walked into the waiting room to get his friend.

"Hey Sarah, your car is ready to go, you should be good for another 3000 miles. I'll see you around."

"Hey Jackson, can I talk to you about something before I go?"

"Sure, what is it?" The two stepped outside for some privacy.

"Becky and John are in a lot of trouble. Some slicked back hair guy from the bank came in and said they are accelerating their loan for the renovations."

"What does that mean?" Jackson asked.

"It means they have to pay the full balance by Christmas time or they will be foreclosed on."

Jackson's eyes widened, "How can they do that? They said they had five more years to pay on that loan."

"John said there was some acceleration clause on their contract, even for one day late."

Jackson's heart was breaking. "That just can't be. We have to do something to fix this mess."

"I know Jackson. John told us not to worry, but they owe over $60,000 dollars. They don't have that kind of money laying around. Running a restaurant is so hard and so expensive. I don't know what they're gonna do."

"They can't do that to them. That restaurant is an icon of Folly Beach. So many people go there."

"Well Jackson, they've got exactly three months to come up with the money or else they are going to take the restaurant. I think it's all a bunch of bull. It doesn't seem legal. I just thought you'd like to know."

"Thanks, Sarah. I appreciate the information. I'll see you later."

Jackson turned and headed back to the garage.

Mr. Willie came out of the office as Jackson was putting his tools away.

"Mr. Willie, can I talk to you for a minute?"

Jackson told Mr. Willie everything that Sarah had said.

"We can't let them lose the restaurant, Mr. Willie. That place means so much to so many people."

"Well, we've got three short months to figure out how to come up with $68,500 or so. Let's put our heads together and see what we can figure out."

"How about a car wash or spaghetti dinner or yard sale?" Jackson asked.

"Jackson, we could do that, but we're talking about $68,500. That's a heck of a lot of money. Those things will bring in a few thousand dollars, but I don't think we could get close to $68,500 in three months with those types of fundraising. We need to come up with some more ideas to make some more money."

Mr. Willie could see the anguish on Jackson's face.

"Don't worry son. We'll find a way."

CHAPTER THIRTY-SEVEN

# Renewed Hope

Jackson barely slept that night, wondering about how and what he could do to help Becky and John keep the Seaside Grille open. After a few restless hours, he awoke to the sweet smell of cinnamon rolls in the kitchen and sleepily made his way to the breakfast nook where his mother sat, reading the morning paper. He explained to her about Becky and John's situation and told her what he and Mr. Willie had planned.

"Only three months to come up with $68,500? That's unbelievable. I can ask some folks about fundraising down at the doctor's office."

"Thanks, mom. My first class isn't until 1 o'clock today, so I'm going to start my art project this morning."

"Okay honey. I'll see you tonight."

Jackson carefully pulled out the picture his professor had given him, and slowly ran his fingers across its glossy surface. He felt the wind blow across his face. Jackson smelled the scent of the fresh-cut grass. He was there at the cistern. That feeling came back again. For the first time in a while, he smiled. The ringing of the telephone startled him. Jackson picked up.

"Hey Jackson, I've got a buyer for that old Mustang Skeeter and Ralphie have been working on. That should make us about $1000 profit. That can be the first dent in that $68,500."

"That's fantastic Mr. Willie, thanks so much."

"Okay Jackson, I'll see you later."

A small smile began to form again as Jackson pulled out his canvas and started to paint. It was magical to watch him work. He blocked out the whole outside world as he entered one of his own, one where he was in control. No distractions; complete focus. He had been working for over four hours and finally put the finishing touches on his first college project.

Jackson arrived about a half-hour early and met Professor Hunt on the way to her class. The warm, muggy air surrounded the courtyard as he walked up the path. He pulled out his canvas and showed her his work. She stared at it in silence and raised her hand to cover her mouth.

"You did this today Jackson?" Jackson nodded.

"I've been teaching art for ten years and been an artist for 25 years, and I have never seen anything like this."

She found a bench and sat down to take in his painting. She ran her fingers over its surface; taking her time. After a while, she looked up at Jackson.

"Jackson, there is nothing I can teach you in this class about painting. You are absolutely the best painter I've ever seen. I know you don't have a degree yet, but how would you like to be my adjunct professor? Maybe, you could even help me along the way."

"Sure, Professor Hunt. I'll be glad to help out."

"Jackson, have you ever sold any of your paintings? You could easily sell any painting like this around here right now for a lot of money, and our December commencement ceremony is just a few months away.

Graduation always brings many families and a lot of alumni, just looking for some nostalgic pictures or paintings to remember their time here at the college."

"Yes ma'am, I've sold some over the years, but that would be great if I sold some. I could really use the money."

Jackson told her the story of the trouble at the Seaside Grille and asked her if she could help him market some of his paintings.

"It sounds like a great cause. I've been there a few times myself. I would recommend that you paint several different scenes from the college and around Charleston like the Battery or Rainbow Row. Our first artist sale is next month. If you can get some paintings ready, you will have no problem selling them."

CHAPTER THIRTY-EIGHT

# Salty

"Salty" Wagner walked the pier outside the Seaside Grille almost every day. He fished, talked to locals or caught a nap in the mid-afternoon sun when he felt the need. His wrinkled face, green eyes and pure white beard helped tell the story of his 70 years. He looked the part of a crew member of Captain Ahab's boat. His old Vietnam vet hat and his disheveled camouflage coat made him look like he just rolled out of bed. No one really knew where he lived. He seemed to show up on his three-wheeled bicycle at different times. For all anyone knew, he was homeless. Sleeping out amongst the stars and laying his head wherever he wanted made him happy. The Folly Beach Police would find him on different benches or camping out in his tent somewhere but left him alone. The locals knew he was harmless, so no one ever complained. Every morning, Becky always asked him to come in and eat breakfast before the lunch crowd began, but he never took her up on her offer. He would always say, "No thank you Mrs. Becky, I wouldn't want to be any trouble to you."

Becky was cleaning the front door glass when she saw Salty coming up the steps toward the pier.

"We made a lot of bacon and eggs this morning, just in case you're interested." The same exchange being repeated day in and day out for several years.

"Thank you, very kindly Miss Becky, but I wouldn't want to be any trouble to you."

"Salty, we're just going to throw it away if you don't eat it. The lunch crowd will be here soon, and we need to get ready for them. We'd be glad for you to have it. Come on now."

Salty just stood there not saying a word.

"Could I come around to the back?" Salty finally asked Becky after some awkward glances.

"Sure Salty, come on around."

Becky had offered Salty breakfast for five years straight, and he had never accepted her offer until today.

Becky walked into the kitchen. "Buddy, please fix up a big plate of cheese grits and eggs, bacon and toast, and I'll take it out to Salty. He's coming around the back."

"He's gonna eat today Becky?" Buddy smiled.

"Yep." Becky grinned and grabbed the plate and headed outside.

A couple of tables and chairs were set up outside the back door for the staff when they took breaks.

"Here you go Salty, please take a seat. I'll be right back with some coffee."

Salty stared at the plate packed full of wonderful food. He didn't know where to start.

"Man, I tell you what, this is the best food I've had... well since I can remember. I sure am much obliged to you, Miss Becky."

Salty seemed a little nervous, so Becky poured him a cup of coffee and left the coffee pot for him. She stared out the corner window and watched him bow his head to say grace. He looked up at the sky, and his emerald green eyes seemed to relax. He breathed deeply almost as a sigh of relief and then he dug in.

John came up behind Becky and hugged her tight. "Wow, he sure loves Buddy's cooking. How did you get him to eat? You've been asking him for years, and he never comes in."

"I just kept asking him. Today he finally said yes. He must eat somewhere because he's got a little bit of a belly. Everybody knows him around here, but some of the tourists don't know what to make of him. I guess maybe he's just misunderstood like we all are sometimes."

Becky turned and looked up at John; "What are we going to do about this loan?"

"We'll figure something out honey. The Good Lord always takes care of us. Don't worry now." John tried to smile as he held her close.

"Don't worry? I'm scared to death. We don't have that much money. I couldn't bear to lose this place. This place has been our life for so many years. It's part of who we are. We've got to figure something out."

John hugged Becky even tighter this time and once again told her everything would be okay. "I promise you things will work out. Please don't worry. We'll figure this out."

Becky was silent, then looked through to the front door. "It looks like some of our lunch crowd folks are starting to show up. We better go see to them."

Becky went in first, then John touched his heart and said a quiet prayer.

CHAPTER THIRTY-NINE

# The Plan

Jackson hadn't set foot inside the Seaside Grille since Hannah told him it was over between them. It was just too painful. So many great memories lingered there. Becky called to talk to him a few times and to see how he was doing. She did her best to encourage him and tell him things would get better. Her kindness was appreciated, but her words just didn't penetrate his heart to make him feel any relief. The sky was as clear blue as Jackson had ever seen it. He patiently waited for Becky's morning ritual to come up to the hostess stand to get ready for the lunch customers.

Becky looked through the glass door and couldn't believe Jackson was standing there. She opened the door as fast as she could and grabbed him and hugged him as tight as her frail arms could manage.

"It's so good to see you Jackson. We've missed you so much."

"I've missed you guys too. You don't know how much."

"Come on in Jackson; we'll make you some breakfast. John is fixing up some pancakes and eggs Benedict."

"That sounds good. I didn't have time to eat this morning. Becky, could I talk to you and John while we eat? I want to discuss something with you."

"Sure Jackson, I'll bring our food out. Have a seat in your favorite spot."

Jackson slowly walked to the corner table with the million-dollar view. He sat down and closed his eyes as he rubbed his hand over the seats and all over the table. Jackson could feel her. His heart pounded faster but the ache he felt deep down far overwhelmed his heart. John came out with Becky and all the breakfast plates. He hugged Jackson and told him how much he missed him.

"I heard about your problem with the bank. I have an idea, and I would like to help."

They sat and talked for about a half an hour and Jackson explained what his professor told him about the opportunity to sell some of his paintings.

"Jackson, we can't ask you to do that. That's your money. Your beautiful paintings are worth a lot of money, that money should go to you. We couldn't take your money." Becky said.

"Sure, you could. You guys fed me almost every day when Hannah and I were together. If it weren't for this place, I would have never met Hannah. We have to keep this place open. I'll do everything I can to help. Do you think I could set up a little area and display a few of my paintings? I have a few already done of the beach and the pier as well as the Morris Island lighthouse. My professor knows a lot of alumni downtown who said they would be interested in my paintings too."

Becky and John hugged Jackson and thanked him for his gracious offer.

"I can set up a nice area for you today Jackson." Becky smiled as she walked him out.

CHAPTER FORTY

# Getting to Work

Jackson got to work painting that afternoon right after class. He had accumulated a large assortment of canvases over the last couple of years. When he sat down to begin the first one, his thoughts raced with each brush stroke. As he painted the beautiful flowers of Middleton gardens, he replayed the wonderful afternoon there with Hannah. The pastel colors of "Rainbow Row" took shape on his canvas, and his heart sank as he remembered showing those exquisite houses to Hannah for the first time.

Jackson shared a quick dinner with his mom and continued bringing each painting to life. By the end of the night, he finished two brilliant works.

Every spare minute, Jackson painted, hardly even stopping to eat. With every stroke, his feelings got stronger and stronger. He was going to make sure nothing happened to the Seaside Grille. So many great memories played through his mind as he worked. Even though he couldn't be with Hannah anymore, some of his fondest memories, well most of his fondest memories with her were spent there, and he wasn't about to let that disappear.

CHAPTER FORTY-ONE

# Christmas is Coming

December's cool winds began to blow. Christmas decorations sprang up all over town as Jackson made the drive to college and back. Marion Square, at the corner of King and Calhoun street, had been decorated beautifully. Scores of people enjoyed the nightly display of all the wonderful trees and the beautiful 10-acre park in the middle of downtown.

Jackson spent every waking moment painting as many Charleston vistas as he could paint. Most nights he finally made it to bed around 2 AM. He managed to do well in his first semester at college, but he just felt like he was running in circles.

Mr. Willie set up an area in the back of the locker room at the garage for him to work when it wasn't busy. He had a donation box set up for customers to help save the Seaside Grille. Jackson had already sold a lot of paintings to the College of Charleston alumni. He managed to clear about $15,000 in the last two months. Still a long way from $68,500. The car sales and donations Mr. Willie received were up around $10,000.

"Hey Jackson, would you mind giving me a hand with this?" Mr. Willie laughed as he came into the locker room with a gigantic box being carried on the tire dolly.

"What in the world is in there?"

"It's our new display this year. A 20-foot Christmas tree that we're gonna put up on the roof. People will be able to see it from miles around. Do you mind helping me drag it up the ladder?"

Jackson made his way to the roof with a rope and pulley system they used in years past to pull up other heavy decorations. An hour later, they both stood on top of the roof staring at the tranquil beauty of their new tree. Up on the roof, the street noise was muffled, and it was so peaceful up there. Jackson looked toward the beach and could see the lights of Folly Beach. His heart sank as he thought about the whirlwind six months he had spent with Hannah and the miserable six months he had spent without her. He could hardly imagine it had been almost a year since he met her. Mr. Willie watched him and saw his heart was breaking.

"Christmas will be here in two weeks. Are you gonna go again with me this Christmas Eve? You know, help me play Santa?"

Jackson thought for a minute. He didn't want to go. It just wouldn't be the same this time.

"I'm sorry Mr. Willie, I don't think I can this year. Everything's so much different now."

"I know things are tough Jackson, but remember how much fun we use to have? Remember those priceless faces? Don't you want to experience that again? You really enjoyed it."

"I don't think so Mr. Willie."

"Well, how about we get a bite to eat? I know your mom is working late tonight. How about the Greek place on Maybank Highway?"

He helped Mr. Willie put everything away and close up the shop. As he climbed into Mr. Willie's truck, Jackson looked back at the garage and stared at all the decorations they put up together. Jackson loved Christmas, but his heart hurt so bad it kept him from enjoying the moment. For those brief seconds, he forgot about his heartache and was warmed inside by the feeling he got from just quietly looking at all the decorations from the Nativity scene to Santa in the Red Corvette, to the giant Christmas tree they just put up. It all looked beautiful, and for once, just for that moment, he was at peace.

Mr. Willie saw what was happening and waited to crank up the truck. He stopped for a minute and took it all in with him.

CHAPTER FORTY-TWO

# Christmas Wishes

Mr. Willie and Jackson made their way to the restaurant and talked about the fundraising efforts for the Seaside Grille as they waited for their food. The owner knew Mr. Willie very well and stopped by to chat for a few minutes. Several other people stopped by to say hi to Mr. Willie. He was well known all over the island. His garage had become a legendary place and was only rivaled by his kind heart.

"It looks like we've got a little over $25,000 Jackson. Your paintings sure have been doing well. We still have a good way to go though. We still have two weeks to raise the $68,500."

"What are we gonna do Mr. Willie?"

"We've got two weeks. That's a long time. Anything can happen, Jackson, you gotta keep the faith.

Jackson didn't say anything, he just looked across at Mr. Willie and nodded.

"Remember Jackson; this is a special time of year. Miracles are around every corner."

Mr. Willie smiled at Jackson.

"Hey, how about you take the next two weeks off and work on those paintings. I'll pay you like it was vacation. Don't forget, there's a Miracle around every corner."

CHAPTER FORTY-THREE

# Almost There

It was December 23rd and Becky smiled at John as they opened the restaurant. The Seaside Grille was decorated more beautiful than she ever remembered it. Lights were all a glow as they covered every window. The biggest Christmas tree they ever had inside was anonymously donated several weeks before. One morning, Becky had turned the sign around like she had thousands of times before and laying out front of the door was a 15-foot Frasier Fir tree with a giant red bow and a card that just said Merry Christmas. John needed all the boys in the back to help him set it up. Over a thousand ornaments adorned the tree. Jackson and Mr. Willie stopped by to bring the last of the money they made from the car sales at the garage.

"Please stay for breakfast." Becky smiled.

The two were seated at Jackson's favorite table as John sat down.

"You don't know how thankful we are for all you both have done for us. We will never forget your kindness."

Seeing Jackson a little choked up, Mr. Willie stepped in.

"John, we are blessed to help you guys. You give so much to our community. How close are you to the goal?"

"Well Willie, with what you guys brought, we have just a little over $58,500. Still about $10,000 left to go."

John's facial expression changed a little as he thought about the looming deadline and what not making it would mean.

Becky had an entire corner of the restaurant set up with Jackson's paintings on display. She sold several in the last few days, and she was optimistic about today. After they finished breakfast, Jackson stopped by the back office to hug Becky and say he would be back later tonight with a very special painting for sale. As he stepped into the office, he caught a glimpse of a picture of him and Hannah after the half-rubber tournament. Her skin was so beautiful, and her smile melted his heart again. Becky saw him and hugged him again.

"Keep the faith, Jackson."

CHAPTER FORTY-FOUR

# The Auction

The day had been slow for customers, and Becky hadn't sold a single painting. She was discouraged and tried to hide it when Jackson showed up that evening with his new painting. He pulled it out of his giant bag and Becky stood there speechless. Jackson had captured a beautiful moonlit night looking out on the pier through the Christmas adorned windows of the grille. The giant wreath at the end of the pier beckoned Christmas visitors. A lonely soul dotted the canvas as he stared out into the deep blue Atlantic.

"This is so wonderful Jackson. It is so real."

Becky stepped down to the best seat in the restaurant and compared it to Jackson's painting. It was difficult telling them apart.

"Your talent is unbelievable. You are such a special young man. I love you so much, Jackson."

Jackson hugged Becky as he held back tears. He worked so hard to make sure the Seaside Grille still belonged to Becky and John. His heart was breaking knowing they were still $10,000 short and that they might lose the restaurant. Jackson walked into the kitchen to say hi to all the cooks and talk to John.

"We have the auction tonight Jackson. Several customers have promised to be here with their checkbooks wide open."

"That's great John. I'm excited."

Jackson tried to put his best smile on, but the uncertainty was killing him inside.

"Hey John, can I use the phone in the office?"

"Sure Jackson, go ahead."

Jackson sat down and dialed the same number he had for the last six months. He went through the same words he usually left every day, but tonight he added a few.

"Hannah, I saw your picture again tonight in Becky's office. I miss you so much. I still love you, and I'll wait for you no matter what. Mr. Willie says this time of year is special and miracles happen. I hope your grandmother is doing better and I'm still praying for you and her every day. I love you. I've never loved anyone but you."

The cold silence at the final beep of the answering machine left a deep dull pain in his heart. How much longer could he do this? Did she even hear his voice? Does she even care? So many doubts crept into his mind as Becky came in.

"Jackson, the auction is about to start."

"I'll be right there Aunt Becky."

A large gathering assembled around Jackson's paintings, and they were amazed at each one. About thirty minutes into it, Becky sold three of Jackson's paintings for $1000 each. The auction was nearing the end, and no other paintings had been sold. Jackson could see the worry in Becky's eyes as she stared around at the crowd. A rattle of the bells on the door turned her attention. It was Salty and another young man in a nice tailored suit.

"Merry Christmas ma'am, my name is Christopher Weeks, and I'm Salty's nephew." John and Jackson gathered around to find out what was going on.

"It's nice to meet you, Christopher. Would you like to have a seat and get something to eat?"

"No ma'am that won't be necessary. Salty wanted to come by and be part of the auction."

Becky smiled. "Is that right?"

"My uncle wants to pay you $10,000 for that painting over there on the easel." He pointed to the painting Jackson just brought in of the moonlit pier at Christmas.

"What? Salty doesn't have that kind of money."

"Well, that's why I'm here. I take care of his finances, and I have a cashier's check for $10,000, and I can assure you this check is real. He said that is him on the pier and he never had a painting with him in it before. I know this may be hard to understand, but when my uncle came back from Vietnam, he was never the same. He never slept inside his house again, choosing to sleep wherever he pleased. He just did whatever he wanted, and he asked me to take care of his money. He comes from a very wealthy family. Salty never had children, so I'm the closest thing he has to a son. Salty wants to buy this painting for $10,000, but he has one condition."

"What's that?"

"That you keep the painting and put it over the mantle above the fireplace, so everyone can see him."

Becky's eyes burst into tears as Jackson and John stood there amazed at what had just transpired.

"Do you know what this means?" John screamed as he swept Becky off her feet in a swirl. They kissed so sweetly and loving that the whole restaurant went quiet. For those brief seconds, time stood still for them. Jackson's heart was elated that they had saved the grille after working so hard for so long. He just stood there rubbing the back of his neck and shaking his head in disbelief as to what had just happened. He looked all around the room at the wonderful customers who helped make it happen. His eyes gazed at each table. Their expressions warmed his heart. One by one he made the rounds through the restaurant, stopping at each table and thanking them. As he stepped towards the last few booths near the door, he was stopped cold. His knees buckled. He did a double take. Was he dreaming? He looked again. Standing outside the front door was Hannah.

CHAPTER FORTY-FIVE

# Redemption

Becky turned to hug Jackson and saw him staring towards the front door. She was silent at first, then blurted out, "I can't believe it. It's Hannah."

She ran to the door and welcomed her inside, hugging her.

"We missed you so much, honey."

Hannah's hair was longer and more beautiful than Jackson remembered. Her skin glowed as if she just stepped out of the sun. She was so beautiful, Jackson couldn't stop staring. Her eyes were uneasy and timid. She hugged Becky and John with a forced smile. All the waitresses and staff came out to greet her. Each one took their turn talking to her and asking her the same questions. Jackson stood in the back and watched her every move as she stared at him. After each said hello, she stepped closer to Jackson and held her finger to her silky pink lips in a play of apprehension. She looked just like the day she left, only more enchanting this time. A long pause of silence ensued as each of them looked at each other, memorizing every line of each other's faces.

She didn't say a word. Jackson couldn't believe he was standing in front of her. Slowly a smile began to form on Jackson's face as he realized he wasn't dreaming. As she saw the sunshine come into his face, her countenance changed immediately back to what he had remembered. So genuine and sweet. His heart swelled with renewed hope. The crowd watched in anticipation as they continued their silence, taking each other in. Trying to find the right words to begin where they left off so long ago. So many words came to his mind, but not one could he convey to her. By now, he was shaking. He wanted the first words he said to her in months to be perfect.

She didn't quite know what to say either. What do you say to someone you have been ignoring for the last six months? Someone you loved so deeply?

Jackson finally broke the silence.

"You look so beautiful Hannah; Merry Christmas."

"Merry Christmas Jackson. Can we talk outside?"

"Sure, let me get my jacket."

Hannah was bundled up in her off-white turtleneck sweater and soft brown leather jacket, being used to the cold Michigan winter.

As the wind bit at their faces, they began the walk down their pier. Hannah's perfume tantalized Jackson's senses and his memories came rushing back. Halfway down the pier, Hannah stopped and turned to Jackson with tears in her eyes.

"Jackson, I know you can never understand what happened over the last six months between us. I still can't believe it myself. When I found out about my grandmother, the world I had known with you was falling apart. You and I were making a new life together, but when I heard about her stroke, I couldn't believe she would be taken away from me too. When the doctors said she could recover, I didn't want to let her down. They said it might take many months or years or she may never recover. I didn't know what to do. Aunt Becky had been so sick, and I couldn't ask her to help. My grandmother's eyes gleamed with hope, and I knew she was still in there and all I needed to do was to help her get back to her normal life. The night I ended it with you was one of the hardest nights of my life. I cried the entire night. I didn't think I had that many tears. I have cried every single day since then. I cry when I wake up and then again after your evening phone call. Missing you, wanting you, needing you. I thought that would be the best thing for you. I was crazy out of my mind with worry about my grandmother and losing her. I had no idea how long it would take or if she would ever recover. I never wanted to lose you. My love for you was so deep; I thought it would be better to let you go and not be held back by waiting for me."

Jackson looked into her eyes.

"I guess I don't understand. I know it was tough, and you didn't know what to do, but why wouldn't you let me help you or let me wait for you. Why did you have to end it like that?"

"At the time, I thought it was the best thing for you. You have your life here with everything and I couldn't take you away from that."

"The best thing for me? How could losing the only girl I've ever loved be a good thing? I haven't been the same since. The sun doesn't shine as brightly as it did when you were here. Nothing is the same. It feels artificial. I still don't understand. I called you every day, and you never answered or called me back. How am I supposed to understand that? What made you show up now?"

"Your calls every day kept me hanging on. Just to hear your voice and to know you still loved me and were waiting for me made things so much better."

"So why now, what made you want to come back now?"

"I guess you can say a "Miracle" happened. Over the last few months, my grandmother has made miraculous improvements in everything she's done. We worked for hours and hours each day in Physical Therapy and Speech. The doctors couldn't believe how much she improved with each visit. My grandmother is completely back to her old self! She is actually checking in at the Holiday Inn next door."

"Really! That's great."

"When she started talking again, she wanted me to leave and come back here, but I had promised her to see her rehabilitation through. When she knew I wasn't leaving, she made me promise to be quiet about her progress until she was ready to come here and see everyone in person. She worked hard every single day, never took a day off from learning to walk again. Now, she hardly even has any limp in her gait. It was her idea to come back here. She wanted to be well by Christmas. The doctors said as long as she took her medicine, she could do anything she wanted for a long, long time. I realize you may never be able to forgive me, but I knew there was only one way to find out, so here I am."

Jackson didn't waste any more precious time. He grabbed her and kissed her more passionately than he ever had before. Everything fell right back into place for them. It was almost like she never left.

"Jackson, can you ever forgive me? Your phone calls every night kept my hope alive that one day we could be together again. If it hadn't been for those calls, I might have never come back."

"I always prayed you would come back to me." Jackson smiled as tears streamed down his face.

"I never gave up hope for us. That's why I always called. I thought that if by chance you were listening that you would always know how much I loved you and know that I would always be here waiting for you."

"Jackson, do you think we could start again where we left off?"

"I thought we just did." Jackson beamed as he wiped his tears away against the cold, clear backdrop of the night sky.

"Jackson, when you kissed me, it felt like I had never left. I just have one question for you?"

"What's that?"

"What took you so long to kiss me? I wanted to kiss you as soon as I laid eyes on you through the front door window."

"I wanted to do a lot more than just kiss you when I saw you. It was my dream come true."

She grabbed him and kissed him again. His heart was once again ignited in full fury. The present he had been waiting on for so long had at long last been delivered.

CHAPTER FORTY-SIX

# Iris

Hannah's grandmother Iris walked through the doors of the Seaside Grille to resounding applause. Everyone in the grille tonight were close friends and knew their story. Hannah made the rounds from table to table saying hello and receiving great praise for all she did to help her grandmother get well. Then her grandmother stopped to talk to Jackson.

"I'm so glad I get to finally meet you, Jackson. For a while there, I wasn't sure if I would ever get to talk to you. The doctors didn't give me a good prognosis for recovery. They said I would never walk or speak again. I guess they forgot about the Head Doctor Upstairs. The Good Lord can do anything, and he sure healed me. They even called me the Miracle Lady when I walked out of that hospital."

Jackson was glad to meet Iris, and he smiled as he listened to her unbelievable story.

"Hannah talked non-stop about you when she would call and talk to me on the phone before the stroke. I want you to know that even when I couldn't talk, Hannah talked to me and told me of her deep and abiding love for you. It was a source of inspiration for me. My husband Jim and I shared 42 years of love together until cancer took him from me. I wanted to fight so she had a chance at that wonderful life. She would sit on my bed and show me magazines of homes and places she wanted to visit with you. I've never seen anyone more truly in love. I hope you can forgive her for how things happened. Her spirit is one that helps others. My health was her main concern above her own life. I couldn't do anything at first. She gave her life to help me. Every day I felt bad that she had put me above her happiness. I prayed that God would let me get back to normal, so Hannah could enjoy a life with you. She was so young when so many terrible events changed her life. It would be difficult for anyone, especially a young person. I made her promise that when I was well, we would come down here and she would try to make things right with you. Please give her the chance. You made it better for her with your phone calls and trying to tell her you would have done the same thing. I heard her crying every day after your call. She tried not to let me hear, but I did."

She hugged Jackson and smiled. "Jackson, true love between two people is very rare these days. Hannah has always loved you. It broke her heart. She would stand and look out the window of my bedroom and just talk. She didn't know if I could hear or not, but she still talked. I couldn't say anything, but I did hear her. Her love for you was so deep. Letting you go on with your life and not having to wait was what she thought would be the best for you. Remember, she still loves you."

Even though Jackson just met her, he felt like he had known her his whole life. Her soft, kind words melted the hurt that had surrounded his heart for so long.

CHAPTER FORTY-SEVEN

# The Question

The next several hours at the Seaside Grille were a celebration of everything that had happened that year. The ups and downs and the triumph of saving the Grille and the reunited love of Jackson and Hannah. The clock chimed 1 o'clock in the morning when Jackson asked her to walk the pier again with him. The few clouds that were present earlier had since drifted away, and the slow pounding of the soft waves echoed high above the surf. The moon hung low and beckoned them to come closer. It was the brightest moon they had ever seen together. They finally stopped at a bench at the end of the pier.

"Hey, guess what? It's Christmas Eve."

Hannah smiled. "I guess it is."

"One year ago, my life changed on this pier." Jackson began.

"I'm hoping it can change again. Hannah, I love you more than I thought any one person could love another. I can't live without you."

He kneeled down on the weather-worn pier.

"Will you marry me? I don't want to spend another day without you."

Hannah's eyes filled with tears of joy.

"You want to marry me, after all, that's happened?"

"I know you were doing what you thought was the best thing for me. I thought about you every minute while we were apart. You still had part of my heart with you. Nothing was the same. I couldn't enjoy anything like I did when I was with you. God healed your grandmother, and now that you're here, my broken heart is almost healed."

"What do you mean, almost?" Hannah looked at him.

"If you marry me, my heart will be whole again."

Tears streamed down her face. "Yes... Yes, Jackson, I will marry you."

She jumped into his arms, and they were so hot for each other, they wanted to begin the honeymoon early.

"My heart is healing now too Jackson. I can't believe this."

"How about we go to the Justice of the Peace downtown first thing later this morning and get married? We can have another ceremony later with all our family and friends."

"For now, can we just keep this between us? I'm so happy to marry you, Jackson. I just want us to work out all the details before we tell Becky and John as well as my grandmother."

Jackson kissed her again "good night and good morning," not believing what had taken place.

On his ride home, he passed by Folly Beach Baptist Church. A stately oak tree stood outside, decorated with brilliant white lights that warmed the church in its glow. Even though the clock was approaching 2 am, he saw a few cars in the parking lot and decided to stop in. During Christmas, the pastor and some of the congregation would keep the church open 24 hours to let anyone come in to pray. "It's a season for miracles," he would always say.

Jackson slowly opened the doors and went inside. Several trees lit the stage covered with beautiful Poinsettias. Sitting down in the second pew, he closed his eyes and prayed. He couldn't believe what was happening after all this time. When he opened his eyes, the young pastor was standing a few feet from him. Jackson and Hannah had been to church there many times earlier in the year, and he knew Jackson.

"Wow Jackson, don't you think it's a little late for you to be out?"

Jackson quickly explained all that had transpired, and the pastor intently listened. He told him they planned to go down to the Justice of the Peace in the morning.

"Why don't you just come here early in the morning and I can do the ceremony for you? Wouldn't you want to be married in God's house?"

"Can you do that for us?"

"Sure, I'm licensed by South Carolina just like the Justice of the Peace is. Only me and God and of course you and Hannah will know you are married. We can do another ceremony later for all the family when you guys are ready."

Jackson thanked him and headed home. He looked out over the Folly River as he crossed the silent bridge, he could see the Christmas star shining brightly while he said another prayer.

CHAPTER FORTY-EIGHT

# The Wedding

A few winks were all Jackson's body would afford him. He was getting married in a few hours after all. You couldn't really blame him. From one extreme to the next, the gamut of all his emotions had been experienced in the last 24 hours. Wow, what a day can make.

Jackson wanted to tell his mom, but at the last minute decided against it. Wanting to have it already done before he sprung the news on her. She loved Hannah, but she had no idea Jackson had asked her to marry him. She was so overjoyed to hear she had returned and to see her "old Jackson" come back. His melancholy state had been tough on her too for these last few months.

"Where are you going all dressed up? I haven't seen you wear a tie since last Christmas."

"Mom, I have to run. I have to pick up Hannah. We're going to a special place. I'll see you later tonight."

He pulled into the parking lot at the Seaside Grille in Mr. Willie's old truck and waiting on the steps was his bride to be. Staring intently, he jumped out and ran to meet her.

"Are you ready to do it? Are you ready to be my wife forever?"

"Jackson, it's all I've thought about since I left to go help my grandmother. I imagined us getting married, having children and sitting on our rocking chairs outside the grille enjoying another perfect sunset. I have been preparing for this day, and I've been praying God would join us together. My heart is connected to yours. You caress my soul. I love you so much, and I'm so glad that you forgave me for all I put you through."

Jackson opened the door for her, and they were off.

"Last night on the way home, I stopped by the church, and it was open."

"At 2 o'clock in the morning?"

"Yeah. It was open. The pastor and some of the congregation take turns keeping it open around the clock during the week before Christmas. I talked to the pastor, and he agreed to marry us and keep it a secret until we can make plans for another ceremony. Would you like to do it at the church?"

"I would love to be married there. I just want to marry you,

Jackson."

She unbuckled her seat belt and leaned over and began kissing him all over his lips and neck.

Jackson parked behind the church to stay out of sight.

"You ready to do this?"

Hannah nodded, and they opened the door, and the Pastor was waiting for them.

Not a soul was around, as they assembled in front of the church.

Jackson began.

"I choose you over anyone else in the world. You make my heart happy. I feel the warmth of your heart when we touch. I want to live my life knowing that reality. I love you for what you are and who you are and for who you make me. I want to be everything for you. I want to be your friend, your lover and the person to share your life with. To experience all that there is to experience together. I will forever love you with all that I have. I will be honest and true to you. When you hurt, I will hurt. Whatever may come our way, I will never give up the love I have for you. God has brought you back to me, and I promise to make you happy for the rest of my life. I will never stop saying I love you until I take my last breath. I won't just say it; I'll show it. This vow I take with you today is a covenant between God and us. I will never break it. I will never give up on you and us. This marriage is a gift from God, and I will treat you as my most precious gift. I will honor and cherish you for the rest of my life."

Tears streamed down Hannah's face as she held his hands. It was her turn.

"I thought I had lost you, but we have returned to each other. I promise to love you with the depths of my soul. I promise to encourage you, to be kind and loyal to only you. I have never loved another. You have the key to my heart. A place I didn't think anyone could get into. I promise to be there for you in the highs and lows. I also promise to never give up on our love and will always work to make it stronger. I will be your friend, your lover and your confidant. I want to build my life with only you Jackson Henderson. My vow to you will be to always love you with all that I am."

"Now with the power invested in me by the great state of South Carolina, I pronounce you husband and wife. You may now... oh well, I guess you know what to do."

Before the Pastor could say his last words, Jackson started kissing his new bride.

They hugged the Pastor and thanked him, and out the door, they went with two cheap wedding bands he had bought earlier that morning. She didn't care. All she wanted was him.

The whirlwind was speeding faster when she asked, "Where are we going next? You know it is Christmas Eve."

"I know, I've got a great place for our first night or for right now, our first day."

The new couple made it to a new hotel on Kiawah Island, about 30 minutes from James Island. Built on the barrier islands, Kiawah Island has seen its share of changes over the years. It's an unspoiled paradise just outside of town. Far from the crowds of Folly Beach, it has such wonderful old-world charm. Being the holidays, there were few visitors as they checked in.

"Please enjoy your stay with us and have a Merry Christmas." The desk clerk smiled.

Jackson grabbed their bags as they boarded the elevator. As soon as the door pulled closed, he grabbed her and held her tight. He wanted to make up for the six months he had lost without her. They were interrupted by the ding at the end of the short ride up. It seemed like they had the whole floor to themselves. He stopped short as he dropped the bags and picked her up. He opened the honeymoon suite door, and a breathtaking view of the ocean met their gaze. He quickly stepped in and nudged the door closed with his foot. As he looked into her eyes, he couldn't believe this was really happening. Just 24 hours before, he didn't think she loved him any longer. Now she was his forever.

"Mrs. Henderson, would you like to take a shower... with me?"

"I believe I would Mr. Henderson. Could you get a nice fire going for us first? I've never seen a hotel with a wood burning fireplace."

Jackson turned his attention to the fireplace, and in a few minutes, the logs were putting out a beautiful warm glow that filled the room.

He was excited about the thought of seeing her naked for the first time; making love to her for the first time. The first for the both of them. He heard the water start, and he could feel his body ache with passion. He laid down two large blankets all around the fireplace and opened the door to the bathroom. She was standing there in only her black lace panties and black silk bra. She had slipped her dress off, and she still had her black high heels on. Seeing her for the first time like that, he almost lost his control. She stared at him too. She looked down and could see how excited he was.

"Would you like to take these off?"

Nodding, he began to gently kiss her neck, savoring every second.

He didn't waste much time. The taste of her was overwhelming. As they entered the shower, they never stopped kissing. They took turns bathing each other and then slipped out into their robes to the awaiting fire. Jackson had drawn the curtains, and the only light was from the burning embers. Hannah laid down with her robe drawn tight. Her long tan legs shimmered against the fire, and her French-manicured toes rubbed against Jackson's. They didn't say a word, constantly studying each other. Jackson ran his hand along her face and held her and kissed her.

"I've been waiting for this day since I met you. I instantly fell in love with you." Jackson smiled.

"I knew on New Year's Eve when you kissed me, Jackson. I had never felt anything as powerful in my life."

She kissed him and then grabbed his hands and laid them on her breasts. Her skin was so soft and warm. Jackson caressed every inch of her as the fire warmed them. He could see her chest rise and lower with every touch. He was trembling as well. While he was busy, she began exploring his body. With every second, the tension multiplied. When they could take it no longer, Hannah looked at him with the deepest eyes and said, "I need you to love me forever Jackson. I can't take anything less."

"No matter what life brings us; I will always be here with you. If you are lost, I'll find you. No matter how far away you are, I'll find my way to you. I promise to love you forever Hannah."

With one swift motion, they united together for the first time. With every move, their hearts and souls entwined deeper and deeper. Every sensation of ecstasy passed over them as they loved each other. Continuing to bask among the waves of pleasure with each act of love, they finally surrendered, and Jackson moved around to lay behind her and held her tight while they enjoyed the embers dancing. Their emotions had been tested so hard these last 24 hours that Hannah drifted off to sleep in the comfort of his arms. Jackson silently watched her and prayed.

"Thank you, Lord, for bringing her back to me. I've never been this happy before. Please keep us together no matter what. Don't let anything come between us. Help me to be the man you want me to be, so I can be the best man for her. Make me strong and wise. Through Jesus, Amen."

A short while passed, and Hannah reached up and pulled Jackson to her again. This time, Jackson began by kissing every inch of her body. He started at her toes and started heading North.

With each pass of his lips along her calves and up along the back of her knees, she breathed deeper and deeper. Slowly he opened her legs and began to please her. With every touch of his tongue, she came closer and closer to him. He continued until she could no longer take it any longer and collapsed with pleasure. Completely sated.

They continued throughout the day and into the afternoon, getting to know one another more deeply with every act of love. The afternoon came too fast, and they knew they should start back to Folly Beach. It was Christmas Eve, and everyone was expecting them. They only had one problem. No one knew they were married.

CHAPTER FORTY-NINE

# A Change of Heart

When they returned to the Seaside Grille, everyone was busy preparing for the Christmas Eve crowd. The suggestion basket still hung by the door as it had last Christmas. Becky smiled, and her heart filled with joy when she saw Jackson and Hannah.

"Did you guys have a great day together?" She asked while setting the table.

They both looked at each other, "It was the best day of our lives."

"That must have been some reunion after six months," Becky laughed with a sheepish grin on her face.

Jackson put his arm around Hannah and held her close.

"Oh, I almost forgot."

"What is it, Jackson?"

"I need to call Mr. Willie. I'll be right back."

Jackson sat down in the back office, and Mr. Willie picked up on the other end.

"Merry Christmas Mr. Willie," Jackson said in the most excited tone Mr. Willie had heard in a long time."

"Hey, Merry Christmas buddy. I haven't heard you sound that happy in a long time. What's going on?"

Mr. Willie was in the kitchen talking to some of the cooks on December 23rd, and he left out the back door after Salty bought the painting. He didn't see Hannah come in.

"She's back Mr. Willie."

"Who's back?"

"Hannah. She's back, and she still loves me. We are ... he stopped himself short. We are together again."

"That's great Jackson. I'm so glad she's back. You sure sound better. Had any change of heart about helping me play Santa tonight?"

"She changed my heart. I would love to go. Do you think we could take her along to help us? She could be a good distraction."

"Can she keep a secret?"

"Sure, she can. Trust me."

"I'll pick you guys up at the Seaside Grille in about an hour."

"See you then Mr. Willie."

CHAPTER FIFTY

# Good News

Jackson hadn't told anyone about playing Santa Claus last year except his mother. One of the most enjoyable experiences of his life was seeing the faces of the people Mr. Willie helped. Now that Hannah was his wife, he wanted to let her in on the big secret.

"Would you come with me and Mr. Willie this afternoon for a little while before Christmas Eve dinner? We need your help."

"What are you talking about Jackson? I'll go with you anywhere."

"You have to promise to always keep this a secret no matter what. You can't even tell Becky or John."

"What is it?"

"You have to promise first."

"Ok, I promise. Now, what's the big secret?"

Jackson told the story of the "Secret Santa" last year, and he watched as a few tears rolled down Hannah's cheek.

"That meant so much to everyone last year. Aunt Becky and Uncle John had been worried all throughout Christmas about how they would come up with the money to pay off their loan."

Mr. Willie picked them up and headed out to a small café that had opened in the summer. It was a quaint place with good food. Business was slow but picking up. The owner was a young single mom with two young children, one boy, and one girl. Nicole Anderson from Maine had escaped the snowy winters for the heat of the South to restart her life after her recent divorce.

The newlyweds and Mr. Willie sat down and ordered a piece of apple pie and coffee. The place was almost full. Nicole was the only waitress. At the front of the store was a life-size Santa and resting in one hand was the handle to a large basket full of Christmas pastries and candy. Nicole's children had been eyeing it since they sat down.

"No sweets until after we eat our Christmas Eve dinner," she smiled trying to make them listen. She had been keeping them out of there all day. They had listened, but their stomachs were grumbling, and they kept staring at the goodies inside the basket.

Mr. Willie handed the envelopes to Hannah under the table and discussed his plan. He walked to the back to talk to the kids, and when he got their attention, Hannah slipped them in Santa's basket in an instant without anyone noticing.

After she brought out their food, Nicole sat with her kids in a back booth to enjoy Christmas Eve dinner. She only had a minute to say grace and take a bite and then she was back up checking on her customers and serving their food.

Her oldest was a beautiful little girl with soft ringlets of sandy brown hair and green eyes named Nikki. She scarfed down her food and headed for the basket. Her mom was a pastry chef in Maine, and it was her specialty. All kinds of pastries and candies filled the decorated basket. The basket was just above the little one's eye level, so she leaned her little arm over and grabbed a pastry. She had a puzzled look on her face, so she went back in for another try. When she did, she pulled out the envelopes. She called out to her mom and ran back into the kitchen to meet her.

"What is it, Nikki? Why all the fuss?"

"Look mom." She held out the envelopes with a crooked grin on her face.

"These are for you."

Nicole took the envelopes and walked back to the table with her young son. They couldn't stop talking while she opened the envelopes. She sat down and slid out the smooth envelope inside with ten crisp $100 bills. Nicole gasped, and her hand covered her mouth. She grabbed her kids and held them tight as she quietly cried into their arms.

"What's wrong mommy? Why are you crying?"

Nicole tried to compose herself and squeezed her kids tighter.

Mr. Willie left the money on the table for their pie, and the group headed out. They walked to the corner of the plate glass window and peeked in to see her still holding her children in a warm embrace.

Everyone was quiet as Mr. Willie pointed the truck to another destination.

"How did you like that Hannah?" Mr. Willie smiled.

She bowed her head in the back seat and sobbed.

Jackson held her. "Are you okay?"

"Yes, I'm sorry, I'm such a mess. Watching that was so wonderful. It's the second-best thing I've ever done on Christmas Eve." Wiping her tears and smiling at Jackson.

"Thank you for including me, Mr. Willie."

"We're glad you came Hannah; we couldn't have all the fun by ourselves." He chuckled.

Two more stops were made, and then they headed back to the

Seaside Grille. Becky and John had invited friends and family for a special dinner to honor Hannah and Jackson being reunited in the side banquet room. She was planning on bouncing back and forth between there and any customers who stopped by for a Christmas Eve dinner.

Everyone was there; Hannah's grandmother, Red and Gina, all the mechanics from the garage and Jackson's mom Leah.

Jackson pulled Hannah aside and asked her if he could break the news to everyone.

"Do you think we should? I mean, it will be a total shock to your mom and Aunt Becky and my grandmother with me showing back up in your life yesterday."

"Everyone is here. What a better way to spread our great news than on Christmas Eve. Plus, they have to be nice to us, since it's Christmas Eve and all."

"I'm okay if you're okay with it."

Jackson stepped to the end of the table and grabbed a glass of Sweet Tea. He picked up the closest spoon and began to ding the side as he gained everyone's attention.

"Merry Christmas everyone, I would like to make a special announcement. All our family and friends are gathered here, and I know you all know how much Hannah has meant to me over the last year. We are back together, and I am so happy for that."

The crowd congratulated him and thought he was done speaking.

"Hold on a minute please, I would like to announce that this morning, Hannah and I got married right down the street at the church. Merry Christmas everyone."

Silence rang out through the room, and no one moved. All eyes were on Jackson's mom and Becky who had been talking before Jackson began.

Jackson's mom started laughing and said, "I'm sorry, I thought you just said you and Hannah got married this morning." Her face grimaced as she looked around to see if they were playing a joke on her.

"That's right mom, that's what I said. We are husband and wife."

Leah and Jackson stepped out of the room, and everyone else was left to contemplate what had been revealed.

"But Jackson, you just started college. How are you guys going to live? You don't have money to support her."

"Mom, I lost her once. I don't ever want to lose her again. I felt like I was dying during those six months. I can't lose her again. She said she was trying to let me go because she didn't know how long her grandmother's recovery would take. At first, she didn't think her grandmother would ever get better."

Leah's eyes began to fill with tears.

"You're too young to get married. The both of you can't live on what you make at the garage and what she makes in tips here. How are you going to support each other?"

Jackson waited a while before he spoke.

"Mom I know you love me and want me to be happy. You know how much I love Hannah, how I need to be with her. We were made for each other. God will help me work it out. I will work three jobs like you did if I need to."

"I didn't want that for you, Jackson. Many years are ahead of you; why couldn't you have waited until you were out of college?"

"What if I died tonight mom and I waited to marry her? I would have missed out on one of the most beautiful things there is in life. Don't you want that for me?"

Jackson hugged her tightly as she cried in his arms. A few quiet moments passed, and Leah wiped the tears from her eyes.

"Well, I guess since you two are serious, we should celebrate."

They walked back in holding hands. Becky, Iris, and Hannah were having the same conversation.

"Hannah, you're married?" Becky began. "You haven't seen Jackson for six months, and now you're married?"

"Hold on a minute Becky," Iris interrupted.

"While Hannah was taking care of me, she talked to me for hours about him. I couldn't talk, but I could hear her. She loves him like I loved your father. I know she's young, but life can be taken from you in an instant. I have first-hand experience. God cured me. There is no other way to explain it. I shouldn't be here right now, but I am. Since we made it back here, Hannah has been a new person. She deserves this. It's a love that can last through anything."

Becky stood quiet, looking at her mother and Hannah. Without a word, she grabbed Hannah and held her tight.

"Are you really sure about this honey?"

"Aunt Becky, I've never been surer of anything else in my life."

"How will you guys live? You and Jackson don't make that much?"

"We will work it out. I just have to be with him. My heart is empty without him."

Everyone was watching as the three women walked back into the room. The crowd erupted in great applause as they saw their tears of joy. Watching from the corner was Mr. Willie. He was smiling from ear to ear.

"Jackson, do you mind if we take a walk outside?"

"Sure, I'd be glad to."

They made their way outside to "Hannah's pier."

"Remember when you first started working at the garage and we talked all the time about everything, including women."

Jackson nodded.

"Remember that I told you that finding the right woman would be the second most important thing you would ever do in your life?"

"Yes, sir."

"I know you love Hannah and I sure am glad that she's back. The change in your demeanor is so much better now. I just want you to be sure you have made the decision to get married for all the right reasons and not just for the euphoria you felt when she walked back into your life."

"Mr. Willie, you have been like a father to me. I've done more things with you than I ever did with my father. I listened to you and all the guys during all those talks. You even helped me make my decision. The picture you painted in my mind of your family was something I didn't want to let pass me by. She makes me want to be a better man. I can't explain it; she helps me in every way possible. When I hug her, I feel more energized, like she's transferring energy to me. I've read about that, and I think it's true. She's the real thing; everything I ever wanted. I'd been thinking about marrying her since last New Year's Eve when we had our first kiss."

"How about we talk some more later about everything okay? Let's go in and enjoy our Christmas Eve dinner."

CHAPTER FIFTY-ONE

# Mr. Willie's Gift

As the new couple walked back in, the whole place erupted again with giant applause and congratulations. For the next half hour, everyone congratulated Becky and John as well as the newlyweds.

The events of the evening had taken their toll on Becky. She was on a roller coaster and needed to lie down. John helped her upstairs and came back down to join everyone and get ready to close up for the evening.

Being Christmas Eve, not too many people were looking to stay out late. John finally ushered everyone to the door, and they said their goodbyes and headed home for the night to get ready for Santa. Hannah turned the sign around. Only John, Hannah, Jackson and Mr. Willie were left downstairs.

"Would you like some coffee, Willie?" John asked.

"Thanks, John, but I better be heading out too. I know you guys have a lot to talk about. Hey Jackson, could you and Hannah walk me out?"

"Sure, Mr. Willie, I'll walk you out."

As they reached the bottom of the stairs leading to the parking lot, Mr. Willie stopped and turned to Jackson.

"Jackson, you were so kind and worked so hard to help Becky and John with the sale of your paintings. I'm so proud of you and how you stepped up to help someone in need. It's the mark of a true man. A man who should be able to drive around in something other than an "old beater" truck."

They took a few more steps and turned the corner and sitting in the parking lot was "Ol' Betsy, restored to her original beauty. She looked like she had just rolled off the assembly line.

"I can't believe it Mr. Willie, I haven't worked on her for so long. How did you do it?"

"Well, me and the boys worked on it while you were painting the last two weeks. They all stayed late every night until we got it done."

"I don't know what to say Mr. Willie." Jackson's eyes filled up with tears.

"You're the best Mr. Willie. I'm so glad you took a chance on me. I will never forget this."

Holding back his emotions, Mr. Willie replied, "Jackson you helped me more than I helped you."

"How could that be?"

"You just did. That's all. I'll see you tomorrow buddy. Merry Christmas. Here are the keys. Be careful Jackson, she is powerful. She might be even more powerful than she originally was. Skeeter put it through its paces and all the guys drove it and adjusted things as we got it ready for you. They are all so excited for you to get behind the wheel."

Jackson watched the truck fade out of sight and looked up at the stars on the clear night. He thought to himself, "I can't believe all that has happened in the span of just a year."

Hannah was speechless. She couldn't believe how good the car looked.

Jackson looked at her, "Well, are you ready to go for a ride?"

The newlyweds hopped in Jackson fired her up. All those horses under the hood made it hard to hear as Jackson revved the engine.

"I still can't believe we're sitting here in this car getting ready to go. This year has been unbelievable." Jackson said.

Hannah buckled up and leaned back against the new seats and grabbed Jackson's hand.

"Ok. Let's go Mr. Henderson."

Jackson took it easy along center street and past the bridge, but once they crossed the bridge and the lanes opened up to two lanes on both sides, he punched it and they sped off into the night. He couldn't believe it was really happening.

CHAPTER FIFTY-TWO

# A New Beginning

Jackson and Hannah opened the door to the Seaside Grille with windblown hair so bad it looked like they had just gone through a tornado. "So, how was the ride? Willie told me he was bringing it tonight. It looks awesome."

They talked to John for a long time about the car and finally John asked another important question.

"Have you two thought about where you are going to live?" John smiled.

"We're still figuring that out Uncle John," Hannah laughed timidly.

"I guess you two could stay here tonight in your room since you are married now. Let me see that marriage license."

Hannah pulled it out of her purse and grinned as she showed him.

"Wow, this has been quite a night. I better go up and check on your Aunt Becky. She was feeling all the emotions of tonight. Goodnight honey."

The fire was still burning, and the soft glow of the flames and the Christmas lights illuminated the scene. Hannah and Jackson sat down on the loveseat and held each other, not saying a word.

About an hour passed when Hannah broke the silence.

"What are your most important dreams, Jackson? I need to know everything about you. We need to make each other's dreams come true."

"I want to be loved deeply, and I want that love to never end. My mom always talked about it, but she never got it. She said her heart wasn't complete without that love. It never was the same for her after the divorce. I always wished she would find that love. She said she would pray that when it came time for me to decide about marriage I would find the right person who would love me forever."

Hannah sat in his lap, staring into his eyes.

"My mom and dad shared that love, and that drunk driver took that love away from her. I hated that guy for stealing her love, and I still can't shake the feeling. After my dad died, my mom talked to me too about those same things. I know I have found that right person. I just have a question?"

"Oh yeah, what is that?" Jackson smiled.

"What took you so long to ask me to marry you?"

"What...?" He laughed and grabbed her and kissed her.

"Are you tired?" She asked as she changed positions and was instantly sitting on his lap facing him.

"Not me. I'm ready for anything."

"Oh, is that so? Well, let's find out how ready you are. We just have to be quiet."

They tiptoed out of sight for their long winter's nap... sleeping optional.

CHAPTER FIFTY-THREE

# Their First Christmas

The most precious gift anyone could receive is the gift of marriage. It must be nurtured, loved and protected. Jackson remembered the words the young pastor told him as they left the church. He would do just that. Protect, love and nurture his gift from God.

Jackson lay still next to Hannah as he glanced out her window overlooking the ocean. He still couldn't believe he was lying next to her. Watching her sleep in his arms was unbelievable. Jackson had dreamed about her every second while they were apart, and now she was his. Slowly replaying their first time together, he recounted how many times they had made love that day.

Seven.

What a lucky number.

What a gift.

Hannah stirred a little and looked up at Jackson. "Are you gonna get some sleep? It's Christmas you know."

"I know, I've already got my present. Can we just stay in bed all day?"

CHAPTER FIFTY-FOUR

# Jezebel

The day after Christmas, Hannah dropped her grandmother off at the airport for her flight back up to Michigan.

"I'm going to miss you so much "grand." Hannah smiled.

"I'm going to miss you too my darling Hannah. How can I ever say thank you for all you did for me these last six months?"

Hannah's eyes were full of tears. "You helped me too "grand," you showed me perseverance, and hard work pays off. You never gave up and worked harder than I've seen anyone work to get well."

"I had to get well. I couldn't let you waste your life there with me."

"I love you "grand," have a safe flight."

"I love you too, my beautiful darling."

When she returned from the airport, Becky sat Hannah down to start planning her wedding ceremony. The breakfast customers faded away, and they had a couple of hours' reprieve before lunch to plan.

"Don't you think you guys should do the ceremony in the spring? Charleston is more beautiful in the spring than any other time."

"You know we don't have to do this Aunt Becky; Jackson and I are already married."

"We have to have a ceremony, Hannah. It's just the right thing to do. It would be good for everyone around here to see you guys happy together again after all that's happened these last few months."

The TV was on, and the gray-haired local weatherman interrupted the programming.

"Well folks, it looks like we have an unusual weather situation we need to report to you. A very rare December Tropical Storm has formed in the Atlantic and is forecasted to come close to Charleston and Savannah. I know Hurricane season is over, but this does happen from time to time. We've had several December hurricanes form, but most never affected land. It is currently named Tropical Storm Jezebel, and it looks to be strengthening. We will continue to monitor this storm and keep you updated. Please stay tuned, and we will let you know what's happening as this storm progresses."

John walked in and heard the last part of the weatherman's discussion.

"Did he say a Tropical Storm? In December?"

Becky's eyes widened, and she nodded her head in confirmation.

He looked at Becky and smiled in an attempt at reassurance as he headed back into the kitchen. "I'm sure it will pass us right by."

Hannah reached across the old wooden table and covered Becky's hand with hers. "It'll be okay Aunt Becky, let's get back to those plans."

Still distracted, Becky tried her best to make wedding suggestions, but instead, cast her eyes out the window into the cold gray ocean looking for answers.

CHAPTER FIFTY-FIVE

# Old Feelings Return

Late that afternoon, Jackson opened the door of the Seaside Grille with a suitcase packed full of his belongings and his painting supplies. He sat them down as Hannah met him at the door and gave him a warm wet kiss.

Jackson picked up his suitcase and headed upstairs.

"Hey, did you hear about the Tropical Storm out there in the Atlantic?"

"Yeah, me and Aunt Becky saw it on the news this morning. She's really worried."

"Oh yeah? I talked to Mr. Willie about it too, and he didn't think we would have too much bad weather. He told me about a few storms they had over the years though. We'll keep checking the weather and see what it's gonna do."

As they stood on the stairs, she passed him and grabbed his hand and smiled back at him.

"I have about a half hour before the dinner crowd gets here." Jackson stopped and looked up at her without a word, then smiled and chased her up the stairs to their room.

The love they shared was intoxicating to both of them. With every minute, they grew closer and closer. The hurt of the past months melted away with every touch of her.

The last rays of sun glistened through Hannah's window as she stared at Jackson, gently running her fingers along his face. "I've never been happier in my life Jackson. It's like all my troubles disappeared when I came back."

As Hannah got ready for the evening customers, she turned and looked at Jackson. "You're not worried about this storm?"

"I guess I'm not worried, but I am a little concerned. We had a bad Hurricane back when I was little, and we lost power for over a week. Our roof got ripped off, and we had to live with our neighbors for about two weeks till we got a new one. It was hard getting food too, so I guess I'm a little nervous."

"We need to go down and see what's going on." Hannah insisted.

"Okay, can you give me a minute? Becky said I could set up my easel in your room if it was okay with you. I'm trying to finish up the painting I was making for Red and Gina's four-year dating anniversary."

"It's our room now Jackson. You can put whatever you want up there. I love to watch you paint. It makes me feel so alive to watch you create those beautiful paintings."

"I'm glad you feel that way. I love to paint. An unbelievable feeling takes over when I'm working."

He stood watching her brush her long blond hair and longed for her again.

"Before you go downstairs, there's something I wanted to talk to you about."

"What is it?" Hannah grabbed his hands and wrapped them around her waist.

"Remember the story I told you a long time ago about when I was in the Fifth grade? You know, the one about how I found the magazine and learned how to paint?"

"Yeah, I love it."

"Well, I don't know if I told you everything that happened that day and the days after."

"What are you talking about Jackson?"

"When I first found that magazine, I touched it and rubbed my finger slowly over every inch of that painting of the beach that was on the cover. When I did, I felt like I was honestly at the beach. The feeling was unreal. I even smelled the salt air and heard the seagulls as they flew around. I felt the sand between my toes. At first, I didn't pay a lot of attention to it, but the next day I touched another painting of the beach that belonged to a lady I had cut grass for, and I had the same feeling again. I was there."

Hannah smiled at him, not quite understanding what he was getting to.

"For years, I had those feelings if I touched some paintings. Sometimes the feeling was there, then for a while, that feeling faded away. I wanted to get that feeling back so bad, but for a long time, I didn't feel anything. I could still paint good, but I had no feeling of being there."

"What are you trying to say, Jackson? Your paintings are so real; I can see how you would feel like you were there. I can look at them for hours."

"I'm trying to say, that since you came back, and we got married, I've been feeling those feelings again today. When I touched my paintings, I felt like I was there again. When it happens, all my senses are affected. It is so real. It had been so long since I felt like that. I missed it so much."

"You mean you really feel like you are in your paintings?"

"That's exactly what I'm saying. It doesn't happen every single time, but when it does, it's wonderful."

Hannah sat there quietly trying to figure out what it all meant. "That sounds like a special gift you've been given."

"It is."

"I don't know what it means or what you are supposed to use it for, but it sounds wonderful. I wonder if I could feel just like you do?"

"You want to try?" Jackson asked.

"Do you have a painting in that bag?"

Jackson slid out a picture of Morris Island at low tide.

"A long ago, you could walk across the mud at low tide and get to the lighthouse. Now the ocean has swept away the path. You can only get there by boat now.

"It's beautiful Jackson. Should I touch it?"

"Sure, go ahead."

She began at the bottom and gently moved her finger across the painting. Her hands were soft and tan; simply perfect. As she kept moving, she would stop every so often. Jackson watched her face, looking for any signs that she might feel what he felt. After every inch was covered, she turned to Jackson.

"It's beautiful Jackson. I imagined myself there, but I didn't have any feeling like you described. I told you, it's a gift you've been given. Maybe it'll come to me someday." She smiled at him and kissed him.

"I better head downstairs, Aunt Becky is probably wondering where I am."

Jackson curled his mouth up tight and looked out the plate glass window to the outline of the pier with the soft lights illuminating the path. He longed for her to feel what he felt.

CHAPTER FIFTY-SIX

# Before the Storm

"Folks, Tropical Storm Jezebel has taken a turn towards Charleston and is increasing in strength."

Everyone gathered around the TV as the weatherman continued.

"The National Weather Service has issued a Hurricane warning from now until Tuesday night. Local authorities are warning residents along the beaches to evacuate and go to high ground. Landfall is expected between Kiawah Island and Mount Pleasant in about 24 hours at the current speed of movement. This is forecasted to be a category 1 and possibly a category 2 storm. High tide is also around the expected time of landfall, and that could make the storm surge more than 15 to 20 feet above normal tides. This could cause widespread flooding and severe water damage to beachfront homes and businesses. Please contact your local authorities and follow the advice of the Emergency Preparedness Facilities."

When he finished, everyone looked at each other in awe. No one there had ever experienced a hurricane in December. They usually celebrated with a sigh of relief every November 30th at the end of hurricane season; now they were in unchartered territory.

"John, what are we gonna do?" Becky urged.

"Well, I guess we will have to evacuate like the man says. We've always put up our hurricane shutters and left every time one was forecast to hit here. It's the best thing. We've been lucky in the past and didn't have much damage. I'm sure it will be like that this time too. We need to close early tonight, so I can put up the shutters."

"I can get started putting them up right now Uncle John."

"Ok Jackson, I'll show you where they are."

Becky stood there in a solemn pose. As John was talking to Jackson, he looked over at her.

"Don't worry honey; God will take care of us. We'll be okay."

Becky managed a brief smile and looked out the windows at the churning sea.

CHAPTER FIFTY-SEVEN

# The Exit

Most of the employees worked through the night helping John and Jackson prepare the Seaside Grille for the impending storm. They all headed up the evacuation route along Interstate 26 towards Columbia in hopes of finding a hotel where they could weather the storm. Traffic was at a slow crawl, and the governor had authorized both lanes of the interstate to be open to help evacuate everyone from the nearby Charleston area. After about 6 hours in the car, they had made it far enough up the road where John thought they would be safe. They were ready to get off the road and began making their way up the exit ramp to find their hotel. The roads were packed in both directions, and John was waiting to turn when he saw it begin to happen. In slow motion, without any warning, he saw the eighteen-wheeler packed full of emergency supplies swerve to avoid another car. He watched the driver's eyes widen as he over-corrected the vehicle, trying to right its path.

It was too late. In an instant, the truck slammed into Becky and John's car on the passenger's side, sending it flipping over and over down the embankment.

CHAPTER FIFTY-EIGHT

# The News

John had been in surgery for 4 hours while surgeons struggled to repair his punctured lung, ruptured spleen and several broken bones. When he finally awoke, 12 hours later, Jackson and Hannah were at his bedside. He was happy to see their faces, but suddenly realized he didn't see Becky's. John yanked out his breathing tube in a fury and screamed, "Where's Becky?"

Hannah tried to be strong but lowered her head into his hand along the bed. Tears streamed down Jackson's face.

"I'm sorry Uncle John, Aunt Becky died at the scene."

"No.... no that can't be!! She was beating that cancer; we were gonna be home free with the last chemo treatment."

He collapsed back into the bed in a rage of tears. The doctors and nurses busted into the room and quickly administered a sedative to try to calm him down.

As the medicine took effect, he fought closing his eyes. A short time later, the room was quiet.

"What are we gonna do now Jackson," Hannah stared at him in the light of the room.

"She was everything to him, and now she's gone. He isn't going to know what to do, and right now, neither do I."

She buried her head into his chest, the tears flowing without hesitation.

"We'll figure it out together Hannah." Jackson whispered into the air, not knowing where their lives were headed now.

CHAPTER FIFTY-NINE

# The Vigil

That night, John slipped into a coma that lasted four days. The storm pounded Charleston, but they hadn't received any damage reports yet. During the four-day vigil, Hannah and Jackson talked about what the future would hold for them. Hannah passed the hours by thumbing through the photo albums she brought in her suitcase. John packed them in her car before they left, and they had been spared from the accident.

In the back of one of the oldest albums, she came across a picture of Becky and John on the day they opened the Seaside Grille. She pulled it out and brought it to her lips and held it close to her chest.

"Could I see it, honey?" Jackson whispered.

Hannah slowly handed him the photo, and he began to run his finger along every edge. He felt the warmth of that summer day and could hear the seagulls outside the front door of the Grille, begging for scraps. She touched his arm, and he was startled back to the hospital room.

"I saw your face shine this time Jackson. Did it happen again?"

"Yeah. It was awesome. I have an idea. Would you be okay if I stepped out for a few minutes?"

"I guess so. Where are you going?"

"I'll show you in just a little while. I promise I won't be long."

Jackson returned an hour later with a bag full of art supplies, and he borrowed an IV pump stand from another room to use as a makeshift easel. Hannah didn't say a word; she knew what he was doing. He outlined the picture, and within a few quiet hours, the photo began to turn into a beautiful reproduction of that wonderful day so many years ago.

Hannah broke the silence of the room.

"What if Uncle John doesn't wake up?"

Jackson looked over at her holding John's hand. "He will Hannah."

"But what if he doesn't?" She screamed.

"He will wake up."

"How are you so sure?"

"Because he's a fighter, just like you."

As they were talking, a faint voice echoed through the room.

"Hannah?"

"I'm here Uncle John."

John had broken his four-day coma and began asking questions about Becky again. As they retold the story, the realization he would never see his beloved Becky again took its toll. For the next three hours, he stared out the window in silence. Hannah tried to talk to him, but he never moved. As Jackson reached for her hand, the door to John's room swung open and Mr. Willie stepped inside. He hugged Jackson and Hannah and laid his hand on John's.

"I'm here for you buddy. We will get through this together."

John turned and smiled a little at Mr. Willie.

"The roads finally cleared enough for us to make it up here. That storm was terrible; it hit directly on Charleston. There was a lot of damage. Trees are down all along Interstate 26, and the power is still out in most areas of the city. I'm so sorry for all of you. I tried to drive up here as soon as I found out, but the roads have been impassable until today."

"Was there any damage to the Seaside Grille?" Jackson asked.

Mr. Willie looked around the room, avoiding eye contact.

"Let's talk about that a little later okay? I came to see if I could help John."

Jackson knew the news wasn't good, so he didn't say another word.

"Willie, how's the Grille?" John broke the silence.

Mr. Willie hesitated for a long time, trying to find the right words. "I'm sorry John, I don't know how to say this. The pier and the restaurant both collapsed in the storm. The storm surge was 18 feet, and it washed most of the restaurant out to sea. It's gone I'm afraid. I'm so sorry John."

The constant beating of the heart monitor and the IV pump were the only sound in the room. Hannah sank to the floor against the wall, pulling her knees to her chest. She cried like Jackson had never heard before. The news devastated them all.

Hannah's tears flowed for over an hour. Jackson didn't know what to do but to hold her. "I promise you we'll make it through this Hannah."

CHAPTER SIXTY

# The First One

The next day, Jackson's mom Leah had made it through the miles of downed trees to reach Jackson and Hannah. A close friend had needed medical attention after the storm, and she wasn't able to come up with Mr. Willie. She cried with them all as she hugged John trying to lend any support she could.

Another few days had passed, and John's condition was improving. He would soon be well enough to leave the hospital. Mr. Willie insisted on taking John home when he was released, and Hannah and Jackson agreed to live at Mr. Willie's place as well until they could find other arrangements. Every day, John's stoic expression had never changed. He barely said more than a few words each day. His heart was broken. Becky was gone, and almost every sentimental possession he shared with her had vanished into the sea.

Each day, Jackson had worked on the painting of Becky and John's first day at the Grille. He had finished it last night and was eager to present it to John, yet apprehensive too. Jackson wanted more than anything to bring a smile and some comfort to John, but he also worried that the painting might make him hurt worse.

Hannah grabbed his hand and nodded her head that he should show John the painting. Mr. Willie smiled and wiped a tear from his cheek as he watched carefully.

Jackson worked up the courage to show John. "Uncle John, nothing I can say to you will take the hurt away of losing Aunt Becky, but I thought this might bring you a little peace."

Jackson brought the painting to John's bedside and John just quietly stared. He showed no emotion for a long time, then slowly the tears began to roll down his face.

"This is wonderful Jackson. It looks so real; it almost feels like Becky is right here with me."

As he whispered those words, he began to run his finger along the outline of Becky's face. Instantly, the room was illuminated with a light so bright they all were blinded. They heard Becky's voice call out to John. Heaven had opened, and they all could see Becky now. She reached out to John and smiled at everyone in the room.

A nurse had walked in just as Becky grabbed John's hand.

"Becky? Is it really you?" John cried out.

"Hi, honey."

Becky held John's hand as she looked around the room.

"We'll see you all again soon. I love you all."

As quickly as it happened, the room went quiet and dark. John was with Becky now. Not a word was uttered. They were all in shock. They had witnessed a miracle. Something none of them could explain.

Jackson turned to Hannah; her face pale, and calm. Her eyes that once glistened now seemed lost. She moved towards the empty hospital bed and laid her head along the small pillow that was left behind.

"I can't believe it. They're both gone." Hannah whispered.

Jackson reached for her and touched her hand. She gently squeezed back.

"She's with him now. They're both at peace."

CHAPTER SIXTY-ONE

# The Explanation

The nurse who had stumbled upon the miracle sat down as they all tried to help her.

"What just happened...? How is that even possible...?"

Everyone was silent. No one could explain what they had just experienced.

"Do you believe in God Miss Avery?" Mr. Willie smiled at the young nurse.

"Yeah... yes, um, yes I do."

"Becky and John were married for over 35 years. They grew up together. They spent every day of their lives side by side. He couldn't make it without her. I guess God reached down and brought them back together. When he touched Becky's face on Jackson's painting, that's when it happened."

"Look, the painting's gone." Hannah said as she ran her hand along the bed.

"As soon as Uncle John touched your painting Jackson, the miracle happened. That painting started it all." A hint of a smile crept across Hannah's face as she looked at Jackson.

"All I did is paint a picture for Uncle John. I didn't do anything else. I didn't make that happen."

Jackson began to pace in the small little room, nervously staring out the window and trying to redirect all the eyes that were concentrating on him.

"I painted a painting. That's it. Nothing more."

Jackson lowered his face into his hands for a few seconds and looked up. The room was eerily quiet. The machines that had been monitoring John and delivering his IV fluids were silent.

"I have to get out of here for a few minutes." He bolted out the door before anyone could say anything else.

"I'll go after him," Hannah motioned for the door.

"Hannah honey, maybe we should give him a few minutes." Leah smiled, touching her hand.

Without a word, Hannah nodded in agreement.

The nurse who had seen everything left the room and quickly returned with the Charge Nurse.

"See... I told you. He's gone. We all saw it happen. It was the most wonderful thing I've ever been witness to." The young nurse smiled as she pointed to the bed that John had occupied a few minutes earlier.

The Charge Nurse stood there in silence like the others, then said. "I'll have to call the Hospital Administrator... and the Police."

CHAPTER SIXTY-TWO

# A Different Kind of News

After several hours of answering questions from the Police and hospital staff, Jackson and Hannah left the hospital. They were emotionally and physically exhausted.

“How do you folks want to handle this when talking to everyone else? The Coroner has agreed to list the cause of death as complications from the wreck. He says he can’t list it as “a miracle.” If word of this gets out, this place will be crawling with reporters looking for the “miracle painter.” Only you folks, the two nurses and the hospital administrator know about what happened. They have agreed to keep this quiet if you want to.”

Everyone agreed that it would be best not to let out what had happened. They weren’t sure what news like that would turn into. Enough trauma had been experienced, and they didn’t want to add anything else to the already difficult situation.

Jackson and Hannah had finally settled into their tiny hotel room to get some rest before attempting to head back to Charleston the next day down the debris-filled interstate. The modest furnishings and comfortable bed were a welcome change for the young couple after the long days spent in the stiff hospital chairs.

"What's gonna happen now?" Hannah looked over at Jackson as she turned on her side.

In a week's time, the newlywed couple had endured more than most couples in a decade of marriage. Jackson struggled for words to comfort her.

"I'm not sure Hannah. I know one thing, and that is I love you, and we will make it through this together."

Hannah cried herself to sleep, wrapped up in Jackson's arms.

The next morning, the ringer of the telephone broke their peaceful slumber. The twenty-year-old clock radio showed 10:01 AM. Jackson and Hannah had managed some rest.

"Hey Mr. Willie, sorry I took so long to answer the phone, but we were still sleeping. What's up?"

"Jackson, I've got some important news for you and Hannah. Can you meet me at the diner at 11:00 AM? I'll call your mom and ask her to meet us there too."

"What is it, Mr. Willie?"

"I'll tell you in person Jackson. See you soon."

Jackson made a cup of coffee from the old coffee maker and tried to put as much cream and sugar into the cup as he could to make it palatable for Hannah. They got ready and headed out to find out what was going on. They opened the door to the cramped diner and saw Mr. Willie and Leah sitting at a table in the corner waiting for them.

"Ok, what is it, Mr. Willie? What's so important that you can't tell me on the phone?"

"Hey, let's order for breakfast before we talk, and then we can head on back to Charleston." Mr. Willie smiled.

"Jackson, I got a call this morning from John and Becky's lawyer."

Hannah interrupted, "Lawyer? I didn't know he and Aunt Beck had a lawyer."

"Their lawyer was a friend of John's, he's Jasper Pinckney. On the day after Christmas, he called Jasper and asked him to draw up some papers."

"What kind of papers Mr. Willie?" Jackson shrugged his shoulders trying to understand. He took a sip of his coffee and sat back in the booth.

"He wanted to change their will. John made Hannah the executor of their will, and he made you and Hannah the beneficiaries of their life insurance policy. He also signed over the title to the Seaside Grille to you both if anything should happen to them. Jasper told me that John wanted you both to continue their business if you were up to it. He knew how much you both loved the place and it was only fitting since it was where you and Hannah met."

Hannah spoke up, "So what are you saying, Mr. Willie? That me and Jackson own the Seaside Grille? Or what's left of it?"

"Yes, you do. John had always kept up great insurance on the grille. He paid a heavy premium, but he knew he might need it someday with all the storms that have passed through over the years. Whatever has happened to the Seaside Grille can be rebuilt."

It took a few minutes for things to sink in. The roller coaster of their lives seemed to be in perpetual motion.

"Do you think we can do it, Jackson? Do you want to rebuild the Seaside Grille with me?"

"There's nothing I would rather do than build a life with you there again. The wonderful place where our life together began. We can make a new chapter in our love story."

Jackson leaned over and kissed her and held her close. The tears flowed again as Hannah tried to handle the news. Leah reached across the table and grabbed their hands.

"I'm so happy that you will be able to start again to rebuild that wonderful place. I hope you get to realize the wonder of true heartfelt love together, and I hope it never escapes you. Jackson, I prayed every day since your father left that you would find your true love and treasure her, love her and grow old together. It looks like John and Becky had the same idea. Promise me that you will always put your relationship above the business or anything else. If there is no relationship, then nothing else matters much. Love each other forever. Never do anything to hurt the other and always think of the other person before yourself. This is my hope and prayer for you both. Take this gift and make it a lifetime of love."

"We will mom. You have taken such good care of me for so long. I've heard you cry at night and I've heard you talk about true love and how it has eluded you. My heart was broken for you. I hope you can find your true love someday. I prayed that I could find that special someone to share my life with and who would love me forever. I know I've found that in Hannah."

Mr. Willie spoke up, "I know this has been such an unbelievable amount of difficult circumstances to happen to a young couple in such a short time. Just know I'll be there to help you along the way if you need it." Mr. Willie smiled.

Leah wiped a tear away as she said, "Thank you, Willie. You have been the father Jackson never had. I can never thank you enough for all you have done."

Mr. Willie lowered his head a little, not trying to show his emotions.

"Is everyone ready to check out? The adjuster can meet us this afternoon at the beach to assess the damage."

CHAPTER SIXTY-THREE

# The Old Seaside Grille

Nothing could have prepared them for the utter devastation they saw as they made their way towards the beach. Center Street, the main crossroads on Folly Beach, was almost unrecognizable. Every structure had some type of damage. Roofs were ripped off; only a few street signs remained, and debris littered every corner. They made it through the army of Red Cross and FEMA vehicles, and they looked towards the Seaside Grille. Where the Grille once stood, a few weary pilings that once held up the restaurant were all that was left. The pier had collapsed, and most of the decking material had been ripped away. They looked along Folly Beach and as far as they could see it was destruction beyond anything they had experienced before. It resembled a war zone. Hundreds of people were aimlessly searching the debris around their property in hopes that something would be spared.

Hannah stood up and looked out to sea. Her eyes weren't focused on anything. "I have no tears left. This is just unbelievable."

Jackson didn't know what to do either. He looked over at Mr. Willie... trying to find some answers.

"This can all be rebuilt. Even better than before." Mr. Willie smiled trying to ease the situation.

"I know this is hard Hannah honey, but in time, this can be new again for both you and Jackson." Leah smiled, hugging her.

"Thank you, Leah."

Mr. Willie spoke up. "How about me and Jackson talk to the adjuster and you two meet us back at the truck? We'll be right there in just a few minutes."

Leah helped Hannah back to the truck and Jackson, and Mr. Willie met up with the insurance adjuster.

CHAPTER SIXTY-FOUR

# The Beginning... Again

A month had passed since they returned to the beach and most of the debris had been cleaned up. Jackson came to the beach every day and helped clean up while Hannah stayed back at Mr. Willie's home. You could look around in a circle and see crews of workers installing new roofs all along the beach front. The fury of the storm affected almost every roof on the island. Jackson managed to find a few decorations from the Seaside Grille. An old lantern and a rustic anchor. He cleaned them up and brought them home to Hannah. She hadn't been able to bring herself to return to the beach yet.

Hannah gently held each piece. Trying to regain her perspective of what she had lost. "Aunt Becky loved this lantern and Uncle John bought this anchor from an old fisherman. He always told me the anchor was a symbol of hope and steadfastness. He said when a ship anchored, it was held tight to its location and that is how he said he and Aunt Becky were; tied to each other. The symbol of hope came from the promise of a new adventure whenever the ship would raise its anchor and head out for another voyage. We used this lantern a few times when the power went out. These can be our first decorations in the new Seaside Grille."

"So, are you ready to get started again?" Jackson smiled with excitement.

"I'm ready."

Later that afternoon, Mr. Willie came home from working at the garage. "I have some great news. Mr. Pinckney called me and said the insurance company would make the final payout on the life insurance policy and the damage to the Seaside Grille."

"So, does this mean we can start rebuilding?" Jackson asked.

"Well, let's talk about a few things first. I highly recommend you hire an accountant before you receive this payout."

"What do we need an accountant for?" Hannah asked.

"This payout is very substantial."

"What kind of money is it Mr. Willie?" Hannah and Jackson asked together.

"It's One Million Dollars."

"What?"

"The payout for John and Becky's life insurance is One Million Dollars.

The building insurance adjuster is ready to settle the claim for the Seaside Grille restaurant at close to $750,000 as well. That should be more than enough to rebuild the Seaside Grille even better than before."

Hannah and Jackson were in shock. A little over a month ago, they were just married with a few dollars to their name. Now they had become millionaires.

"That accountant is very important. I have a really good accountant. I've been working with him for over 25 years. He's honest and knows his job well. I'll put you guys in touch with him if you want me to or you could find someone else on your own."

Hannah reached for Jackson's hand. "I need to go lie down for a little while. You finish talking with Mr. Willie."

CHAPTER SIXTY-FIVE

# Construction Begins

Six weeks after the fierce winds of Hurricane Jezebel blew through Folly Beach, construction began on the new Seaside Grille. The construction of the new county fishing pier had begun a week earlier. The massive wooden pilings that would support the pier began to make their way from land out to more than a thousand feet out into the wild Atlantic. Mr. Willie was helping Jackson manage the construction. He helped enlist the services of an experienced beach architect Eliot Dodge and well-known general contractor Ed Rainey.

Jackson spent countless hours with Hannah going over the details of the construction and the layout of the new restaurant as well as the loft of their new home. The old plans from the initial construction were referenced because they both wanted the windows to be set up the same way as before. They added a couple more fireplaces and many other improvements to make it cozier. Jackson and Hannah had rented an apartment close to the beach that recently opened after the storm. It allowed Jackson to be there every day checking on the progress. In their quaint little apartment kitchen, Hannah opened up.

"Can we have some windows in the corner of our room that wrap around so you can see down the beach without anything in the way?"

"I'm pretty sure we can. I'll talk to Ed to make sure he can get them made."

"How about a big balcony outside our bedroom with a pergola and a swing and a place for you to paint when you want? I want to be able to go to our little private spot up above the noise to relax."

"Whatever you wish my dear. I'll make sure it happens. We are meeting Ed later today. We can talk about those changes with him then."

"You are so sweet, Jackson. This has been one of the most difficult things to get through in my life. Just when things got better, life took us for another ride. I didn't think I could hang on, but you held on to me the whole time and never let go. I'm ready to move on and build our life together."

The loss of Becky and John, along with the Seaside Grille had taken a massive toll on Hannah, almost to the point of a nervous breakdown. She and Jackson hadn't been intimate since the day they evacuated the island. Hannah had a hard time sleeping, and the nightmares were frequent.

Jackson was comforted by Hannah's recent change of heart, and he continued to pray hard that things could be like they used to be very soon.

CHAPTER SIXTY-SIX

# Healing Begins

The morning light broke through the windows of Hannah and Jackson's apartment and gently woke Jackson. He quietly stretched and did his best not to wake Hannah. Jackson wanted to slip out and do his morning run before she got up and then they could share breakfast together. He got dressed, brushed his teeth and was catching a quick glimpse of the morning news when he heard Hannah stirring in the bathroom.

"Oh Jackson..." Hannah called to him.

"I'll be right there Hannah." Several minutes passed, and he was still watching the weather forecast.

"Jackson! Now please."

Startled, Jackson made his way into the bedroom to see what the commotion was all about. He was stopped cold. With two flicks of her wrists, the pink lace nightgown she was wearing quickly found its way to the floor, and she stood there with the morning light shining on nothing but her tan skin. They stood there smiling at each other. He ran to her and grabbed her and in an instant, they reconnected after so long. As he looked down to kiss her, she laughed.

"What took you so long?"

"I'm sorry. It won't happen again."

They stayed in each other's arms for the rest of the morning. Noon came, and they sat together around the small circular wooden table in their tiny kitchen.

"Do you think we should finish college now?" Hannah asked Jackson as she took a bite of her toast.

"Well, I really do think we should give it a lot of thought. We have a lot of money, and we have to be responsible with it. Maybe we could go part-time and still run the Seaside Grille. Or one of us could go full time and the other work at the Grille, I don't know. It's a lot to think about."

"My mom and Aunt Becky always wanted me to go to college and get my degree. I've always wanted to get my degree as well, but I don't know how we would do that with all the responsibility of the restaurant."

"We'll figure it out. We don't have to plan everything right now."

Jackson looked across the table at his beautiful bride and smiled.

"How about Round two after brunch?"

She smiled at him and grabbed his hand. "I think that can be arranged."

CHAPTER SIXTY-SEVEN

# An Unwelcome Surprise

Four long months had passed, and the final touches were being completed on the Seaside Grille to be open in time for the beginning of summer. Things were finally getting back to normal on Folly Beach, and only a few visible remnants of the hurricane's damage remained. Jackson walked into the kitchen to check on the new terrazzo floor that was being laid and he caught a glimpse of a worker in the corner and instantly recognized him as the hairs on the back of his neck stood up.

"Well if it isn't the old painter boy. Oh yeah, I guess it's the rich painter boy now."

"Billy Barbatt! What the hell are you doing here?" Jackson couldn't believe he was standing in their restaurant.

"I'm putting your floor in. Do you have a problem with that?"

As Jackson stood there fuming, he couldn't help but remember all the run-ins with Billy over the years, and now Billy was working for him.

"Is there anything else Mr. Henderson?" Billy laughed with a nasty grin on his face.

"Oh yeah, when is that hot wife of yours gonna come around and take a look at the place. I sure would love to show her around."

Billy's boss Frank heard his comments as he stepped into the kitchen. Jackson charged Billy and landed two punches to his face before Billy knew what happened.

Frank jumped in the middle. "Alright, alright!! Enough is enough."

He pushed them both apart.

"I want this jackass off my property now," Jackson yelled.

"But he's not done with the job yet."

"I want him out of here this instant. Get his ass out of here now!!"

Billy's boss shook his head and told Billy to pick up his tools and head home. He would call him for another assignment when one came available.

"You think you can throw your money around huh Henderson. I just need to talk to that Hannah and I'll be glad to take her off your hands and show her a real man."

"You come back here again, and you won't be walking out of here on your own power." Jackson stood there with his fists clenched as tightly as he could as Billy turned and walked out.

Billy turned and looked back at Jackson. "Oh, don't worry painter boy. I'll get you back. Don't you worry now. I'll get you back."

"Go on Billy and get out of here before more trouble happens. What happened Mr. Henderson?" Billy's boss Frank Thomas asked. "What was that all about?"

"Why did you hire that guy? Don't you know what kind of person he is? Didn't you check him out? He's been in and out of trouble his whole life. That guy has been bothering me ever since I can remember. And now he thinks he's gonna talk about my wife? I'll break every bone in his freakin' body if he ever so much as comes near her."

"I'm sorry Jackson. I know he's had some trouble, but I just wanted to give the kid a chance to redeem himself. He does good flooring work."

"Just make sure he never sets foot in here again okay?"

"I got it. He won't be back."

CHAPTER SIXTY-EIGHT

# Almost Done

Everything was set for a July 4th grand opening that was only a week away. Jackson and Hannah had managed to rehire almost all the old kitchen staff and waitresses. Hannah and Jackson had been working tirelessly with a local designer, Sharon Carpenter, to decorate the restaurant and their upstairs loft. They had both agreed to only see the restaurant and leave the upstairs loft up to her. She promised it would be a paradise retreat for them both.

"Hannah honey, Sharon called and said she would be ready for us to move into the loft tomorrow, so we could have time to get set up before the Seaside Grille opens."

Hannah opened the bathroom door and stepped out as she finished toweling off her hair. As she stood there in her light pink robe, Jackson couldn't think of anything else.

"You are so beautiful Hannah. I still have to make sure I'm not dreaming every time I see you. Especially like this."

She smiled and enticed him over for a kiss. "I sure am ready to move out of this tiny bathroom. I can't wait to see what Sharon did for us upstairs."

"We get to start our life again, fresh. It's gonna be great. Our walk-through is this afternoon with the builder to finish the punch list, so we are ready for Saturday's Grand Opening."

"I still can't believe this day is finally here." Hannah stood there with only her pink robe on, and Jackson watched as she dried her wild waves of blond hair.

"Not a day goes by that I don't wish Aunt Becky and Uncle John were still here. Sometimes I dream about that Christmas almost two years ago when I got here. They made me feel so welcome. I'm so happy you agreed to make as many things as we could like the old place. Just like I remember it."

She paused and looked at Jackson. "Did you hear me?"

A few seconds of silence passed then Jackson quietly acknowledged her.

"Yes beautiful, I heard you. It's just a little distracting and hard to pay attention when you're standing there like that. Hey, you know, we have about two hours before we have to meet her."

She smiled and said, "Oh is that right? Well, I guess we should make some lasting memories of this little apartment before we leave."

CHAPTER SIXTY-NINE

# The Final Unveiling

As Jackson and Hannah arrived at the Seaside Grille in the beautiful Red Corvette, they met Red as he was helping the builder finish up the last-minute items before the walk-through.

"Hey Red, did you decide to take the job at the construction company that me and Mr. Willie are starting?"

"Yeah man, I thought about it. This job you gave me has been great, and you helped me out a lot. It's a fantastic offer, but I think I should be my own man. Since being on the shrimp boats didn't turn out to be my thing, I've been thinking about going to the police academy and then becoming a Police Officer here on Folly Beach. Chief Townsend said he would hire me when I graduate."

"You'll be your own man. I won't be a crazy guy to work for. You're my best friend."

"I know man, but I feel like I need to do this. I really do."

Jackson lowered his head a bit and then looked up at Red. "This job will always be yours if you want it, man."

"Thanks, Jackson. Why did you and Mr. Willie want to start a construction company anyway?"

"Since I was little, I liked to build things and make things. I always wanted to be able to build my mom a house for all she's done for me, and I hope I get to do that soon."

Just then, Sharon Carpenter pulled up in her shiny Mercedes and greeted Jackson and Hannah. They were anxiously awaiting the move into their new home. The suspense was killing them.

"Hi guys, are you ready to see your new loft?"

Hannah smiled, "I thought you'd never ask. I've been doing a lot of dreaming lately."

"Well, let's go up and see our new place." Jackson grabbed Hannah by the hand.

"Okay, close your eyes," Sharon pleaded as she opened the door to their new loft. She guided them in, and the sound of the waves crashing, and the feel of the Atlantic breeze beckoned them in.

"Ready... ok, open your eyes."

The young couple opened their eyes and stood together holding hands. Their emotions overcame them both as their eyes moved from the beautiful golden floors to the windows that never stopped. Each corner of the whole loft was decorated with the utmost care. Jackson's paintings lined the hallway with plenty of space left for new arrivals. The front of the loft faced the beach, and giant French doors invited them outside as the waves crashed against the shore. Jackson turned and walked into his studio, his fingers running across all the supplies and a beautiful giant easel. He stood rigid and stared down the beach as far as he could see. It was just as he imagined it would be. Hannah wrapped her arms around him from behind and kissed his neck.

"I can't believe we're finally here. I'm so at home."

Jackson turned around and pressed his lips to hers and held it. "It's a dream come true."

"Sharon, this home is so wonderful! How could you know everything we would want? It's absolutely perfect."

Sharon smiled, "I listened. Don't you remember those questions I asked you months ago?"

The only detail about the whole loft Jackson asked for specifically was the corner windows that provided a clear view of the beach. The curved windows were so massive and clear; it felt like you were outside. Jackson and Hannah turned around, breathing in their new surroundings. The beauty Sharon captured in all the colors and furnishings made for an unforgettable experience. She had taken some part of each of their lives and intertwined them together to make a home.

After thanking Sharon over and over and waving goodbye, the young couple was at last alone in their new home with the sweet sound of the ocean playing in the background.

"Let's go sit on our new porch Jackson." Hannah led Jackson outside, and he sat down beside her and slid in tightly next to her on their giant hammock style porch swing. The loft was high above the restaurant, and the windbreaks on each side made their little retreat feel like they had the beach to themselves. Jackson rested his head on her shoulder and closed his eyes and tried to let the whirlwind at least slow down a little.

"We're home Hannah, and a new chapter in our life has begun. We won't ever be the same after this; we'll be stronger."

The passion between them had been rekindled back at that little apartment, and Hannah sought to make their first moments in their new home something Jackson would never forget. She didn't have to say a word as she grabbed his hand and led him down the hall to their new bedroom.

CHAPTER SEVENTY

# The Grand Re-Opening

The grand re-opening day finally arrived, and everyone was excited. Newspapers and radio stations from around Charleston ran advertising about the opening for over two weeks. Phone calls came in every day inquiring about the new menu. A few small establishments opened their doors after the hurricane, but the Seaside Grille was the first restaurant on Folly Beach to re-open. It was good for the community to see things returning to some semblance of normalcy. The wounds of the storm were slowly healing.

Everything was in its place on every table. Not a detail left out. Some of the new furnishings were made from the old wood they salvaged after the hurricane. The anchor and lantern Jackson recovered were on display at the hostess stand at the front. Hannah had picked up an old open and closed sign for the door that looked just like the original one Becky turned around thousands of times.

"Jackson, are you ready? I still can't believe we're gonna do this."

"I'm right here with you Hannah. It's been so long. I can feel Becky and John with us."

CHAPTER SEVENTY-ONE

# The Unexpected Visitor

Hannah turned the sign around as she waved goodbye to the last "Opening Night" customers. She latched the glass door and turned towards the kitchen as Jackson greeted her with a warm, wet kiss. They held their embrace and didn't speak. Each knew what the other felt. Jackson leaned down to kiss his bride again and noticed a young woman standing outside all alone.

"Hey Hannah, someone's outside." Jackson unlatched the door.

"Hi ma'am, we're closed for tonight, are you okay? Is there something I can help you with?"

"I'm not here to eat Mr. Henderson."

Surprised she knew his name, Jackson turned and looked at Hannah then back to the young woman.

"Can I help you, ma'am?" Jackson muttered again.

"Could I speak with you for just a minute? It's very important."

Jackson paused for a minute, then invited her in.

The young woman's eyes were streaked red, and her mouth drawn up from what appeared to be dehydration. The ponytail she pulled her hair into was twisted and jagged, and her dress was stained and wrinkled.

"What can I do for you Mrs....?" Jackson tried to open the conversation as he and Hannah sat down with her in the first booth.

"It's Jennifer, Jennifer Thomas."

"What can I do for you, Jennifer?" Jackson asked, his voice cracking a little. He didn't know what to make of this situation.

"I know who you are Mr. Henderson. I know you're that Miracle Painter. It took me a while to find you. I've ridden the bus all the way from Washington state."

A tidal wave of nervous emotion crashed into Jackson. The secret they shared from the hospital was out. Jackson didn't want any part of fame or notoriety. He wanted his simple life with Hannah.

"I'm not sure what you mean Mrs. Thomas."

"Mr. Henderson, please help me."

She reached across the table and grabbed his hand as her eyes welled up with tears.

"My little boy Josh died last month from leukemia. It was just him and me. Now I have nothing. Absolutely nothing. I can't sleep, I can't eat. I want to be with him again."

She squeezed his hand and stared into his soul.

"Please help me get to him. Please paint this picture of us and let me be with him again."

She pulled out a recent 4 x 6 print of them together at a playground. His little smile brought a smile to Jackson and Hannah.

"Please don't be mad Mr. Henderson. My cousin was the nurse who witnessed the miracle after you painted that painting for your wife's uncle. She promised to keep your secret, but she saw how devastated I was. She couldn't keep it in and was only trying to help me. At first, I didn't believe her, but everything she told me turned out to be true. She promised she didn't tell anyone else."

Jackson's heart raced, and he felt like he'd been kicked in the stomach. He looked down at the table and closed his eyes. Silence fell across the room.

Jackson raised his head and said, "I'm sorry Jennifer, I can't help you. I haven't painted since that happened. I don't know if that can happen again. The emotional risk to you and to me for that matter is too great. What if it didn't work? How could I live with myself knowing how much you counted on me and what you had dreamed of never happened? The police also wanted us to keep it a secret because they feared people wouldn't believe what happened. What about your family? Wouldn't they miss you?"

Jennifer grabbed his hand again and stared into his heart so deep she started to unlock his deepest apprehensions. In her other hand, she held the picture close to her face and struggled to smile.

"Please Mr. Henderson. Please help me be like this again. He was the only thing that gave me hope in this world. Let us be together again. I don't have any other family."

Hannah grabbed his other hand and squeezed it and rested her head on his shoulder. Jackson sighed deeply and reached both hands across the table to Jennifer's.

"What if it doesn't work? Are you prepared to handle that? I just painted the picture. God did the miracle in the hospital. Maybe it's not your time right now?"

"Please just try for me. Every day without him is so empty. I have even thought about ending it myself, so I could be with him, but I know God doesn't want me to do that. God is a God of miracles, and I'm just asking you to try. If it doesn't work, then I'll have to deal with that if it comes. I know it will work though. I can feel it."

Jackson still hadn't agreed to paint her picture. He was scared; he turned to Hannah and looked into her eyes.

"Jackson, please at least try to paint her back to her little boy Josh. If you don't try, we'll never know." Hannah smiled.

"Ok Jennifer, I will do everything I can to paint this picture and let God bring you back to your little boy."

Jennifer leaped across the table and hugged them both as the tears fell from all their eyes.

"Could you come back in three days about this same time after we are closed, and all the customers have gone home? I can have it finished by then."

"Thank you so much, Mr. Henderson. I know I will see my Josh real soon."

"Please Jennifer, call me Jackson. I'm younger than you."

"Ok, Jackson. I'll see you and my Josh in three days."

CHAPTER SEVENTY-TWO

# The Details

Jackson hardly slept as he worked hour after hour on the young mother's picture. Detail after detail he perfected, taking great pains to recreate it just as it was. His favorite critic Hannah was always close by watching from the sofa in the corner of his studio or checking on him during a quick break when the restaurant was open.

Three days had passed, and Jackson had put the finishing touches on the painting. Hannah had been his official judge and sounding board, and he asked her to come upstairs to have the first look.

She made her way up the stairs from the restaurant, and as she reached the top, she saw Jackson's masterpiece.

"Wow Jackson, you did it again. It is unbelievable how close these pictures are. It's almost impossible to tell that this is a painting."

She grabbed him and kissed him so sweetly his heart melted.

"It's two hours until we close Jackson. How do you feel about tonight?"

Jackson shook his head in uncertainty.

"I don't know. How am I supposed to feel? It's not me doing it. I'm just the copy artist, remember? God has to show up tonight to make this miracle happen."

"I'm sure he will, I have a good feeling." Hannah said as she grabbed his hand.

"C'mon, we still have customers downstairs to take care of. How about come down here and give me a hand?"

"I'm right behind you." Jackson smiled.

CHAPTER SEVENTY-THREE

# The Answer

Everyone had gone home, and Hannah and Jackson stood at the door waiting for Jennifer.

"Do you think it'll happen again, Jackson?" Hannah squeezed him as they held each other searching in the darkness.

"I don't know. I felt confident while I was painting. We'll have to wait and see."

Suddenly Jennifer appeared from the shadows. This time, her hair was done, and her dress was a beautiful flowing pink. They all looked around to make sure no one saw them, then headed upstairs. Jennifer reached the loft and burst into tears as soon as the picture came into view.

"It is so beautiful Jackson. I can't believe it."

She looked at them both and wiped the tears from her eyes as she stepped closer to the painting. Jennifer didn't wait for Jackson's cue, she walked right up and held her petite index finger just slightly from the surface of the painting, just above little Josh's face. Slowly she moved her finger around and caressed the outline of her little boy's smile. Tears streamed down her face as she began to gently stroke his chubby little cheek.

Jackson and Hannah waited for the wonderful white light they longed for, but the only light that shone on the painting was the small lamp Jackson left on in the corner.

Jennifer looked at Jackson and Hannah.

"Am I doing it right?"

Jackson nodded in agreement and Jennifer feigned a smile while she continued touching the little boys face. She lowered her head and began trembling but trying to touch the painting ever so softly. Jennifer's tears of joy turned into sadness as she realized her miracle wasn't to be. The young mother collapsed on the floor; completely devastated.

Jackson and Hannah gathered around her, trying to find some words of comfort.

After almost an hour, Jennifer stood up.

"Thank you, Jackson." She hugged him and Hannah and headed downstairs.

"Can we take you home Jennifer?" Jackson asked.

"I'll be ok."

"Are you sure?" Hannah said.

Jennifer nodded, then disappeared into the night the same way she came.

They had their answer.

CHAPTER SEVENTY-FOUR

# "What now...?"

Jackson couldn't sleep as he tried to lay still, holding Hannah. Jackson's heart was broken too.

The image of Jennifer's face rolled over and over in his mind, and he couldn't find rest. Every time he drifted off, he was startled awake by the sound of the heartsick sobs of Jennifer realizing her miracle wasn't going to come true.

Hannah laid quietly next to him, comforting him every time he woke.

The next morning, Hannah awoke to the incessant pounding of the waves as she saw the curtains blowing in the breeze. She looked out and saw Jackson standing out and looking into the deep blue. Hannah stepped out and wrapped her arms around him. Jackson leaned down and kissed her, but his eyes were still filled with tears and regret.

"I'm done painting."

"Excuse me?" Hannah questioned.

"It's too painful. I'm done painting."

Hannah looked at Jackson and then looked back into their loft at all the beautiful paintings lining their home and all the art supplies in the corner.

"You're gonna leave a lifetime of painting?"

"I have to; I can't take the pain of not being able to paint the picture good enough to be a miracle. To be acceptable to God."

"Jackson, God accepts you for who you are. Jackson, you're the one who said it yourself, God is "The Artist." You are copying his work. It's not Jennifer's time to go yet. It's not your fault. She'll see her son again someday, just not right now."

"I just knew the miracle would happen last night. I could feel it. My heart felt like it was breaking as I heard her cry. I couldn't imagine feeling that way again."

"Jackson, I'm so sorry, honey. I wish I could take the pain away from you. It's not your fault."

CHAPTER SEVENTY-FIVE

# Another Twist

"Jackson, I'm gonna be sick. Please help me to the bathroom," Hannah screamed as they awoke around 5:00 AM the next morning.

"What's wrong honey?" Jackson asked, scared to death.

Jackson held her hair as she repeatedly vomited, retching in pain.

"Hannah, what's wrong? Did you eat something that made you sick?"

"I don't know. I feel horrible."

"Let's get you to the Emergency Room to check you out. I've never seen you get sick like this."

"We don't need to go to the ER. Just let me lay here until I feel better."

She got sick three more times, then finally agreed to go to the hospital.

When they made it back into one of the ER rooms, Jackson pleaded with the nurse for her to bring Hannah some medicine for her nausea.

"We have to run a few tests, so we can find out what's going on. I'll bring her back some ginger ale and crackers to help with the nausea until we know what made her so sick."

Another hour passed, and the nurse came back in.

"Well, Mrs. Hannah, we know why you're sick."

"That's great." Jackson butted in.

"You're six weeks pregnant my dear."

Several minutes of silence enveloped the tiny room. The older nurse stood there contented, waiting for the news to sink in.

"Pregnant!" Hannah and Jackson shouted in unison.

"That's right. You are about six weeks along little lady." The sage nurse smiled.

The new parents looked at each other and Jackson jumped up and hugged and kissed his new mother to be.

"Can you believe it, Jackson? We're gonna be parents!

I can't wait to tell your mom."

CHAPTER SEVENTY-SIX

# Boy or Girl?

Over the next three months, Jackson and Hannah were busy picking out the furniture and accessories for their baby on the way. The busyness kept his mind off the sorrow of the miracle not happening for Jennifer. That afternoon was Hannah's ultrasound appointment to tell them if they were having a boy or a girl. Jackson hadn't touched a paint brush, and Hannah didn't pressure him.

"What do you want Jackson? A boy or a girl?"

"Hannah, I've told you over and over, as long as the baby is healthy, it doesn't matter to me. If I had my choice though, I would love a sweet little girl like you."

"Well let's go find out."

"Hi, you two. I'm Peggy, and I'll be your ultrasound tech. I bet you guys are excited."

The ultrasound room was dim and comforting as Peggy began. Jackson looked at the blurry pictures on the screen but couldn't make anything out.

Peggy kept stopping and taking pictures and finally looked at the two parents.

"Do you want to know what it is?"

"Yes!" They both shouted.

"It's a girl."

"Are you sure?" Jackson asked.

Peggy laughed loudly.

"Jackson, I've been here going on 18 years now, and I've seen a lot of little babies. There ain't no stem on that apple. You're having a little girl."

They couldn't believe it. Their hopes and dreams were continuing to come true, and Jackson's heart was healing from the emotional pain of not being able to help Jennifer.

"Hannah honey, could you hold still for a few more minutes? I have to take some more pictures of the baby's heart and lungs."

Peggy continued rolling the ultrasound probe over Hannah's protruding tummy. She stopped and repeated several scans of a small area and then laid down the probe.

"I'll be right back you two. Hold on a minute please."

She slipped out, and Hannah and Jackson wondered what was going on.

A few minutes later, she returned with a radiologist. He greeted the two and ran the ultrasound probe over Hannah's belly again and again.

Jackson interrupted. "Doctor, what is going on?"

"Well, Mr. and Mrs. Henderson, there looks to be a small defect in your little baby's heart. It appears she has a hole in her little heart that didn't close up. It is possible that it will heal on its own, but we need to do an ECG to determine that. Dr. Peterson is the best pediatric cardiologist around. We will give him a call and get you an appointment to see him."

The radiologist left the room, and Peggy thought to give them a few minutes alone before she returned to the room.

In the soft glow of the room, Jackson struggled for a comforting word to encourage his young wife.

Hannah smiled at Jackson. "I know everything will be okay Jackson. I feel it in my heart. We just have to have faith."

Jackson's eyes met hers and smiled back. "That's it."

"What's it?" Hannah asked.

"We should name her Faith." Jackson didn't say another word. He waited for Hannah and seconds later, the biggest smile broke across her face.

"Faith it is."

A couple of days had passed, and Jackson and Hannah had met with Dr. Peterson, and he ran a battery of tests on little Faith in the womb.

"Well Mr. and Mrs. Henderson, in my experience, the defect that little Faith has in her heart won't repair itself on its own. Surgery is the only option."

"When would she need the surgery?" Jackson looked up at Dr. Peterson.

"Normally we perform a series of operations in the first years of a child's life. The first one is generally right after the baby is born. Sometimes we have to do surgery before the baby is born."

"You mean while she's still in Hannah's womb?"

"Yes. It's not always required, but it is possible. We will know after a few more weeks of growth and monitoring to see how well she is doing."

Alone again. The young couple held each other in the silence. Happy with the prospect of bringing a beautiful little girl into the world and scared to death at the same time of what was ahead in surgery.

CHAPTER SEVENTY-SEVEN

# The Results

Dr. Forrester gathered the young couple in his office to explain the test results. Hannah was eight months along now and eager to deliver her precious baby. She had worried all pregnancy that her little baby Faith would need surgery before she was born, but Dr. Forrester checked her every week and was confident she could go to term.

"Well Hannah and Jackson, I know this has been a difficult pregnancy for you. Little Faith has hung in there and is continuing to develop normally. I know this will be difficult, but Faith will need surgery very soon. The prognosis is very good and once we make the repair, she should have a normal life."

CHAPTER SEVENTY-EIGHT

# Birthday Number Five

Jackson stood outside on the deck with a soft breeze coming in from the ocean. The sun hadn't quite peaked its head across the horizon and he stood there deep in thought. His cup of coffee was warm and as he took a sip, he began to roll through the memories they had shared over the last five years.

Hannah had been in labor for almost 12 hours before Faith finally decided to introduce herself to her parents. Jackson had done everything he could to comfort Hannah, but the pain was unbearable at times, but when little Faith arrived, the glow appeared on her beautiful face. He remembered Faith's first surgery and how they both were so scared. Little Faith walked very early and they quickly had to baby proof their loft to keep those little hands from getting into trouble. Five years went by like a blink. Summer vacation trips to the mountains, Disney World and Hawaii scrolled quickly across as he tried to re-experience each one. He thought about his time with Hannah too. They had planned on waiting a few years before having kids, but God had other plans for them. They still were hot for each other and every chance they got to make love, they did. Most weekends, they would try to break their record, but never quite made it to seven. Jackson was deep in thought when Hannah grabbed him from behind and squeezed him.

"Can you believe our baby is gonna be five today? I dreamt of every birthday party she's had since she was born. I still can't believe everything that has happened."

Jackson spun around and kissed her. "I've been thinking too. These five years have flown by too fast."

The two enjoyed breakfast together as little Faith slept. They talked for almost two hours before Faith got up.

"I have to get a few more things ready before the party. Let's go wake up our little birthday girl."

Later that afternoon, the sun began to sink a little and cool things off just a bit. Jackson finished putting up all the decorations and balloons and had started the grill out on the deck, getting ready for the hamburgers and hotdogs.

Hannah was busy with the final touches on the birthday cake. She stopped for a second and looked around at her little girl drawing at the kitchen table; turning five today. How she had prayed that she would see this day. Some of the doctors didn't think she would make it past three. Little Faith had endured seven surgeries over the years to repair her heart and just last month had been released from the hospital after her final surgery. Hannah walked out the sprawling French doors to Jackson, who was concentrating on the grill and she covered his eyes with her hands.

"Guess who?"

Hannah's perfume intoxicated him, and he was instantly captivated by her, like always. He turned around and grabbed her and kissed her neck and then made his way to her lips where he was greeted with a warm wet kiss.

With her lips pressed against his, they turned to look at Faith. Sitting at her little table, Faith was intently working on her picture. They stood there watching her complete her work. Her wrists were turning and twisting as she kept looking up at her parents.

"What are you drawing honey?" Hannah asked her little girl as she walked back in.

"I'm drawing you and daddy."

"Can I take a look?" Hannah smiled.

"Sure. How does it look?"

Little Faith turned the picture over and in blue pencil was a very good picture of Jackson and Hannah. The outline of their faces and the proportions of their bodies was even good.

"Wow Faith, this is beautiful. Can I keep it?"

"Sure mommy; could we put it on the refrigerator?"

"I'll put it right at the top for everyone to admire. Come on, help me put it up there."

They walked into the kitchen and Hannah displayed Faith's beautiful drawing of her parents.

"Everyone is going to be here in a few minutes for your birthday party. Can you go help daddy while I finish up a few things in here?"

Little Faith walked out to the deck as Hannah finished up the last-minute details for the party. As she was searching for the candles, the first guests showed up.

Jackson's mom and her new husband James, Mr. Willie, all the guys from the garage, Gina and a host of other family and friends from the restaurant piled into their loft. As everyone mingled saying hello, Leah caught Hannah alone and hugged her.

"I'm so happy we get to celebrate this day Hannah. I was so scared for so long with little Faith. You and Jackson have been so strong with her and everything y'all have been through. My heart is just bursting with joy."

They both cried together for a quick minute.

"Thank you for being there for us. All the prayers and all the helping out at the restaurant. We can never say thank you enough for all you did for us."

Mr. Willie found his way into the kitchen. "Now, now. What's with all the water works. This is supposed to be a day of celebration."

He hugged them both as their tears continued to fall.

Gina stopped to talk to Jackson. "Hey Jackson, what a big day this is."

Jackson smiled as he hugged Gina. "Hey Gina, is Red coming to the party?"

"He's still on shift for another two hours, and then he'll be headed over."

Hannah had finally dried her tears and was looking for the candles again.

"Hey Jackson, have you seen the candles for Faith's cake?"

"I forgot to pick them up when I got her cake at the store. Let me finish cooking these burgers, and I'll run up to the corner store to get some."

"That's okay Jackson, finish cooking the burgers. I'll go right now. Your mom said she would take care of everything until I got back."

"No honey, I forgot them, let me go get them." Jackson pleaded.

"I need you to not burn the hamburgers and save me one, so I can enjoy it when I get back. I'll be gone ten minutes tops. I love you, Jackson."

CHAPTER SEVENTY-NINE

# In Motion

Down at the corner bar on Center Street, Billy Barbatt sat alone at the glossy bar, watching the game. Billy had occupied this stool for years. His eyes were blood red and glassy. He could hardly stay on his barstool. A blueish bruise was forming around his right eye, and his top lip was swollen; a result of an altercation over a game of pool an hour before.

"Billy, it's only 5:30 PM and you've already had five drinks. You need to slow down," implored Joe, the bartender. "You look a little rough Billy, what happened to ya?"

"Just give me another shot and shut-up, why don't you?" Billy yelled.

"That's it, Billy, I'm cutting you off. I'll call you a cab. You need to go home and sleep this one off."

"I ain't going anywhere; now pour me another drink!"

"You're done, Billy. That's it." He looked at Joanie, one of his best waitresses and asked her to call Billy a cab.

"I'm sorry Billy, but you gotta go. You're too drunk, and you're causing a scene around here."

Billy stood up and slammed his glass down and kicked his stool as hard as he could and began his tirade of curse words as he made his way to the door.

"Joanie called you a cab. It'll be here in 5 minutes. Just wait outside."

Drunk Billy held up his middle finger as he busted through the front door almost running over some customers coming in.

He stumbled to his truck and poured himself in. He sat there for a minute, fumbling for his keys, then he cranked it up.

CHAPTER EIGHTY

# Twists and Turns

"Hey, Donna, what aisle are the birthday candles on?" Hannah smiled as she rushed through the little corner store.

"Hey Hannah, they're on aisle 7. How old is little Faith gonna be?"

"She is turning a very bright five today. She is taking after her daddy."

Hannah got back into her old Mustang and headed back home making her way down Center Street.

Billy started down one of the side roads and was headed towards Center Street. His truck was swerving all over the road, and he never slowed down as he plowed right through the big red STOP sign.

CHAPTER EIGHTY-ONE

# The Wreck

Red busted through the door of the loft with his police uniform on drenched in sweat. "Jackson, you have to come with me right now. Hannah's been in an accident."

Jackson almost passed out as a wave of pain poured over him. He glanced up at his mom. "Please take care of Faith."

As Jackson and Red ran to his squad car, Jackson kept screaming. "What's going on? What happened to her?"

They turned the corner and Jackson saw her car lying on its side, at least a hundred feet from the road she was traveling on.

Slow motion set in as Jackson ran towards the car.

"No..., no..., this can't be."

He made it to her and saw her bloody face. She was pinned against the steering wheel and the dashboard, and the car had been smashed from the side.

Jackson laid down on the hot asphalt and slid in to hold her hand.

She whispered to him. "What took you so long?" She mustered a small smile.

"You're gonna be alright Hannah; the ambulance is on its way. Just hold on honey. Just a little longer."

He held her hand as his tears poured down the side of his face. "Now you hang on honey, I can hear the sirens coming. Just a little longer."

"Jackson, take care of Faith for me. She's part of both of us."

Jackson screamed. "I need you to take care of her with me; I can't do it without you! I need you! Please don't leave me, please don't leave me."

Jackson sobbed and sobbed as Hannah drifted in and out of consciousness.

As she took her last breath, she squeezed his hand. "Jackson, paint me back to you. I know you can do it baby. I love you."

"I will Hannah, I promise. I'll find a way."

CHAPTER EIGHTY-TWO

# The Reaction

"Who did this to her?" Jackson bawled as he stumbled around the crash site looking for Red. He kept screaming it over and over.

The immensity of the situation made it difficult for him to breathe and he collapsed on the ground in front of Hannah's car. Through the smoke and emergency vehicle lights, he saw Red handcuff Billy Barbatt and put him in his patrol car. He didn't have a scratch on him.

Red leaned over to Billy and told him he was being charged with felony DUI and read him his rights.

Jackson looked up from the hot pavement, and the most horrible feeling he'd ever felt overtook his body.

"No!!!!!!!! It can't be." He screamed and screamed, but he couldn't move. He felt paralyzed.

Staggering over to the patrol car, he swung open the door and snatched Billy out of the car by the throat. "I'm gonna kill you, you son of a bitch."

As Jackson pounded Billy in the face, Red and another officer grabbed Jackson and pulled him away.

Red screamed. "Jackson, stop! He's gonna go to prison; you can't do this. It ain't gonna bring Hanna back."

Jackson collapsed again, sobbing. "He took everything from me... Everything."

Red picked Jackson up and held on to him, trying to calm him down.

Jackson's mom arrived and ran to him and held him.

"I'm so sorry, honey."

Her embrace did little to console him. The incessant waves of emotion continued to erupt all over him, and he couldn't catch his breath. The paramedics finally convinced him to lay down on a stretcher and breathe some oxygen and gave him a sedative to try to help calm him down.

Mr. Willie pulled up in his Silverado, and the lights and the sirens brought back those haunting memories of the fateful night he lost his family to that car crash. His heart was pounding as he searched the scene for Jackson.

He saw Red towering above the others and shouted out to him.

"Where's Jackson?"

Red pointed over to the ambulance, and Mr. Willie headed that way. With tears in his eyes, he grabbed Jackson's hand. For a while, he couldn't say anything. He just held his hand and cried with him looking at the wreckage as the police conducted their investigation.

"Jackson, there's nothing I can say that will help make this any better. I'm so sorry, son. We will all be here to help you get through this."

CHAPTER EIGHTY-THREE

# Reality

Jackson's hands trembled in the cold, sterile hospital room and he dropped the pen three times while he signed the papers for Hannah's final arrangements.

Jackson's mom Leah put her arm around him.

"Come on Jackson, let's go home. Little Faith needs you right now honey."

The desolation of it all was unbearable as he opened the door to their home. Jackson couldn't bear to go back into their bedroom. Little Faith curled up under her soft pink sheets, and Jackson laid down beside her. They lay quietly facing each other, tears running down their faces.

"Daddy, is mommy in Heaven?"

Jackson's eyes filled completely as he struggled to speak; his throat swollen and sore.

"Yes honey, mommy's in Heaven, smiling down on you right now."

Little Faith reached her little finger out and wiped the tears from her daddy's cheek.

He held her hand and traced the lines along her fingers until her eyes drifted shut. Her favorite Teddy Bear lamp illuminated the room with a warm glow as he laid on his back and tried to close his eyes. Sleep eluded him; every time he tried to let himself slip away, the crash replayed in his mind.

Jackson looked around Faith's quaint little room. Hannah had decorated every inch of it, and her fingerprints were on everything. A picture of the three of them on the pier rested on Faith's bedside table. Jackson picked it up and ran his finger along the outline of Hannah's face. He longed so deeply to hold her again. To smell her sweet scent, to caress her beautiful warm skin.

When his body could finally take no more, he closed his eyes.

CHAPTER EIGHTY-FOUR

# The Funeral

After the funeral was over and everyone had left, Jackson was completely lost. Leah stayed over to help him care for Faith. Once Leah and Faith were both asleep, Jackson went down to the restaurant and pulled out a bottle of vodka and made himself a drink. He had never been much of a drinker. As he took his first sip and looked around, everything reminded him of her. The feeling of loss was crushing him. He knew trying to sleep would make it much worse for him. The darkness brought on the anxiety with such intensity that he couldn't bear turning the lights off again. Every memory of her cascaded through his mind and then, he got an idea. It had happened before. Couldn't it happen again? Her last words set him on a mission.

He snuck back upstairs and quietly picked up the photo of the three of them from her nightstand and closed his daughter's door, so the light wouldn't wake her and then he headed to the studio.

He hadn't painted anything in over five years since the painting of Jennifer and her son. Working all night, he painted and painted. It felt good again. Finally, around 5 am, he was done. He knew this was the right thing to do.

Jackson sat down next to Faith's bed, and that cute Teddy Bear lamp still burned brightly. He was ready for all of them to be together again. Jackson placed the painting on his lap and slowly began to rub the outline of Hannah's face. His paint splotched fingers trembled as he waited for the miracle to occur. Touching ever so softly, he longed to see her again.

Nothing...

No miracle was to occur this morning. The pain slowly crept in, then became overwhelming. The pain became anger, and he lifted the painting up to smash it as his little girl woke up.

"What are you doing daddy?" Faith rubbed her eyes as she sat up in her bed.

Realizing what he was about to do, he caught himself and quickly brought the painting down to her eye level.

"I painted a picture of us. Take a look."

Faith rubbed her little finger around the outline of her mother's face, and she jumped back like she'd been shocked.

"What's wrong honey?" Jackson exclaimed.

Little Faith looked up at her daddy. "I thought I was back there when we took that picture. I could feel mommy's arm around me."

Excited about the possibility of "what could be," Jackson asked her to touch it again.

Once again, the tiny little tan finger traced the outline of Hannah's face. This time, nothing happened. She kept trying and trying, moving even slower to see if it would happen again. Still nothing.

Jackson was heart-broken but couldn't let on to Faith. They both laid back down and drifted off to sleep.

CHAPTER EIGHTY-FIVE

# Grief

It has been said, "Grief is overwhelming. The beast lingers around and won't let go. Grief feels like the ever-pounding ocean. As soon as you try to stand, another wall comes to knock you back down."

Only a few hours of sleep a night is all Jackson could seem to manage for almost the first year. He never turned the lamp out on the table next to the sofa in his studio. The few winks he did manage to get, he slept on that sofa. Jackson hadn't slept in their room since Hannah's death. The room was just as she had left it that fateful day.

It was a week before the anniversary of her tragic death, and he'd done everything he could to try to keep Faith occupied and not concentrate too much on the terrible loss they both had suffered. Trying to smile for the teachers at school and people at church took its toll on him.

Everyone said that things would get better with time. Not for Jackson. She was his whole life. Every thought was of her. Nothing seemed to help, because everywhere they went, he was reminded of her in some way. It was inescapable. One thing was certain though, Faith was growing up, and he needed to be a dad to her.

CHAPTER EIGHTY-SIX

# Moving Forward

"Daddy, can you teach me how to paint?"

Jackson turned around from the stove while making dinner and smiled at little Faith. The sun was sinking, and the sky was bathed in a multitude of colors that Jackson hadn't seen in a while.

"You want to learn how to paint?"

"Yeah, just like you." She leaned back in her chair and pointed to all the stunning artworks that adorned their home.

"Mommy told me a bedtime story before she went to heaven and you were the star. She said you could make the paintings magical. She said God helped you make them magic."

Jackson just stared at her as his heart sped up.

"Is that true daddy? Can you make magic paintings? Can we really go to wherever you paint? Mommy said you had a special touch that made you able to go where your paintings were. She said you were the artist with a special touch. Mommy said you could paint so good, that the touch of your hand made your paintings come to life and take you there."

Jackson couldn't believe his little girl was telling him this. He had asked everyone, including Hannah to never talk about what they had witnessed long ago.

"Faith, daddy can't make magic paintings. I just try to paint the best picture I can, but whatever happened long ago, God did that, not me. He is the real artist with The Special Touch. Just look outside. See how unbelievably beautiful the sky is with all its colors. I try to mimic that on my canvas, but nothing comes close to the real thing.

Faith didn't quite understand. "Remember, anything is possible with God, right?" Jackson managed a smile.

Little Faith shook her head in agreement.

All the rush of emotions flowed back with a fury when Jackson thought about painting again. "Ok then, you can have your first lesson after we finish dinner."

CHAPTER EIGHTY-SEVEN

# Growing Up

As the years slowly passed, Jackson did his best to help Faith grow up as normal as a child can without a mother. When it came to fixing her hair, Jackson was hopeless. He did his best, but she would frown when she looked in the mirror and had lop-sided ponytails. Her grandmother Leah helped quite a bit, and Jackson would take Faith fishing and boating every chance they got. He had taught her how to swim at the YMCA, play soccer in the spring and softball in the summer. The busier they were, the less time he had to think.

Before he could blink, she was turning 16. High school was something Jackson wished he didn't have to deal with. The crazy drama with friends, the boys with hormones, and a million other stresses of life during the high school years he would love to have avoided. Every day was a struggle.

A few young boys were interested in dating Faith, but Jackson did his best to run them off. Most of them were punk kids just looking for one thing. Long ago, He and Hannah had prayed that Faith would meet a nice young Christian man that would care for and respect her.

"Daddy, can I take your car for a drive when I get my license tomorrow?"

"Old Betsy? You want to drive my Corvette?" He was surprised she would even ask. She knew how much he loved that car and how much it meant to him. Jackson washed and detailed it every Friday morning. It was one thing that he enjoyed. He felt close to Hannah there. They had taken so many trips in that car and he loved to watch her hair dance in the wind as they sped through town.

Faith had been practicing driving since she was 14. They would go out on the backroads every Sunday afternoon and he would have her drive one of his trucks and he even bought an old beater stick shift car, so she could learn on that. By the time she got her real license, she was able to handle a car very well.

"If you pass your license test on the first try, I will let you drive ol' Betsy around town, with me along for the ride of course."

"Deal. Make sure the tank is full today dad, cause we'll be going for a long ride."

Jackson laughed. He liked that confident personality that was developing in her. He had tried to do everything he could to help her learn and become independent. She worked at the Seaside Grille right along with him. She was one of the most popular waitresses.

The afternoon came, and Faith bolted out of the DMV with her shiny new license in hand.

"Hand me the keys "Old Man", let's go for a ride."

"Old Man? I can still outrun you young lady. Let me see that license."

Faith smiled as she snatched the keys from his hand. She hopped in and fired up all those horses as the pistons opened wide.

"Faith, take it easy now, this car is powerful. It's not like driving your car."

"Ok dad, I know. I'll be careful. You ready?"

Jackson reluctantly nodded the best he could sitting in the passenger's seat with a 16-year-old driver behind the wheel of his prized Corvette.

Faith was careful as they made their way from the beach and out to Folly Road, headed for town. Once she passed the bridge and the lanes widened up, she popped the clutch and the engine roared. She jammed on the gas and threw them both back in their seats. Faith let out a wail just like her mother used to do when Jackson would do the same thing with her riding shotgun. Jackson remembered the first drive he and Hannah shared in just this same spot.

His little girl was growing up, and his heart was breaking because her mother wasn't there to watch.

CHAPTER EIGHTY-EIGHT

# The One

"Daddy, he's the one."

Jackson was stopped cold. "What are you talking about?"

"He's the one I want to marry."

"What?" Jackson almost fell over.

"You're still a junior in college."

"I know, he hasn't actually asked me yet, but we have talked about it a lot. We talked about getting married as soon as we graduated and found a job."

"I don't even know this kid very well and he hasn't come to talk to me."

"Dad, I've been dating John for almost three years now. He comes on all our summer vacations. He practically lives here in the summer."

Jackson shook his head. "But marriage Faith? You don't even have a job or your degree yet."

"I will dad. We are planning a long engagement. I promise we'll give you plenty of notice before we decide on a date."

"Well, he better come talk to me if he's thinking about marrying my daughter."

"He will dad. You still make him nervous after all these years."

CHAPTER EIGHTY-NINE

# The Opportunity

Jackson put the mail on the kitchen counter and saw a letter from a college he didn't recognize.

"Faith, there's a letter here for you. It's from that college in NC."

His bright-eyed college senior busted out of her room and tore the letter open. Jackson tried to wait patiently as he watched her eyes light up.

"I got in! I got in!"

"Got in what?"

"The Masters Art Program I applied for 6 months ago."

"I thought you were just kidding about that. You said there's no way you'd get in."

"That's what I thought, they only let the top talent get in. There are so many talented artists who can paint better than me."

"Well, I guess they saw something they liked in your work."

"Dad, I can't believe it. I just applied on a whim. I never expected to even get a denial letter back. Anyway, I can't go."

"What are you talking about? This is a chance of a lifetime!"

"I'm not leaving you dad. I can go to the College of Charleston's program. It's good too."

"Faith, you can't turn something like this down. It's what you wanted. I'll be okay. The restaurant is as busy as ever and I have to keep Mr. Willie busy since he retired."

"I could never leave you dad. It's just been me and you for so long. I would miss you too much."

"You're going. We'll visit every chance we can."

CHAPTER NINETY

# Leaving Home

Jackson packed the Tahoe with the worst feeling in his gut that he'd had in years. He smiled every time he passed Faith as they loaded the SUV to the brim. He didn't want to let on that the last thing he wanted was for her to leave. She was growing up and looking more like her mom every day. He wasn't sure that he could leave her once they made it to North Carolina. She had never been away from him for more than a couple of days when she spent the night with friends. Now, she'd be four hours away.

He didn't know it, but Faith felt the same way too. She was excited to start her new program, but she did everything with her dad. She was going to miss him like crazy. Her boyfriend was finishing up his degree this year and would be starting his new job at a prestigious engineering firm the day after graduation. John Connor was a great kid. Jackson tried everything to run him off too like he did the others, but his love for Faith was so strong, he kept coming back no matter what. Jackson had finally realized that she would be twenty-one soon and she was an adult. Some parts of him didn't want her to leave, but he knew deep down he had to let go. Jackson was even a little comforted that he finally had someone to count on to take care of and protect his daughter.

As they were just finishing up the last boxes of her shoes, John pulled up in the driveway.

Mr. Henderson, could I talk to you sir, his voice crackling a bit.

Hannah looked at her dad and flashed that beautiful smile. "Don't be rough on him dad, okay?"

"What?" He gestured with his arms in the air as they walked inside and went upstairs to the loft.

CHAPTER NINETY-ONE

# The Question

"Mr. Henderson, I'm sorry for showing up like this, but I've been thinking about this for almost three years now and I've been practicing what to say to you."

Jackson stared at him and didn't say a word.

"What I'm trying to say sir is that I love Faith. I love her more than anything else in the world. My parents have been married for over thirty years and they have always shown me what love was and they showed me the model for how a marriage should be. Hannah had the same example with you and her mom. She remembers so much about her and she remembers how close you both were. You have been there for Faith in every way and she has seen how you handled the single most difficult situation a person could be put in."

Jackson's face was somber, and a tear began to trail down his cheek.

"John, what are you trying to say?"

"Mr. Henderson, I would love to have your permission to marry your daughter. I promise to put her first in everything and always be there for her and make her happy for the rest of our lives."

"John, my daughter is the most important person in my life on this earth. She is half of me and her mother. I would be trusting you with my life, since whatever happens to her would happen to me too. Do you know what that means?"

John was trembling, but he stood firm.

"Yes sir. She means everything to me. I promise to always be someone she and you would be proud of."

Jackson stood there for what seemed like an eternity, while John was so nervous he was almost hyper-ventilating.

"John, I would be proud for you to be my son-in-law."

As soon as those words left his lips, Faith busted into the room and hugged her dad and then John.

"So much for privacy." Jackson laughed as she saw her daughter kiss her husband to be.

They had set a date for the wedding as soon as Faith graduated from her master's degree program. As she drove off, he just stood there until he could no longer see the lights of her car. He made his way back to the loft and as he looked around at everything, he began to sob. He walked into the room he and Hannah shared and laid on the bed while he thought about what life was going to bring for him now. About an hour passed and he knew they needed him in the restaurant; he turned to get up and on the nightstand beside the bed was a photograph taken of Jackson and Hannah on the balcony on the day of the accident. He had never seen it before, and the flood of emotions returned as he sobbed once more. Faith must have put it in there he thought. He ran his fingers over the outline of her face and longed to be with her. Touching the picture over and over... he had an idea.

CHAPTER NINETY-TWO

# The New Artist

Jackson had taught Faith to paint very early and she had been painting for many years now. She was an artistic sensation at her North Carolina college. Her work hung in many of the nearby restaurants in Asheville and she'd won some local art contests. The pace of school and her projects kept her so busy, she hadn't come home in quite a while. Faith had been able to make a lot of the wedding plans over the phone and Jackson had did his best to help make sure she had everything she wanted. It was going to be a grand affair.

Faith and John had rented a condo a few miles down the beach and she would be staying there as soon as graduation was over. John was finishing up a big project for his company and would be moving down after the wedding. Jackson was still trying to wrap his head around his daughter getting married. Faith and Jackson talked every couple of days on the phone, and she could tell he was getting sad.

CHAPTER NINETY-THREE

# The Wedding

As Jackson walked his baby down the aisle, every glimpse of Hannah ran through his mind. He remembered them both standing in that church with only God, and the preacher watching. The church was full when Jackson turned around to take his seat for the service. His tears flowed freely now. Faith looked so much like her mother. Jackson couldn't believe the resemblance was so close. As Faith and John said their vows, Jackson remembered his and he remembered his promise.

CHAPTER NINETY-FOUR

# The Special Touch

Jackson made it through the father-daughter dance and did his best to enjoy the reception as he made the rounds thanking their friends and family. And now it was time for Faith and John to go on their honeymoon.

He kissed his beloved daughter on the cheek and hugged her as she was about to get in the car all decked out with "Just Married" decorations. She held on to him for a long time and whispered in his ear, "I love you so much daddy! I'll be back soon."

He did his best to smile as they slowly drove out of sight.

Mr. Willie did his best to get Jackson to come to dinner with him, but he declined and said he just wanted to go home and rest.

Jackson opened the door to the loft and he was almost unable to breathe. He couldn't believe Faith was gone. Jackson looked over to his studio and to the painting on his easel that he'd finished earlier that morning. Jackson lost count of the number of times he had painted that picture of them on that fateful day. Each and every time after the paint dried, he would sit down and begin to touch Hannah's sweet face; he so longed to be with her again.

Nothing.

No feelings of being in the picture with her ever came again. Each time, he felt like his heart would burst, and his spirit would be shattered. The hurt was so deep, he would throw the paintings as hard as he could.

Jackson wasn't going to give up, he would keep trying to keep that promise he made to Hannah so long ago. He sat down next to the easel and stared at the painting and prayed.

"God, little Faith is with John now, and he will take care of her. Please let this painting be good enough and let me be with Hannah again. I need your touch. The Artist of the Universe. The real Artist with the Special Touch."

He reached his finger to begin to touch her face; he longed for that feeling so much. Jackson continued and ran his finger over every square inch, but his miracle was not to happen.

When he finally realized his miracle was not to be, he broke down in tears and collapsed on the floor.

Another hour passed and then he finally picked himself up and sat in his chair as he looked out at the crashing waves of the ocean. He heard the rattling of the door below.

Jackson wiped the tears from his eyes as the door opened that led up the stairs to his art studio. The familiar creaking of the steps in just the right spot told him it was Faith. She always stepped on the same spot that creaked just a little. Before she made it to the top of the old staircase, he stood up from his easel and again gazed out across the beach and into the ocean. He tried his best to regain his composure before she saw him.

Faith reached the summit of the stairs and stared at her father without uttering a sound. He was still looking out the window and running his fingers through his hair as she watched him. Jackson's "little girl" looked stunning in her light blue and white polka dot dress. Her long sandy blonde hair framed her beautiful face perfectly. Her warm, tanned skin glistened in the sunlight coming off the window.

Jackson turned to her and smiled. "You look so beautiful Faith, you look just like your mother."

Faith smiled and looked around the room.

Jackson spoke up. "Faith, honey what are you doing here? Shouldn't you be on your honeymoon?"

She kept looking around the room, "Our flight doesn't leave for a few more hours, and I wanted to see you one more time before we left. How are you doing?"

"I'm fine, honey."

The art studio revealed a different story. It had been so long since Faith last visited her father's art studio. Faith turned away in anguish when she realized how long it had been since she last visited him here. She had been so busy finishing her master's degree in North Carolina, finding a job and planning a wedding. When she had finally looked around the entire room, her eyes widened in disbelief. Hundreds of damaged canvases lay littered on the floor and in every corner. They were all torn apart or painted over. When she focused on each one, she realized they were all the same familiar painting.

The art studio had never been in such a mess. Jackson had always been meticulous about keeping things neat and clean; she couldn't believe he let it get like this. Jackson had scores of custom cabinets built to store all the paints, brushes, and canvases and each one had its specific place. The cabinets and their shelves were in terrible disarray as she took it all in and tried to make sense of it. He noticed her looking at the condition of the studio when their eyes met.

"I know it's a little messy around here, but I've been a little tired lately, and I haven't been able to keep everything cleaned up."

Even though the wedding reception ended several hours earlier, Jackson was still wearing his black tuxedo.

"Faith, you didn't have to come here... Dad's okay."

She said to herself, "Yeah, I can see you're okay."

"Daddy, I brought you something... I'll be right back."

As she disappeared back down the old staircase, the visions of her whole life ran through Jackson's mind. Teaching her how to paint, swimming lessons at the YMCA and the first adventure on her bike. He was there for every single one. Every moment played through his memory like the slow winding frames of a movie, each with bold clarity. He was so deep in thought, he didn't hear her return up to the loft.

She walked over and placed the large brown package down on the worn, gold pine floor in front of him. He picked it up and slowly ran his hands along the edges. He sat down and removed the packaging, revealing its contents. When he slid the last of the covering away, his heart sank as his eyes met her gift. He stared at it without saying anything. Faith stood close, waiting for his response. As tears trailed gently down his cheeks, a smile broke across his face, and he looked up at her.

"How did you know?"

"How could I not know? Just look around here. With all the things I've experienced in this place and all the things you taught me, and all the stories mom told me. I remember them. And when I see you so lost without her, I just had to try. Daddy, I think it's time."

Jackson smiled as he looked at her painting. It was the picture that Jackson had discovered on the bedside table. She had painted such a masterpiece of her parents, Jackson could hardly tell it was a painting.

“Honey, this looks better than any painting I've ever done.”

Jackson got up and hugged her once more. He sat back down and began to touch the outline of Hannah's face. As he gently traced the outline, that warm wonderful light that he so longed for, illuminated the room so brightly they both couldn't see. Their eyes adjusted slowly and then there was Hannah smiling at both of them.

“You look so beautiful my darling Faith. I'm so proud of you.”

Faith and Jackson couldn't believe it was her. Hannah reached out her hand to Jackson. “I knew you would find a way baby.”

Jackson grabbed her hand and pulled her to him as they were whisked away to Heaven. Hannah spoke up as she kissed him, "I just have one question my darling Jackson."

Jackson smiled, "What is it honey?"

"What took you so long?"

# The End

## THANK YOU

Thank you, dear reader, for reading this book, my debut novel. I hope you enjoyed the journey. It has been my dream to write this book and touch your heart with emotion. If you enjoyed this book, please leave a review on the site where you purchased it and Goodreads.

If for some reason you didn't like it, please let me know why at riverwildusa@gmail.com.

Please be on the lookout for my follow-up novel coming early 2019. It is titled "The Sacrifice of our Youth." This story chronicles several service members as they realize what they have given up serving their country.

## ABOUT THE AUTHOR

River Wild grew up in Charleston, South Carolina where he fell in love with Folly Beach and all the surrounding Charleston area. He met and married his high school sweetheart in Charleston. He served in the military for more than 20 years and has two children. River and his family live in South Carolina.

COPYRIGHT

This book is a work of fiction. Names, characters, places, and incidents are the product of the author's imagination or are used fictitiously. Any resemblance to actual events, locales, or persons, living or dead, is coincidental.